CRITICS ARE
THE VAM

"Good-natured fun . . . Elr

—*Locus*

"Elrod's sharp vampire's-eye view of the powers of the undead goes a long way . . . Excellent . . . Intriguing . . . Tight and effective!"

—*Dragon*

"The pace is fast . . . intriguing . . . an updated version of the old pulp novels!"

—*Science Fiction Review*

"Well done . . . Original . . . Fleming makes a powerful and charming detective . . . You won't want to miss this series!"

—*Cemetery Dance*

"A pleasant addition to the growing number of vampire hero series . . . Entertaining!"

—*Science Fiction Chronicle*

"Builds to a frenzied climax leaving the reader almost gasping for breath. Be prepared to read the last half of the book in one sitting . . . Should satisfy even the most demanding adventure-lover's appetite for breathless, nonstop action and excitement."

—*Big Spring Herald*

"The twists and turns of the story are reminiscent of *The Maltese Falcon* or *The Big Sleep* . . . Excellent!"

—*Tarriel Cell*

Ace Books by P. N. Elrod

The Vampire Files

BLOODLIST
LIFEBLOOD
BLOODCIRCLE
ART IN THE BLOOD
FIRE IN THE BLOOD
BLOOD ON THE WATER

RED DEATH
DEATH AND THE MAIDEN
DEATH MASQUE

Coming in Summer 1998
from Ace Books

A CHILL IN THE BLOOD

LIFEBLOOD

P. N. ELROD

ACE BOOKS, NEW YORK

This book is an Ace original edition,
and has never been previously published.

LIFEBLOOD

An Ace Book / published by arrangement with
the author

PRINTING HISTORY
Ace edition / June 1990

The Penguin Putnam Inc. World Wide Web site address is
http://www.penguinputnam.com

ISBN: 0-441-84776-5

Check out the Ace Science Fiction/Fantasy newsletter,
and much more, at Club PPI!

ACE®
Ace Books are published by
The Berkley Publishing Group, a member of Penguin Putnam Inc.,
200 Madison Avenue, New York, New York 10016.
The name "ACE" and the "A" logo are trademarks
belonging to Charter Communications, Inc.

PRINTED IN THE UNITED STATES OF AMERICA

10   9   8   7

A special thanks to Ben, for being so patient.

"BE A SPORT," I said to the bartender, not quite meeting his eye, "I'm nursin' a broken heart."

"Yeah, yeah," he replied, and continued polishing a glass with a gray rag.

"No foolin', I got the money." And I fumbled five singles from my shirt pocket and let them flutter onto the damp black wood of the bar. "Come on, that's worth a bottle, ain't it? I won't make no trouble."

"You can make book on it."

He had a right to be confident. We were nearly the same height, but I'm on the lean side and he was built like a steam shovel and just as solid. He thought he could take care of me.

He stopped polishing the glass and put it down next to the bills. I smiled and tried to look friendly, which was a hell of an act under the circumstances. This was one of those cheaper-than-two-bit dives where you take your life in your hands just by going to the men's room. From the smell of things, the facilities were located just outside the front door against the wall of the building, gentlemen on the left, ladies . . . I renewed my hopeful smile and rustled the bills temptingly.

He looked at them, then gave me a fishy eye, gauging my apparent drunkenness against the lure of the money. It was a slow night and the money won. His hand made a move for it, but mine was a little faster and covered three of Washington's portraits first.

"Wise guy," he said, and took a bottle of the cheap stuff down from the shelf behind him. Hell, it was all cheap, but that hardly mattered to me, I only wanted an excuse to hang around.

"I've had some, but not that much." I left two bucks on the bar, took the bottle, glass, and remaining money, and tottered to the second booth in line along the wall. With my back to the front door I settled in, using the careful movements of a drunk who wants to show people he isn't. I spent a lot of time counting my three dollars and putting them away before pouring a drink and pretending to imbibe. Ten cents for the whole bottle would have been an overcharge; the stuff smelled like some of the old poison left over from before repeal. I brought the glass to my lips, made a face, and coughed, spilling some of it down my well-stained shirtfront.

While I was busy dabbing at the mess with a dirty handkerchief, a big man in dark gray came in and went straight to the bar. He was in a suit, which was wrong for the neighborhood, and he was in a hurry, which was wrong for the hour. At one in the morning, nobody should be in a hurry. He ordered a whiskey with a beer chaser and took a look around. It didn't take long; except for me, seven booths, and the bartender, the place was empty.

He studied me like a bug. I pretended real hard that I was drunk and simple-minded and hoped he'd buy the act. It helped that I wore rough work clothes that stank of the river and past debauches with the bottle—just another country kid corrupted by the big bad city.

Apparently I was no threat. He knocked back the whiskey and took the beer to the last booth next to the back door and sat on the outside edge, where he could see people coming in from the street. I used the tilted mirror hanging over the bar to watch him. It was an old one with flecks of tarnish like freckles, but his reflection was clear enough. He hunched over the beer and drained it a sip at a time, with long pauses in between. His soft hat was pulled low, but now and then his eyes gleamed when he used the mirror himself. I kept still and enjoyed his slight puzzlement when he couldn't spot my image in the glass.

Another man walked in from the night and hesitantly approached the bar. He was also too well dressed, but was a bit more seedy and timid. He had a tall, thin body with a beaky nose that supported some black-rimmed pince-nez on a pastel blue velvet ribbon. He wore a cheap blue suit, the cuffs a little too short and the pants a little too tight. His ankles stuck out, revealing black silk socks peeking over the tops of black shoes with toes that had been chiseled to a lethal point. He affected a black cane with a silver handle, which would buy him eternity in this neighborhood if he waved it around too much.

He tried ordering a sherry and got a look of contemptuous disbelief instead. He had better luck asking for gin, then made a point of wiping the rim of the glass clean with his printed silk handkerchief before drinking. After taking a sip, he dabbed his lips and smoothed the pencil line under his nose that passed for a moustache.

He looked around, as nervous as a virgin in a frat house. He noted me and the man in the back booth, and when neither of us leaped out to cut his throat, he relaxed a little. He checked the clock behind the bar, comparing its time to a silver watch attached to his vest and frowned.

The bartender moved away, no doubt driven off by the scent of dying lilies that the newcomer had doused over himself. A cloud of it hit me in the face like exhaust from a truck, and I gave up breathing for a while.

He looked at the watch again and then at the door. No one came in. He removed his hat, placing it gently on the bar, as though it might offend someone. From a low widow's peak to the curl-clustered nape, his dark hair had been carefully dressed with a series of waves that were too regular to be natural. He removed his gloves, plucking delicately at the fingertips, then absently patted his hair down.

The bartender caught the eyes of the man in the booth and shrugged with raised brows and a superior smile as though to say he couldn't help who walked through the door as long as they paid. The man in the booth hunched closer to his beer and watched the mirror.

Two minutes later a lady walked in, probably the first one to ever cross the threshold. She was small, not much over five feet, wearing emerald green with a matching hat and a heavy dark veil that covered her face down to her hard, red lips. She carried a big green bag trimmed with beads that twinkled in the light. Her green heels made quite a noise as she crossed the wood floor to the tall man at the bar. He straightened a little, because polite men do things like that when a lady comes up to them, and he did look polite.

She glanced around warily, her eyes resting on me a moment. She must have been pretty enough to be noticed even by a drunk like me; at least she had a trim figure and good legs. I gave her an encouraging, if bleary leer and raised my glass hopefully. After that she ignored me and tilted her chin expectantly at the tall man.

He frowned, worried, but gathered up his hat, cane, gloves, and drink and followed her to the second-to-last booth at the end. She sat with her back to me and the man slid in opposite her with his back to the big man in gray, who was now pressed tight against the wall. She seemed not to have noticed him.

The gin placed his cane across the table, the curved handle hanging over the outside edge. His hat went next to it and the gloves were tucked into a pocket. I could tell he was nervous again from the way he fussed with things. He quietly asked the woman if she cared to have a drink. She shook her head. He repeated the gesture to the bartender, who then moved down to my end and picked up another glass to polish. He was watching me, but I was in a slack-jawed dream, staring into space, at least at the space occupied by the mirror behind him.

The man in gray leaned to the outside and craned his neck. He could see the bartender and was now worried that he couldn't see me as well, but it was too late to investigate the problem without calling attention to himself.

The woman stared at her companion, her breath gently ruffling the veil. Her voice was pitched low, but even at that distance I had no trouble hearing the conversation.

"Do you have it?"

The man cocked his head to one side, favoring her with the stronger lens of the pince-nez. "I might ask you the same question." His voice was flat and breathy, as though he were afraid the let the words out.

She didn't like him or his answer, but eventually lifted the purse from her lap to the table. With her left hand she pulled out a slim leather case and opened it for his inspection. It was no larger than a pack of cigarettes, and she held it ready to pull back if he grabbed it. He peered at the contents a moment, then drew a jeweler's loupe from his pocket.

"May I?" He extended a manicured hand. She hesitated. "I have to verify that it is genuine, Miss . . . er . . . Green. Mr. Swafford was very clear on that point."

She put the case on the table, her right hand lingering inside the big purse. "Just as long as you know that this is genuine," she told him, and turned the bag to let him see inside.

He stiffened, his eyes frozen on her hidden hand. He licked his lower lip. "V-very well." Slowly he picked up the leather case, removing the pince-nez and screwing the loupe into one eye. He examined what was in the case for ten seconds and reversed the motions, replacing it back onto the scarred tabletop.

"Well?" she said.

"It is genuine." He settled the pince-nez back on his nose.

"I knew that, let's get on with it."

"Y-yes, certainly." From his coat pocket he produced an envelope and gave it to her. She opened it and examined the contents in turn, pulling out one of the hundred-dollar bills from the center. A second later she looked up and grabbed the leather case.

"You can tell Swafford it's in the fire," she said in a voice like ground glass.

His eyes darted unhappily from the empty spot on the table to her veil. "But why?"

"These bills are marked. If there's cops outside you're a corpse."

"No, please, I didn't know about this, please wait!"

She didn't look like she was ready to move, but the man was unnerved. Behind him the big guy had shifted a hand to the inside of his coat, which explained why she hadn't noticed him; there'd been no need to notice her partner.

"I-I don't understand this. Mr. Swafford entrusted me to verify the stamp and to pay you—nothing more. I assure you that I had no idea—"

"I said it's in the fire."

"But wait, please, you have no idea how valuable it is—"

"Five grand. I only asked for half."

"I can help you. I know other collectors, ones who would

ask no questions. They'd be glad to pay you its full worth. If
I had the money, I'd buy it myself.''

She took in his cheap clothes, her mouth becoming small
and thin. ''I'm sure you would.'' Her hand shot up and
knocked the pince-nez from his nose, and his head snapped
back a fraction too late to avoid it. They hung from the velvet
ribbon, swinging free and hitting the table edge with a soft
tick.

In turn his gray eyes hardened and his cowering posture
altered and straightened. ''We may still come to an equitable
arrangement, Miss Green.'' His breathy manner of speech
had been replaced by a precise English accent, and the prissy
mannerisms dropped from him like sour milk.

''Like hell we will, Escott. Stand up and follow Sled out
the back door.''

Escott glanced up as the big shadow of the man in gray
loomed over him. ''I meant what I—''

''Shut up or you get it now.''

He shot her a glum look and stood. He put on his hat and
reached for the cane, but Sled grabbed it first, grinning at
Escott's discomfiture. Sled opened the back door and started
through a short, dark passage that served as storage space
and led to the rear alley. The bartender watched me and pretended not to notice his other customers.

I gave up my drunk act and vanished into thin air. Maybe
he could pretend not to notice that, either.

Escott moved slowly through the passage after Sled. The
woman was behind him, presumably with her hand still on
the gun in her purse. For the moment I was only aware of
their bodies and general positions. The woman shivered as I
passed her, the way they say you do when someone walks
over your grave. Escott paused when I brushed past him and
had to be urged on; it was his way of letting me know he was
conscious of my presence.

Sled was out the back door now, waiting as Escott emerged
with the woman. I didn't know if Sled had his gun ready yet,
but hers was, so she'd have to be dealt with first.

I melted back into reality and solidified. From her point
of view I just came out of nowhere, which was essentially
correct. I slapped the gun from her grip, put a hand over her
mouth, another around her waist, then half lifted her away

into the dark. She made a nasal squeal of outrage, her heels flailing against my shins.

Sled's attention cut from Escott to her, and the gun jumped from the shoulder holster to his hand like magic. Escott grabbed it, forcing it down, and used his body to ram Sled against the brick wall of the dive. He was stronger than his thin frame promised, and the bricks did nothing for Sled's looks or disposition. He hit Escott with the cane, but it was at the wrong angle and he couldn't put his full strength in it. There was a meaty thump and gasp as Escott slammed the man's gun hand hard into the bricks. The gun dropped. The cane came down again. Escott took the blow against his side and at the same time led with a right that went halfway to Sled's backbone.

While they danced around, I tore the purse from the woman. Holding on to her was like trying to give a bath to an alley cat. I pushed her away from the melee, hoping she would have the sense to run. We wanted the stamp, not her. She was agile, though; one second she was getting her balance, the next she was making an unladylike tackle for Sled's gun.

She got it.

Her index finger slotted neatly over the trigger on the first try and she rolled and brought it up like an expert, firing point blank at me as I lunged. The yellow flash filled my whole world. I didn't hear the thing go off, maybe at that range it was too loud to hear. I felt the wrenching impact as the slug struck over my left eye and sent me on a slow, breathless tumble into white-hot agony.

Its duration was mercifully brief. I was writhing and solid one instant and weightless and floating the next. The shock and pain had knocked me incorporeal, temporarily releasing me from the burden of having a body full of outraged nerve endings. I wanted to stay in that non-place, but Escott's voice, distorted as though through layers of cotton, was dragging me back. He shouted my name once, and then the gun went off again.

I reappeared in time to see the smoke flaring away from its muzzle. Sled launched himself away from Escott, grabbed the protesting woman on the run, and dragged her off the battlefield.

Escott was leaning against the wall and had made no move to stop them. He was doubled over, struggling to breathe, with his arms curled tight around his stomach. His pale face stood out from the shadows like a fun-house ghost. Even as I found my feet he lost his and sank to the ground.

I was kneeling by him in a second, heart in my throat. "Charles?" My voice was all funny, as though it were borrowed from some stranger.

"Minute—" he gasped. He shut his eyes, let his mouth sag, and concentrated on drawing in air. I eased him more comfortably against the wall and tried to check his damage, but he shook his head.

"How bad?" I asked.

He showed a few teeth, but I couldn't tell if it was a grimace or a smile: with him it could go either way. His breathing evened a little and his eyes cracked open. "Where's the stamp?" he whispered.

Stamp? What the hell did that matter? "I'll get an ambulance."

"No need, I'm not hurt."

"You're doing a good imitation of it. Just hold on and—"

One of his hands came up. "Give me a minute and I'll be fine."

"Charles . . ."

The other hand came up. Clean. "I'm only winded."

"What the—"

"My bulletproof vest," he said with an air of stating the obvious.

I checked; under the rumpled clothes was a solid-feeling something encasing his torso.

"Unlike you," he continued, "I have no supernatural defense against flying bits of metal and must provide an artificial one."

I was stuck exactly at the halfway point between relief and rage. He wisely chose not to laugh at the expression I must have been wearing.

"I think I shall purchase a more effective vest for the future, though, this one seems a bit too thin for the job. Now, where is the stamp?"

Mutely, I handed over the beaded green bag. I didn't trust myself to say anything yet as it probably would have been too obscene. While he rummaged for the leather case I got up and checked the alley exit, putting some distance between us for a minute. On top of everything else, the son of a bitch didn't need a punch in the chops from a friend who was glad to see him alive.

Sled and the woman were long gone. It seemed like a good idea for us as well; their bartender friend might come out any minute, and we'd had enough excitement for one night.

Escott found and checked the case with its faded smudge of blue paper. "Philately is not an especial interest of mine. I fear I am quite unimpressed, even if it is worth five thousand American dollars."

"Yeah, well, let's make tracks before that girl remembers and decides to come back."

He saw the sense of it. "Would you help me up? I fear the bullet caught me near that knife wound, and things are still rather tender there. What rotten bad luck."

"I'd say it was pretty good since it missed your head." I got him to his feet and retrieved his cane.

"Heavens, are *you* all right? I saw you—"

"She was using lead, not wood, so I'm just peachy."

He decided to ignore the sarcasm. I was justifiably annoyed with him and he knew the best thing was to let it run its course.

He leaned on my arm for support as we gingerly picked our way out of the alley. Though his was pretty fair, he didn't have my night vision and relied on me to keep him afoot. We found his big Nash a block away. He insisted he could drive, so I shoveled him behind the wheel and took my place on the passenger side with a sigh.

"What went wrong back there?" I asked.

"She recognized me, for one thing, but that's all right because I recognized her."

"Okay, I'm holding my breath."

He spared me a sideways look, started the car, and pulled into the street. "I can believe that. She still might have been willing to deal, but the whole business went wrong because of Swafford's marked money. I should have checked it earlier."

"You really think she would have chanced a deal, even after spotting you?"

"It was a possibility. Even knowing me, she might have taken the money and given you the chance to follow, but then the best-laid plans and all that. Swafford has his precious stamp and cash, but he's going to hear a few words from me about it." He suddenly swung the car in a wide turn. "I think we shall visit him now while I'm still angry."

He didn't look angry—a touch gleeful, but not angry.

"It's after one," I pointed out.

"Good, then it is unlikely we will be interrupting any of his other appointments."

He drove to a suburb that had the kind of big houses with hot and cold running servants, precision-cut lawns, and cars that always started in the dead of winter. He picked out a lumpy stone specimen, sailed through the decorative iron gates, parked, and motioned me to follow. Some lights were showing through the downstairs windows, but they were only to discourage burglars and to keep Jeeves from tripping over the Chippendale while answering the front bell in the very early morning.

The bathrobed butler opened the door, decided we were strictly servant's-entrance material, and was about to close it, but Escott got past him and requested to see Mr. Swafford.

"Mr. Swafford has gone to bed," he informed us in chilling tones.

"Then I suggest you roust him or I shall have the unpleasant task of doing it myself."

Both of them had English accents, but Escott's was genuine, and the butler knew when he was outclassed. He sniffed at us, a bad mistake, because Escott still smelled like a stuffy church on Easter Sunday, and retreated upstairs. After a brief wait, Swafford came down under escort and gaped at us.

"Who the hell—"

"You engaged my services to recover your stamp," Escott reminded him.

Swafford squinted, trying to peer through the disguise. "Escott?"

"And my assistant, Mr. Fleming."

"What is all this, Escott?" he demanded in a small, thin voice that didn't suit him.

"We merely came by to return your property and discuss some details on the case."

"Then you have it? Where is it?"

"I see you have a library. Perhaps we shall be more comfortable there." Escott led the way as if it were his own house. Swafford glared at his back and then at me, ineffectually. I just waited until he got tired of it, then followed him into the next room.

He was wide and stocky all the way down to his slippered feet, and even a fancy silk bathrobe had a difficult time making him look society smooth. My guess was he made his money the hard way and was using it now in an attempt to make people forget about the work. His library bore this out, and was done up like something out of a movie, with an eye to impress the audience. There was a Renoir over the fireplace, but its function was to hide the safe and not to express the owner's tastes.

"Where's my stamp?" he asked, planting himself at one end of an acre of desk.

Escott was busy admiring the Renoir. "I rather like this one. What do you think of it, Jack?"

"Nice colors," I said noncommittally, keeping an eye on Swafford. He was awake enough now to know something was wrong and to try dealing with it.

Escott drew out the envelope full of hundreds and tossed it on the desk. Swafford grabbed it up and counted them. While he did this, Escott discovered a gold-plated candelabrum on an overvarnished table and lit all five of its candles. He carried it to the painting.

"Yes, either by diffuse daylight or by candlelight, that was how it was meant to be viewed." He placed the candelabrum on the desk. "I trust it is all there?"

"Yes, now where—"

"Then you may regard this case as closed."

Swafford looked up slowly and tried some hard thinking. "What happened to the stamp?"

"You signed a contract with me for my services, you should have read it. A good contract is designed to protect both parties should one attempt to defraud another. You defrauded me of your trust. Our association is ended."

"What are you talking about? Explain."

Escott gestured at the money. "That should be explanation enough. You had it marked and rather clumsily marked at that. The thief spotted it easily enough, realized I was not the philately expert, and gave me this.'' He exhibited the new ventilation on his coat and vest. ''You should have trusted me; your money and the stamp would have been returned as promised. Now you have only the money. You've forfeited the stamp.''

Swafford flushed a deep red that slowly faded to a muddy pink as he thought things over. ''All right, what do you want?''

''A telephone call to have the charges against Ruthie Mason dropped.''

''What else?''

''First the phone call.''

''But it's—''

''I know. Wake up your lawyer, that's what you pay him for, have him set things in motion.''

''If I do this, will the stamp be returned? Do you have it?''

Escott dropped the case on the desk. It thumped once against the thick blotter before Swafford grabbed and opened it.

''Empty!'' He froze. Escott held up a slip of paper folded into quarters. He waved it dangerously close to one of the candles.

''For God's sake be careful. That's worth five thousand—''

''Get on with the call,'' he snapped.

Swafford got on with the call. Since he couldn't argue with Escott he took it out on the lawyer, and before five minutes were gone another Chicago citizen had had his night's sleep broken up. Knowing how fast some cops liked to work, it was a good bet that the lawyer would be tied up until well after breakfast. For that he would certainly gift Swafford with a whopping fee. Escott knew the art of a properly administered low blow. While Swafford was on the phone, Escott turned up some paper and a carbon from the desk and wrote out several lines.

Swafford hung up. ''There, I've done it. Ruthie will be out in the morning.''

''I doubt she'll wish to continue her employment here. Should that be the case, she will need references, and good ones.''

"I'll have my wife do that—it's her job. The girl will have no trouble finding work."

"I also suggest a decent monetary gift to counterbalance her precipitant arrest."

"All right, you have my word . . . and there's your witness." He nodded confidently at me.

"Excellent. Now there is only the matter of my fee—"

"But you've been paid!"

"A retainer only. Under the terms of the contract I am within my rights to cover my expenses." His thumb emerged from the hole in the vest and wiggled. "Had I not taken precautions, you most certainly would have paid for my funeral, since your interference nearly caused it."

Swafford's face closed in on itself warily. "How much?"

He indicated the twenty-five hundred-dollar bills lying on the blotter. "I think that should cover it, but this time they're to be unmarked."

"But that's extortion," he grumbled.

"Earlier tonight you seemed eager enough to hand it over for the return of the stamp."

"At least then I might have gotten the stamp back."

"You may have that chance now; it depends upon how quickly you can open your safe. Our thief threatened to burn this when the marked bills were found; it occurs to me to be a very good idea. What a lot of fuss over a bit of blue paper the size of my thumbnail. Would the world stop spinning if I should commit it to the flames, I wonder?"

Before he could wave it near the candles again, Swafford had the Renoir swung to one side and was spinning the combination with nervous fingers. There was plenty more in the safe than twenty-five hundred, and he must have been worried we were after that as well. He gave me a wall-eyed look, and with good reason—I was still dressed like a hard-nosed punk, and the cheap booze stinking up my dirty shirt added to the image. I shifted my weight forward and tried to look tough. He quickly drew out a bundle of bills and hastily shut the safe.

Escott stood very close to the candles, their light and shadows making his minute smile look evil. "Would you mind counting it, Jack?"

I didn't. It made a tidy little pile: twenty hundreds and ten fifties. "It adds up right," I said, and pocketed it.

"Good. Now you will sign this, Mr. Swafford. It is nothing more than a receipt for my services, with a promise to pay that sum to Ruthie by tomorrow. I'm sure you'll find it as useful for your tax records as I do."

Swafford signed it and threw the pen down. Escott tucked away the original. He considered the folded paper between his two fingers, then suddenly put it into the candle flame. Swafford's eyes peeled back and he choked, one hand raised as if he were taking an oath. The scrap burned down to nothing and Escott dropped the ashes onto the desk. He looked thoughtful.

"Odd, I had imagined five thousand dollars going up in smoke would look much more impressive."

His former client was beyond speech and looked ready to have a coronary.

"Well, no doubt your insurance can cover it—oh, dear, you mean it is *not* insured? How careless of you to have something so very valuable and portable lying around uninsured. On the other hand there are taxes to pay on these things. But surely as a good citizen you pay your taxes?"

"I'll sue you," he whispered. "I'll have your hide—"

"Next time, Mr. Swafford, I suggest you follow instructions to the letter when they are given to you. It is simply good business practice, especially when not doing so can cost you dearly. I hope this has been a lesson to you. Remember it."

Escott swiftly crossed the room and we let ourselves out into the hall, leaving Swafford frozen in place by the desk. The butler was waiting and locked the front door behind us. Escott paused, counted to five, and went back to use the bell.

The butler was too sleepy to be annoyed. Escott extended his hand and gave him a folded paper identical to the one that had been burned. "I forgot to give this to Mr. Swafford. Please present it to him with my compliments."

He took it without comment and locked the door with a solid and final click.

Escott was still chuckling as we drove away.

"One of these days it'll be one of your own clients bumping you off for that kind of showboating," I said. "That's no way to attract business, either."

He shrugged. "His sort of business I do not need. Swafford nearly got me killed tonight. I thought I'd give him something equally unpleasant in return. For his sort, being deprived of money by his own folly is the worst kind of torture imaginable."

"Okay, he goofed in a big way, but then I nearly got you killed when I got optimistic about her brains and let her go too soon."

"An accident, nothing more. In the dark she could have just as easily shot her partner."

"She also could have run, but didn't. The lady wanted blood, Charles. She tried to kill us both."

"Through no fault of your own," he insisted. "I'll admit to underestimating her professionalism, but I place no blame upon you or your actions tonight. Even if things had gone according to plan, I daresay she might have tried to kill me anyway. Had you not been along, I would certainly be lying in that alley this very minute."

I shook my head. "I'm too dangerous to have around; I'm only an amateur to this gumshoe business—"

" 'Gumshoe'? Really, Jack." He looked pained.

"All right, private agent, then. I'm supposed to be a journalist."

"I don't hold that against you."

I let that one pass.

He tilted the rearview mirror, stretched his upper lip, and peeled the tiny moustache off, rubbing the area with evident relief. "That's better, these things drive me mad. Would you mind opening your window? You may not breathe, but it's still a habit with me."

I cranked it down. "Between your cheap perfume and my cheap booze, it'll take a week to air this buggy out."

"Possibly. I hope it washes off." His nose twitched.

"The suit?"

"My skin. I'm considering the suit might be better off in the furnace."

"Isn't that a little extravagant?"

"You're right, I'll see if I can't have it fumigated and repaired, as this is an amusing persona; it's based on someone

I saw once—the best disguises always are.'' With one eye on
the road and the other on the mirror, he carefully removed
his wig, lifting first from the base of his neck and bringing
it forward.

''But she still saw through it.''

''Not right away. She knew my name from Swafford's
household, but had never seen me close up and had no reason
to make the association. If he hadn't marked the bills . . .''

''So who was she? You got Swafford so upset he forgot to
ask.''

''Dear me, you're right. She was his wife's new personal
maid, the one with the unimpeachable references.''

I recalled a photo of the house servants he showed to me
earlier tonight when he asked me to help him. The idea was
to keep my eyes open should any of them walk into the bar
where the exchange had been set up. ''That little thing? She's
hardly more than a kid.''

''Yes, a mere child of twenty-seven, with a demure manner
and a youthful complexion. The Swaffords were correct to
suspect one of the servants, but I fear their accusations against
Ruthie were purely racial in origin. The other girl worked
and waited until someone new had been hired onto the staff;
Ruthie came along, the stamp was stolen, and she got the
blame. The thief's real name is Selma Jenks, and she's done
this sort of thing before.''

''You got a police blotter for a brain?''

''Just about. Anyway, Ruthie called Shoe Coldfield's sister
for help and Shoe called me. Swafford may have hired me to
recover the stamp, but I really consider Ruthie to be my true
client.''

''I wondered how you got the job. Swafford isn't your
type.''

''Too shady?''

''Too rich.''

It was close to two when Escott turned the car into the alley
behind his house and eased into the glorified shed that served
as a garage. The interior was too narrow to open the car door
very wide, and rather than struggle squeezing through, I disappeared and sieved out. I was sitting on the back bumper
when Escott finally emerged.

He gave a start and caught himself with a sigh. "Damn, but that's—"

"I know—unnerving. Sorry."

"Quite all right. Let's go inside, I'm in need of something liquid and soothing."

"Like a bath?"

"Yes, that, too."

He cursed sedately as he struggled with the rusty lock on the back door. It finally gave way and we walked into his large high-ceilinged kitchen. His house was a big, roomy place; a three-storied pre-fire relic that in its better days (or worse) had been a bordello. As his time, money, and health allowed, he was gradually cleaning, painting, and restoring it into a livable home. But the kitchen was not high on his priority list and still retained an air of cobwebby disuse in the corners. Except for replacing the old icebox with a stream-lined new refrigerator that crouched and hummed between sagging cabinets, he'd pretty much ignored the room.

In silent and common consent we peeled off our coats and dropped them on the battered oak table that had come with the house. An invisible cloud of booze and dead lilies filled the room and grabbed my throat.

Escott suppressed a cough. "Horrible stuff, that. Should I ever assume that persona again, I shall substitute something less lethal."

"Why use anything at all?"

"Attention to detail is the key to a good disguise."

"I think you poured on too much detail this time. You must have gotten perfume mixed up with cologne."

His brows went up. "There's a difference?"

"A lot, I think."

"What is it, then?"

Now I was stuck. "Uh . . . maybe you'd better ask Bobbi. She knows more about that kind of thing. All I know is there's a difference; one's stronger and you need less, or something like that."

"Hem," he said neutrally. "I know better than to offer you liquid refreshment. Do you mind if I indulge?"

"Go ahead. Just hold a glass under my shirt and I'll squeeze some out for you."

He declined with a polite but decisive head shake and

smile, and went into the dining room. There was no dining table yet, just a stack of cardboard boxes that hadn't been unpacked and a large glass-fronted cabinet on one wall holding a modest collection of bottles.

''Think I'll go and change. It's getting late,'' I said.

''You're welcome to use the bathtub if you like. The water heater is almost reliable now.''

''Thanks.'' I left him pouring out a gin and tonic and trotted upstairs. I'd scrub my face and hands off, but total immersion in a tub of possibly cold water was an experience I could do without.

My clothes were in a narrow bedroom next to the bath. The bed was long gone, leaving some holes in the floor where it had been bolted down and some rub marks from the headboard on the once florid wallpaper. There was no closet; my stuff was draped over a spindly wooden chair and more unpacked boxes.

Now that I was alone and changing back into familiar things, I felt a delayed reaction from the shooting tonight. I could avoid death in that manner, he couldn't. It didn't seem to disturb him, but I'd been thoroughly frightened, and I was far less vulnerable. If Escott hadn't been wearing that vest . . . Maybe he could treat the whole business casually, but not me. He hadn't seen the gun swinging up in his face and the muzzle flash searing his eyes. I touched the spot where the lead slug had passed through; all trace of pain was gone, the flesh and bone were smooth and unmarked.

My hand was trembling as it came away: half in wonder of what I'd survived and half in fear of what I'd become. A small mirror still clung to one wall, reflecting only the empty room, and nothing more. I shivered the length of my spine, turned away from it, and finished dressing.

Respectable again, I joined Escott in his downstairs parlor, where he'd stretched out on the sofa. He looked tired.

''This should cheer you up.'' I put the money on a low table next to his glass.

''What?'' He turned his head just enough to see. ''Oh, I'd forgotten.''

I dropped into a leather armchair. ''How can you forget twenty-five hundred bucks?''

''Twelve hundred fifty. Half of it's yours.''

"Come on, Charles, I didn't do anything except get in the way."

A faint smile twitched in one corner of his mouth. "As you insist. But whatever tonight's outcome would or would not have been, you are still entitled to something for your services to the Escott Agency. I'd give you all of it, but thought you wouldn't accept it."

"Don't be so certain."

"I'll fill out some kind of receipt later."

"For tax purposes?"

"Of course. I have always been impressed by the manner in which the government finally managed to take care of Capone."

"What's that have to do with me?"

"With both of us, my dear fellow. Undeclared income and income without employment are things that are certain to be noticed sooner or later. A person with your particular condition need not call attention to himself."

"Okay, I see what you mean. What about that bundle we picked up from the Paco gang in August?"

"I said then we should consider it the spoils of war, but I plan to declare my half. I wonder if there is some sort of penalty in padding one's records in favor of the government?"

"In a bureaucracy do you think they'd notice? And it's gotten a lot bigger and more complicated since Roosevelt got in."

"I see, yes, what a ridiculous question. Still, I suppose the best thing is to store the lot in a mattress and declare it a little at a time over the years. Ah, well, here's to crime." He drained off his glass and grimaced.

"You all right?"

"Probably. I shall be stiff for a few days. Bad coincidence getting hit in the same spot."

"Let's have a look."

He'd already taken off his suit vest. Now he shucked the shirt and I helped him ease out of the bulletproof vest underneath. On his left side just below the line of his ribs was a thin red scar about four inches long where a thug's knife had cut him up not so long ago. He probed the area gently with his long fingers and winced a little.

"There, it caught me a bit lower than I thought. Nothing more than a bad bruise and some shock. Quite lucky, considering how close the gun was."

"Charles, about all you had going for you tonight was luck. If her aim had been a little better or worse she could have taken your head off."

"So you mentioned earlier."

"I'm gonna mention it again. You scared the shit out of me tonight."

"I truly appreciate your concern, but after all, nothing really happened, and I do intend to be more careful in the future."

"You mean that?"

"Certainly. This was an isolated incident. Before I met you the most violent encounter I'd ever experienced was a director with a vile temper who tried to kill me with his blocking of a stage fight."

I was verging on exasperation, but too curious to pass up the opening. He rarely spoke about his past. "What happened?"

"It was the difference between his opinion and my facts. The man had concocted some ridiculous fencing movement and I tried to point out something safer and more natural for the circumstance. Since I was only a very junior member of the company at the time, he got his way. On dress-rehearsal night I slipped in my felt costume shoes, fell into the orchestra pit, and broke the poor violinist's collarbone and nearly my own neck when I landed on him. I was never able to convince that director I hadn't done it on purpose just for spite."

I pulled my mouth shut to control the laugh. "Now you're changing the subject—"

"But I have not. My point was that tonight was an unfortunate set of circumstances, nothing more. In all fairness, how could the director or I have known that the stage floor had just been waxed? How could you have known the young lady was so murderously and athletically inclined? Believe me, if any future jobs like this should come my way, there is no one else I would rather have to back me up. I know you have doubts now, but you've a quick, observant eye and with a little training . . ."

I shot him a suspicious look. "What have you got planned? A little extra paint on the office door saying Escott and Fleming, Private Agents?"

"That would be interesting, but not possible. It takes several years of training to qualify for a license, and then you have to show up for the exam—in daylight. No, in practical terms that's quite out of the question for you."

"Then what is in the question?"

"I'm only proposing the odd job now and then, like tonight. I know you really consider this as just doing me a favor, but there's no reason why you can't make something for yourself out of it." He looked at the money and then at me.

"You trying to bribe me? Because it's working."

The faint smile appeared again in the same corner. "I had hoped you would consider it seriously. Of course one never knows what the future may bring; not all of my clients are as well off as Mr. Swafford, nor as easily bullied, but there should be enough coming in to keep gas in your car and so forth."

I put my half of the cash in my wallet. "This should buy a lot of so forth."

He smiled again at this obvious acceptance of his offer, briefly, this time in both corners.

▲
2
▼

It was nearly three when I left Escott's, but Bobbi would be awake. She may have left her job and her room at the Nightcrawler Club, but she still kept club hours. Her new home was a suite in a respectable hotel that provided maid service, meals, and a bribable house detective—everything a girl could want.

I crossed the marble-floored lobby, waving at the night clerk, who knew me by sight. The kid in the elevator was sound asleep on his stool, so I charitably took the stairs up to the fourth floor. Her rooms were to the left of the stairs, taking up a corner block of windows that fronted the building. Light was showing under her door. I knocked softly, heard her bare feet patter close, and a single hazel eye peered through the peephole. I winked back and the door opened.

"Hello, stranger, I was beginning to think you'd never show up." She pulled me inside and locked out the rest of the world.

"So you're taking me for granted, huh?"

"Uh-huh, just like the laundry."

"You dress up like that for the laundry?"

"This is dressing down; something informal, yet intimate." She was wearing some baby blue satin lounging pajamas that made it difficult for me to think straight. When she walked, her legs made a pleasant susurrous sound. Slightly hypnotized by the rhythm, I followed her into the living room as we curled up on the sofa. At least she curled—

I stretched my legs out and hooked an arm around her shoulder.

"What kept you so long?" she asked.

"Charles needed some help tonight."

"What did he do, drag you backward through a distillery?" She sniffed my hair critically.

"Just about. Thought I'd lost the atmosphere of the place when I'd changed."

"Into what?"

"What do you mean 'into what'?"

"A bat or a wolf—"

"What are you talking about?"

She pulled a thick book from under a pillow and tapped the lurid red letters of the title with one nail. "It says in here . . ."

Then I had to laugh and shake my head. "Bobbi, you nut, you can't be taking that seriously."

"Well, it's the only book I knew of about vampires."

"There are lots of others, but they're not necessarily right, either. Why are you looking at that stuff? You've already got the real article."

"I wanted to know more. According to this, you'll be turning me into one any time now." She said it like a joke, but I could see a real concern underneath. She waited for my reaction.

I took the book and flipped through until I found the right page. "There, read that part and try to ignore the scary language. Until we do this there is no chance of you ever turning into a vampire." I waited, listening to her soft breathing as she read, my arm close around her shoulders. She finally let the book droop.

"*That* scene wasn't in the movie."

"Too erotic."

"Erotic?" She sounded doubtful.

"Don't let the description put you off until you've tried it."

She looked speculative. "You want to do that?"

"Not unless you want to. It's your decision."

"What would happen?"

"One hell of a climax for both of us."

"And that's all? Not that there's anything wrong with a great climax," she quickly added.

"I'm glad you think so."

"Come on, Jack. What else is it?"

I rubbed absently at that spot over my eye. "Okay, it's got to do with reproduction . . ."

"You mean I could get pregnant?" That possibility alarmed her.

"No, I mean you could get like me. My taking from you is one thing, but if you should take any of my blood, there's a remote chance you could be like me after you died."

"Would it kill me?"

"No, of course not."

"How remote a chance?"

"I don't know. As I understand it, it almost never works because nearly everyone is immune. They'd have to be or there'd be more people like me around."

"Maybe there are and you just haven't noticed them. You don't exactly look like a vampire, you know."

"Not the Hollywood kind, anyway."

"I mean you don't stand out in a crowd."

"Oh, thank you very much."

She swatted my shoulder.

"Okay, okay, I know what you meant."

She settled in again. "This kind of reproduction . . . is that why we don't make love the usual way?"

"Yes," I said shortly.

"Hey, don't clam up on me, I was just asking."

"I know, honey."

I tried to relax and succeeded to some extent. She'd hit a sore spot, but it wasn't an unexpected blow. I wasn't—to put it delicately—fertile in the way that men are usually fertile with women. The pleasure centers and how they operated had drastically shifted. Oddly enough, I did not feel deprived, physically or mentally; I just felt that I *should* feel deprived, or that maybe Bobbi was losing out on things. There was no justification for it, so far our relationship was as mutually satisfying as anyone could wish for.

She snuggled closer under my arm. "If you want to know, I really prefer it your way."

"You mean that?"

She lifted my hand and pressed it against the soft, warm

skin of her throat. "When you do it this way, it just goes on and on. . . ."

That was how it felt to me. As a breathing man, I'd had some great experiences, but they were hardly an adequate comparison to what I now enjoyed.

"Sometimes I think I'll go crazy from it," she murmured, kissing my hand.

My lips lightly brushed her temple, the small vein pulsed beneath them. Of their own will, my hands began to undo her buttons. "You sure you like it this way?"

"Yes, and for another good reason: I don't have to worry about getting pregnant."

"Hmmm."

She sat up straight, her top open almost to the waist and her perfect red lips curled into a sleepy, roguish smile. She nodded her head once toward the bedroom. "Come on, let's go get more comfortable."

Bobbi made a contented growl in the back of her throat, turned on her side, and burrowed close with her back to me, out bodies fitting together like two spoons. I draped an arm over her, and if my hand happened to end up cupping her left breast, nobody minded. We were in a lazy post-lovemaking afterglow and life was good.

"It's funny how you can get used to things," she said.

"I'm boring you?"

"I didn't mean it that way, and no, I'm anything but bored with you."

"Thanks for the reassurance. What is it you're used to?"

"I was remembering the time when I first noticed you didn't always breathe. It bothered me and now it doesn't. I just thought it was a funny thing to think of as normal."

"For me it is normal."

"Oh, I know that now."

"What else are you used to?"

"Umm . . . the no-heartbeat thing. But if you live on blood, how does it get through your body?"

"Beats me. Charles is speculating it's some kind of osmosis."

"What's that?"

I'd asked Escott the same question and tried to repeat his

answer to her. It must have been garbled—laboratory biology and chemistry had never been my best studies—but she took in enough to understand.

"It sounds like the way a root draws water up into a plant," she suggested.

"Maybe so, just as long as it works."

"What about mirrors? Have you figured out why you don't show up?"

"Nope."

"Let me know when you do, 'cause I'm not used to that, yet."

"If it's any comfort, neither am I."

"You mean you can't even see yourself?"

"Nope."

"Do you know you need a haircut?"

"Hum a few bars."

She groaned. "That stunk."

"It's old enough. Anything else?"

"That's it for now."

"Until you can think of something else to analyze?"

"If you want deep intellect, go to bed with a philosopher."

"Thank you, no."

"I thought you'd say that." She was quiet for a while, resting her head comfortably on my extended arm. I nosed into the platinum silk she had for hair and began kissing the nape of her neck. She squirmed. "You want to go again?"

"It might not be good for you. Your body has to adjust gradually, even to a small blood loss. Too often . . ."

"But you don't take much."

"Neither did those doctors who killed a king from too much bloodletting."

"I heard of that, I think he was English. But this is different and I'm very healthy." She twisted up on one elbow to look at me. The satin sheet slipped down quite a bit.

"Yes . . . I can see that."

She made a face. "I'm serious. I've been eating liver like crazy, and I hate liver."

"I had no idea."

"So do you want to go again?"

"It's very tempting, but better for you if we wait."

She thought about it, decided not to push the issue, and

wiggled back into my arms again. "Who taught you all this restraint?"

I pretended it was a rhetorical question and resumed nuzzling her hair. It smelled lightly of roses.

She went on. "I can't help but be curious about her. I won't ask anymore if you don't want me to."

"But you'll still wonder."

"Uh-huh."

"Her name was Maureen." The words dropped out like lead, as always when I talked of her in the past tense.

"I can tell you loved her a lot. It's the way you look when you think about her."

"It's that obvious?"

"Sometimes. You'll be looking at me and then I'm not there for you, and I know you're seeing her instead."

"Sorry."

"It's all right. Are we much alike?"

"Her hair was dark and she was shorter."

"I didn't mean like that."

"She needed love," I said lamely.

"Everyone does."

"She needed it like . . . I don't know. It was all that mattered to her."

"And you loved each other a lot."

"God, yes. But I didn't realize how much until—we were both happy, a long time ago."

"I'm glad you were, that you had something like that. I never did—until now." Her voice was soft, I thought she was drifting off to sleep.

I tried to remember Maureen's face, but it was like recalling a dream. The harder I tried, the farther it slipped away.

"I hope you believe me," she said.

"About what?"

"About liking your style better."

"Thanks. Are you sure you don't miss the old way, though?"

She shrugged. "Not much. It's apples and oranges; I like 'em both when it's done right."

My hands began wandering again. She rolled on her back and we did some serious kissing. Her breath came faster and her heart rate went up.

"I thought you weren't going to take any more from me tonight."

"I'm not, but maybe you'd like some oranges?"

"What?"

I kissed her again, one hand passing over her smooth flank, dipping at the waist and pausing briefly just below her navel.

"Oranges," she murmured. "Handpicked, of course."

Asleep, she looked younger than her twenty-four years. Sleep lent vulnerability and vulnerability brought youth. I watched her protectively, feeling a fierce, quiet joy at the sight of her relaxed features. A little makeup clung to the pale skin, a trace of powder high on one cheek and the faint line of drawn-on brows. Her own had been carefully plucked away to follow the current fashion. I had seen many pretty faces, but few classic beauties, and fewer still with brains and personality. She was beautiful, at least as I perceived it, with the kind of looks that artists sometimes capture, if they have the talent.

Her blond head turned on the pillow, the lips parting slightly then closing. They were light pink now; all the lip rouge had been kissed away quite awhile ago. From previous experience I could guess that if any were left it would be on me. I didn't mind a bit.

It was a hard chore to leave, but necessary—the sunrise was coming and with it my daytime oblivion. I eased out of bed, got dressed, and kissed her forehead in farewell.

Her eyes opened, but she was still nine-tenths asleep. "Are you a dream?"

"Yes."

"Thought so." There was a sigh and she slipped under again.

After being with Bobbi, it was always a rude jolt to come back to my own spartan hotel room. The essentials were there: a bed, rarely used, a chest of drawers, a chair, a bath, even a radio. For $6.50 a week it was luxurious, but not really a home.

Bobbi knew where I hung my hat, but had never been invited over. There was little reason for it since her own place was more comfortable and larger. For one thing, she did not have a three-by-five-foot steamer trunk taking up most of the floor space. More than once the bellhop had asked if I wanted to have it stored in the basement. I tipped well so he was always alert to do me a favor. A basement might be better to avoid sunlight, but was not as safe. During the day I needed a DO NOT DISTURB sign hanging from the doorknob and the door firmly locked against curious eyes. The trunk was locked as well, the key on a chain hanging from my neck. Once, after getting back too late, the sun had caught me out. I'd been unable to sieve inside as usual and suffered a painful and panicky search for the key, an incident I planned never to repeat.

I drew a hot bath, cleaned the remaining booze smell from my hair, and tried to get comfortable on the lumpy bed. The bellhop had left my regular pile of newspapers outside the door. I filled in the remaining time before dawn flipping through them. Nothing in the news held my attention, and that felt odd since it had once been my bread and butter. Times change, people change, and I had certainly changed more than most.

Automatically, my eyes scanned the personal columns, but as ever, there was nothing to see. Five years had gone by without a response.

The papers went into the wastebasket. I thought of Bobbi, and with a sharp twist of guilt, I thought of Maureen.

I remembered the touch of her body, smaller and stronger, with dark hair and light blue eyes. I remembered the long nights spent loving her and our hope that it would last forever. Together we decided to at least try to make it so. I had no guarantee that it would work for me, but the hope was there; it would have to be enough. After taking from me, she tilted her head back, drawing the skin taut, and used her fingernail in a deft movement over the vein in her throat. She pulled me close and I tasted the warmth of what had been my blood, filtered through her body and returned again. Its red heat hit me from the inside out like the rush of air from an open furnace. A shock of fire, a flash of inner light, and then the shimmer of her life filling me . . .

My hands clenched. There was no comfort in remembered passion, it was all gone. Maureen was gone.

But Bobbi was here, vital and loving. I wanted and needed her just as much. It was hardly fair to her to have my mind drifting back to Maureen at awkward moments, nor was it fair to myself.

I found paper and wrote out instructions. It took less than two minutes, and another three passed downstairs as I explained what I wanted to the night clerk. He promised to fix everything. A minute for each year of searching and waiting, and that was how long it took to break off my last hope of contacting her. I felt empty, but no worse than usual. With Bobbi to help I could put the memories away for good. It was time to let the past rest; let it rest or it would continue to tear me up inside.

Let it rest, because God knows I was tired.

"Mr. Fleming?" It was the bellhop's voice, sounding faintly worried. His knuckles rapped on the door. "Mr. Fleming?"

I had no twilight moment of grogginess; I was either awake or totally unconscious. I faded from the interior of the trunk, re-formed outside, and answered the door, pretending to look sleepy.

"Yeah, what is it, Todd?"

"Sorry to wake you, but you got this phone message and the guy said it was urgent. He's been calling all day. You never answered, so we figured you were out." He gave me a slip of paper.

I unfolded it and read Escott's name and the phone number of his small office a few blocks away. He wanted me to call or come over immediately.

"You say he's called earlier?"

"A couple of times since I came on at four. It sounded important and I've been trying—"

"Okay, thanks for bringing it up. Did Gus get around to that stuff like I asked?"

"Yessir, got 'em all, he said to tell you. You still want your usual delivery?"

"Yeah, go ahead with that," I said absently, rereading the brief note. Escott certainly knew better than to try contacting me during the day, so he must be in some kind of trouble. I dressed and shot down to wedge into the lobby phone booth.

He answered on the first ring, sounding perfectly normal.

"Hello, Jack, I've been trying to reach you."

"What's up?"

"Something extremely interesting. Another case, as a matter of fact. I'd like to talk it over with you right away."

"Sure, I'm on my way."

"Have you dined yet?"

"Well . . ."

"We could talk details over dinner—my treat."

I struggled to keep alarm from my tone. "Sounds great. Meet at your office?"

"Certainly."

My premature relief was blown to bits. His perfectly normal manner had not been for me but for the benefit of whoever was in the office and listening to the call. He knew I no longer required ordinary food and was unavailable before sunset, but the listener did not. It did indeed look like the start of an interesting case.

Dusk was taking its own sweet time; the sky was still harsh and bright to me when I started my Buick. I fumbled on my sunglasses to ease the light down to a comfortable level. It didn't take long to cover the distance to Escott's office and park around the corner from his door. I wanted to check things out first before barging in.

He had two modest rooms on the second floor, each with a window fronting the street. Both were wide open because of the warm weather, but the blinds were drawn. Slices of light showed through the right-hand room. The left, which served the back room, was still dark. Without hurry I walked until I was positioned directly under it, and since the street was momentarily clear, partially vanished.

By concentrating, I could control the degree of transparency. My body took on all the solidity of a double-exposed photo and about half the weight. My hand went out and I could see the bricks of the building through it. Like a helium balloon, but with gripping fingers, I went up to the second story. I did not look down. I hate heights.

I made it to the window and thankfully slipped inside, but retained my current state. This semi-solid form left me visible—if alarming to any witnesses—but did not deprive me of sight and speech and gave me agile and perfectly silent movement.

The connecting door between the rooms was wide open. A bright fan of light spilled in from the front, so I took care to avoid it and folded the sunglasses away for unrestricted vision.

Escott was seated behind his desk, his back to me and his head turned slightly to the right. A chair stood on that side, and from his posture alone I could guess it was occupied.

I vanished completely and got close enough to him to give him a chill. After a moment, he stifled a shiver and cleared his throat. I drew off to one side to see what he wanted of me.

He cleared his throat again. "May I go get some water?"

A woman answered him. "No."

"I thought perhaps you might want some as well."

There was no reply.

"You might not be able to get us both, you know. My associate is extremely fast when he wants to be."

"I remember how fast, but no one's this fast."

"Perhaps. The first shot will be the most important. After that . . . well, homemade silencers are notorious for problems."

"Not this one."

Escott was taking a hell of a risk apprising me of the situation in this manner. She could get the idea to shoot him first and then wait for me to come along later. If my scalp had been intact, the skin would be crawling.

Their conversation died, but had lasted long enough for me to get an idea of their relative positions. She was seated with her back to the wall next to the open window, about seven feet from Escott, close enough not to miss hitting him, but not so close that he could try taking the gun from her. There were also a few seconds of critical time in her favor, since he was seated so firmly behind the desk. As far as I could tell from a swirling sweep of the office, they were alone.

The problem wasn't too complicated. I could appear and grab the gun away before she knew what hit her. It was something I'd managed before, but a dark alley was a different situation from a well-lit office. She would wonder where I'd come from and how I'd gotten so close without being seen. If the cops got involved there might be more complications, and I could *not* risk coming to official attention.

"Where is he?" The ground-glass quality was back in her voice.

"Please be patient. It won't be long."

"It's been too goddamned long as it is. Call and see if he's left."

"As you wish."

I heard dialing sounds. Her attention would be fully focused on Escott. I got into place in front of the window. She was right-handed and that would be the one to grab. I readied my own hands—or what would become my hands—over hers.

Just as Escott said hello I re-formed and twisted the gun from her grip. The hammer had been cocked back and the safety off. Hardly any pressure was needed to finger the trigger; my attempt to disarm her was more than enough. The thing suddenly jumped and coughed, and a neat hole appeared in the far wall. I yanked the smoking rod free and let it drop. It decided not to go off again.

She jumped up and both my hands were full, one cutting off her surprised and angry shriek and the other pinning her arms. Escott hung up the phone, came stiffly around the desk, dodged her kicks, and grabbed her ankles. We shoved her back down in the chair by weight alone, needing every pound because she squirmed and bucked like a hooked pike.

"I must confess that you are a most welcome sight," he told me, still struggling with her legs.

"Anytime. Now what do we do with her?"

"The police, I suppose. They still want her for that robbery."

"Can you leave me out of it? I'm in no shape for a court appearance."

"Yes, as you wish. But without you for a witness, this incident could end up as my word against hers, that is, if I press charges."

"With her record do you need to?"

"Let's put it this way: after what I've been through today, I would very much *like* to. Hang on a bit. I've some cuffs in the desk."

He released her ankles and dodged another kick as he picked up the dropped automatic. He took it off cock, removed the magazine, emptied the firing chamber of its bullet, and put it away in his desk. From the same drawer, he drew out and opened a set of cuffs.

I put pressure on her shoulders to keep her in place and

nimbly kept my fingers away from her teeth. Escott clicked the cuffs over her wrists, then produced a washcloth and a long strip of bandage from the tiny bathroom in back. Between us we shoved the cloth in her mouth and tied it firmly in place so that her outraged screams wouldn't bring well-intentioned, but misinformed help. Some of the fight went out of her by then, but I wasn't going to relax my hold.

Escott was puffing. "This is certainly no way to treat a lady."

"I could debate that," I replied, sucking a finger. She'd managed to lock her teeth on it for a few seconds while we were gagging her.

Selma Jenks, alias Miss Green, glared hard and hatefully at each of us, and I hoped the daggers she was throwing remained wishful ones. Today she wore a now-rumpled blue dress; the remains of a matching hat were on the floor. The skirt part had hiked up in the struggle, revealing a nice stretch of leg and the gartered tops of her blue stockings. I made a move to pull the skirt down, but she threatened to start up again, so I left things alone.

Escott excused himself and went back to the bathroom for his belated glass of water and other things. He returned, his tie loosened a little, and painfully eased his cramped limbs.

"She walked in at two o'clock and kept me sitting there all bloody afternoon. Five hours in one spot is certainly brutal on the lower spine."

"You sat there for five hours?"

He shrugged. "It was that or get shot. She was quite upset on how we'd crossed her last night and even more upset that we survived. She looked my name up in the phone directory and came a-hunting. It is my admittedly inexpert opinion that she is more than a little loony."

"Loony?"

"That's the word." He sighed deeply and drew a handkerchief over his face. "She kept me calling your hotel to get you over here, I did what I could to warn you."

"It worked."

"Thank heaven. Spending the day a bare two yards from a nerved-up woman holding a hair trigger is not my idea of entertainment."

"It isn't?"

He shot me a considering look and let it pass. "Well, I suppose it's time to call the police."

"What about her partner, Sled?"

"From the little she dropped in conversation, I got the impression he doesn't know about this, nor, I think, would he approve."

"That's something. So maybe he's not down the street waiting for her."

"Quite likely. He'd have been up here ages ago to find out what was taking so long."

"All the same, could you go out the back way and take a look around just to be sure? He might guess where she is, and if he's down there any cop car will spook him off. You could spot him better than I, you know the street."

"Well, just to be safe . . . I'll be back shortly." He went to the back and I heard the sounds of his exit. He'd equipped the bathroom with a hidden panel that opened onto the up-stairs storeroom of a tobacco shop that faced the next street over. He used it now to make a discreet exit outside without exposing himself to anyone watching his regular doorway.

As soon as he was gone, Selma launched from her chair for the door, slipping from my grip like a greased eel. Catching her was no problem, but she was stubborn and full of fight, and in the end I had to lift her bodily and swing her down on the floor with a thud. She was small and that helped, but it was a hell of a lively wrestling match. I threw one leg over her knees, pinning them flat, used one hand to keep her nails out of my eyes, and the other clamped across her forehead. By a little twisting, we were intimately face-to-face. Her eyes were wild, the whites showing all around, but not from fear; her skin under the powder was flushed beet red from sheer fury.

She abruptly stopped fighting, her breath loud and labored through her nose, and stared at me with pure loathing, waiting for my next move. She knew nothing about me, Escott was gone, along with any protection his presence offered. I was someone unknown to her and taking advantage of the opportunity while it was available. No doubt from certain points of view I would be guilty of a kind of rape, but for me it would make things a lot easier.

My eyes on hers, I said her name.

* * *

Escott returned from a clear street in ten minutes and found
us as before in the office. I still held her shoulders, but she
had calmed down considerably.

"May as well call the cops," I said as soon as he came
in. He dialed the number and asked for someone by name.
He explained the situation and was told to expect a car to
come right away.

"All the business at the station will take a bit," he said
after hanging up. "I suppose a late supper will have to do for
me."

I nodded in sympathy. "I'll wait till the cops are at the
door and go out the back. You can handle this wildcat for
that long."

"She's not so wild now," he observed.

"Probably tired herself out."

"Indeed. Thank you for coming. I hope it didn't disrupt
your evening unduly."

Bobbi and I were going to the movies, we'd still be able
to catch the second feature.

The cops showed up in due time. At the last second, Escott
cut away her gag, tossed it to me, and I slipped into the back.
I waited long enough to hear the opening questions, then
went out the window the same way I entered. My car and I
were long gone by the time they were ready to take her away.

Bobbi had wanted to see *Last of the Mohicans* because she
liked Randolph Scott, but Escott's accent had given me a taste
for Shakespeare, and I talked her into going to *Romeo and
Juliet* instead. Much to her own surprise, she enjoyed it.

"You can understand what they're saying in this one," she
commented during intermission. We'd arrived late and missed
the newsreel and cartoon, but were in no particular hurry to
leave. I bought her an extra soda and popcorn while we waited
for the next cycle of features to start.

"Why not? The sound's good."

"Well, I saw this once as a stage play and it was awful.
The actors were bellowing to reach the back row and talked
so fast you couldn't understand a thing. This kind of stuff you
gotta talk clearly so you know what's going on. I like it as a
movie better than on the stage."

"I should get you and Charles together to discuss it."

"Oh, yeah, but he's a good egg, he'd let me win just to be polite."

"Don't be too sure, he's got some pretty firm ideas about the stage and Shakespeare in particular."

"Staging I don't know, but I could give him a tough time about Shakespeare."

"How do you mean?"

"Like this show, it was good, but the girl was a nitwit for not running away from home to start with. That's what I would have done. She was wearing enough jewels to live off of for years."

"It wouldn't have been a great tragedy, then."

"Romeo could have swiped her money, left her stranded—anything could have happened."

"That's kind of a negative view."

"It's more believable than gulping down drugs to fake your own death. I think it stinks that Shakespeare didn't let them get together in the end like they wanted, after all the trouble they went through. What made you want to see this instead of Randolph Scott?"

"He makes me jealous."

"No, really."

"They had the biggest ad in the paper and this is a fancier theater. I wanted to impress you."

She glanced at our opulent surroundings. "It worked. They could show a blank screen and people would still pay admission to sit here."

"They do."

"What?" She was half-wary for a joke.

"No kiddin', I knew this usher who swore to me that the ticket is for the chair you sit in, the movie itself is free."

"That's crazy."

"Nah, that's just the way it works out. This usher also told me that theaters make most of their money off popcorn sales."

"It must take a hell of a lot of five-cent bags to pay the rent on this joint."

"Eat up, then, I'll get you another. I like this place."

Another evening ended very pleasantly and as ever I was reluctant to leave. When I dragged my feet back to my hotel room in the small hours, though, I found Escott waiting for me. He was drowsing in my one chair, his feet propped up on the trunk.

I shook his shoulder. "Anything wrong?"

He blinked fully awake and alert. "I think not. Did you enjoy your movie?"

"How'd you know I went to a movie?"

He indicated the paper I'd left on the bed, opened to the entertainments section. "Or perhaps you went to a nightclub, but I recall hearing Miss Smythe state she was fed up with them for the time being."

"She is, but how'd—"

"Her rose scent is quite distinctive, and traces of it linger on your clothes. What film did you see?"

"*Romeo and Juliet*. It was pretty good."

"Yes, the principals were decent enough, if a little old for their parts, but the fellow playing Tybalt seemed to know what he was doing."

I had no illusions that he'd been waiting all night to deliver a review. "Charles . . ."

He straightened, putting his feet on the floor and fixing me in one spot with his eyes. "I came by to have you satisfy my curiosity."

"About what?" I tried to sound casual, but it wasn't working. He was far too sharp for me to lie to him, but I wasn't going to make it easy.

"About Selma Jenks . . . It was very odd, but when they began questioning her, she made a complete confession."

"She did?"

"In fact, she confessed to every robbery and extortion she and her partner committed since they teamed up. She then told the police where he could be found. They lost no time bringing him in, though he was not nearly so cooperative as Selma."

"Sounds like a good thing, though."

"Yes, an excellent bit of luck. But now I'm curious as to what you said to her after you got me out of the room."

"I want you to know that that was a legitimate request."

"I don't doubt it, but it was convenient for you. Did you hypnotize her?"

My tie suddenly felt too tight. I tore it loose and tossed it on the bed. He waited patiently, knowing there were some things about my nature I was reluctant to discuss.

"It seemed like the easiest thing to do. I didn't want her talking about me or giving you more trouble than you needed. I just calmed her down and gave her a few suggestions."

He was amused. I'd expected reproach. "Suggestions? Good Lord, you should be in the district attorney's office with that talent. You'd never lose a case. I doubt if a priest could have gotten so thorough a confession."

I shrugged. "But it showed. You knew."

"Only because I got so well acquainted with her that afternoon. Her behavior at the station was normal enough, but such a flood of information was hardly in keeping with her personality."

"You said she was a loony," I pointed out.

He got up, stretching his muscles with small, subtle movements. "Why were you so reluctant to tell me about this?"

I shook my head. "I don't know. I didn't want to tip her off to any funny business, I didn't want an audience, stuff like that. What I did, it's not something . . . well, it's . . ." I broke off with a tired and inadequate gesture for my feelings.

"Nothing you need be ashamed of," he quietly concluded. He let that sink in for a thick moment, then picked up his hat. "Well, this has been a long day—and night."

I grabbed at the change of subject. "You wait long?"

"No more than an hour."

"You could have called me at Bobbi's."

"It was hardly a pressing issue, I'd no wish to disturb you. Phone calls at late hours are bad for the heart."

"Thanks." I meant it for more than just his consideration.

He echoed my reply from earlier. "Anytime."

3

IT WAS ONE in the morning and the same pair of headlights had been bumping around in my rearview mirror for most of the night. I noticed them first when I left Chicago, assumed they belonged to a fellow traveler on the same route, and forgot about them.

I stopped briefly at an all-night service station in Indianapolis, stretched my legs, and bought some gas. Owing to a wrong turn and getting lost in some downtown streets for a while, I didn't get back on the main road immediately. There wasn't much traffic at that hour, but my eyes were occupied with things in front of me, so the car hanging fifty yards off my rear bumper went unnoticed. Finally on the right road again and mentally congratulating myself for getting unlost, I settled in for the last leg of my drive, starting with a routine check in the mirror.

Until the night I woke up dead, I'd never been very paranoid, no more than anyone else, so the familiar look of the car took awhile to penetrate my thick skull. It wasn't a conscious thought process; more like a gradual dawning. When the realization finally came it left me wondering how I could have been so slow.

My night vision allowed me to see past the glare of the headlights to the occupants of the car. There was little detail at this distance, I could only make out their figures: the slightly hunched posture of the driver, and next to him, a shorter man in a hat. They were in a black car, fairly new. I thought it was a Lincoln, but couldn't be sure from the fore-shortened image in the mirror.

Not quite ready to believe that they might be following me, I decided a little testing might break up the monotony of the trip. Easing slowly off the gas, I dropped my speed to ten miles below the limit. Most drivers will keep coming right up your tail until they get impatient enough to pass. But this guy was on the ball and his speed dropped as well. When I came to a hill and crested, I hit the gas and let the momentum bring me up to the limit and over. I gained half a mile on him while he was on the other side, but when his turn came he easily caught up. There was a lot of power under his hood.

It could have been coincidence, but I was disturbed. If they really were following me, I wanted to know why.

About twenty minutes later I signaled a right turn and leisurely pulled off the road onto the shoulder. The black car—it was a new Lincoln—went past without the men inside turning to look. I saw only a dark, blurred profile that could have been anyone. They continued on until a long, wide curve took them from sight.

Just in case they'd stopped and were watching from a distance, I got out, stretched, and walked into some sparse trees that sheltered the side of the road. As I walked, I made fiddling movements with my belt and fly. I didn't have to go, but could pretend, and stood with my ears wide open. My hearing was extremely sensitive now, but the wind was blowing in the wrong direction for me to pick up any motor noises ahead. For the sake of my nerves, I dawdled another five minutes, leaning against the car and superficially puffing a cigarette for something to do.

Once back on the road, I eased up to speed with my eyes peeled, but there was no sign of them. I was still edgy. It had only been a couple of fast weeks since my life had been completely disrupted by some of the more violent members of Chicago's gangland. The thought that some grudge-bearing survivors of that fracas might be after me was not a comfortable one. They'd killed me once already, once was more than enough.

Briefly, I thought about turning back, then vetoed the thought. More than half the journey was behind me, and if it came to it, I could handle two jokers playing road games. I had an errand in my hometown that I wanted to get done. If I ran into a little trouble along the way, I could always rag Escott about it later. The trip was originally *his* idea.

The second night after our match with Selma Jenks, I woke up and again found him sitting in my old chair. I never minded his drop-in visits because he always had a good reason behind them.

"Good evening," he said. "At least I hope you will find it so. Things have cooled off a bit."

Fairly indifferent to temperature changes, I couldn't really tell, and found it hard to gauge the weather from the way he dressed. It was the middle of September, and though his suit was lightweight, every button on his vest was secure in its buttonhole. His neck was encased in a heavily starched detachable collar, which gave him a stiff and formal posture. He looked like a banker or a teacher of the old-fashioned sort. The intent was to boost the confidence of his clients.

"How's tricks with you?" I greeted in return, getting out of my trunk.

"I have no complaints, though I've been busy."

"New customers?"

"Old business. Since the influx of Mr. Swafford's cash is legally declarable, I've been able to afford a few modest home improvements and to clear some other details up."

"What details?"

"Your own case, for one. I've been tracking down the names on the infamous list you acquired—"

"I thought you were going to destroy it."

"I will, but not until I've provided a little peace of mind for some of my fellow pilgrims."

"Oh, yeah?" My tone asked him to enlarge on the subject while I brushed and gargled. My exclusive diet of whole blood sometimes made me subject to a slight breath problem. Thanks to modern hygienic products, I could still be socially acceptable, but had to be regular in habits.

The list had cost several lives, including my own. My breathing life and all the potentials that went with it were forever gone and I never wanted to see those scraps of disaster again. I should have been purposely disinterested in it, but a couple of weeks can be a long time. As Bobbi had observed, it was funny how you could get used to things.

Escott had long since broken the code it was typed in, revealing over two hundred names with skeletons in the closet. A smart blackmailer could make a fortune or wield considerable power, for without exception the names were those of important politicians, judges, lawyers, and cops, with a few big businessmen thrown in for good measure. Along with the names, the list provided the locations of the blackmail items, either incriminating documents or embarrassing pictures. Most of the stuff was stashed in a scattering of bus and train depot lockers throughout the area. He'd been collecting some of it today, and his briefcase bulged with enough scandals to keep the tabloids busy with hot headlines for months.

"I'm only halfway through it all; the hand delivery is what takes so long," he said. "It is sometimes very difficult to set up an appointment with some of these fellows."

"You've been giving it all back personally?"

"It's no great hardship. Posting it would be easier, but allows the chance that a letter or parcel might be innocently opened by a third party. The victim's life is either ruined by exposure, or they are still stuck with a blackmailing problem, but from a different quarter. It is not for me to judge the follies of my fellows, so I simply return the item, suggest they destroy it, and advise them to be more cautious in the future."

"But they might think you're the blackmailer, or in league with him if you run around doing that."

His eyes crinkled and he shook his head. "Hardly, because I don't look a bit like myself when I return the things."

"What do you look like?"

"Perhaps I shouldn't say, I might wish to try it on you sometime."

"Oh, thanks. What kind of stuff did you pick up today?"

"The usual run of evidence of extramarital affairs, illegal business dealings, and tax frauds . . . Nothing really outstanding, though the names involved are surprisingly interesting."

"Come on and drop one, I'm not a reporter anymore."

"Well, I could mention the name of Hoover, but I shan't tell which one or the nature of the blackmail article."

He looked smug and left me guessing which Hoover: Herbert, J. Edgar, or the vacuum cleaner. I finished dressing and someone knocked on the door. It was the bellhop with my regular pile of papers. I tipped him and shut the door.

"Good heavens, you read all of those?"

"I'm addicted, but trying to taper off." I opened the top paper to the personals page and checked the column of fine print. My notice was missing, but I was still hoping for a reply. I went through the rest of the stack in short order and dropped them to one side.

"What were you looking for?"

In answer, I fished an old paper from the trash, opened it to the right page, and pointed.

" 'Dearest Maureen, are you safe yet? Jack,' " he read. "I'd wondered if this were yours. This was the lady you knew in New York?"

I nodded. "That's from the other day. I've had the ad canceled."

He didn't ask why, not aloud anyway, but he was curious.

"If she were alive . . . she would have . . ." I wanted to pace, but the room was too small. Instead I took the paper from him and shoved it back in the trash. As an afterthought I threw the rest of them on top with it. "I *looked* for her. I'm no amateur, I know how to look for people, but this was like she dropped off the face of the earth."

"You still have doubts," he said kindly.

"I shouldn't after all this time. I've got Bobbi to think of now, I've got a different life ahead of me."

"And an unresolved question in your past. I would like to help, if you'll allow me."

"The trail's five years cold. I couldn't ask you to do it."

"I'm volunteering. I'm planning to go to New York, anyway. If nothing turns up you're no worse off than before, and if I do find anything, pleasant or not, it's better than not knowing at all."

"You know what it's like, don't you?"

His eyes flickered and settled. "I have an imagination." Whatever it was, he didn't want to talk about it, and changed the subject. "How is Miss Smythe doing these days?"

"Better since she quit the club. They put Gordy in charge of it."

"How fortunate for him."

"Anyway, she's been busy doing some local broadcast

shows and stuff. Next week she's going to be on her first national broadcast. I'm going to drive her down to the studio.''

"How delightful. I'm truly happy for her. She appears to have fully recovered from her . . . uh . . . adventure.''

"I guess, she doesn't talk much about that night, and I don't bring it up if I can help it.''

"For all concerned, it's probably for the best. Well, I did come by to ask a favor of you.''

"What?''

"I shall be out of town for a few days next week—my business in New York, you know—and was wondering if you would mind staying over at my house while I'm gone. I'm expecting a shipment from overseas and would be glad to have someone there to receive it.''

"They deliver after dark?''

"I could arrange that, yes.''

"Sure, no problem.''

"Thank you, I appreciate this. I'll have a duplicate key made up for you.''

"Were you serious about looking for Maureen?''

"I can try, but I'll have to have her full name and description, where she lived at the time, and any other facts about her that could possibly be useful. Have you a photograph?''

"No.''

"A pity, it might have helped.'' He shrugged his eyebrows philosophically and changed the subject again. "I've been reading Stoker's book—''

"You have my sympathy,'' I said dryly.

"Indeed, it does become turgid in spots, I had to completely skip over the correspondence between the two female characters—such a letdown after those terrifying scenes in the castle. But the idea of the multiple boxes of earth strikes me as very clever, and I came by to recommend it to you. You are quite vulnerable with just the one trunkful.''

"It's not even that much, but I see your point. I've been thinking about that, but putting it off. After all, I'm hardly being chased by Van Helsing. Who believes in vampires in this day and age?''

"Myself, Miss Smythe, Gordy, and anyone else who might notice your lack of a reflection in a mirror or window and think it peculiar. Consider it a safety measure. Suppose there's a fire, or someone steals your trunk?''

''I'm sold already, but where do I stash all this extra dirt?''

He had a ready answer. ''I've plenty of room in my cellar until you can work out your own places. Are you planning to acquire a second trunk as well? The one you have is a bit large.''

''You noticed. I'll look around for another tonight and see if I can locate something like a feed sack.''

''What about some canvas bags?'' He pulled one from an inside pocket and unfolded it. It was about eighteen inches long, with a rounded bottom six inches across. Around the opening were some things like belt loops. ''They were originally made to hold sand, but should work just as well for your earth.''

With that as a clue I realized it was the kind of bag that theaters used to counterweight curtains and stuff backstage. The loops were to be threaded with rope to attach it to lines.

''I have several dozen of these, you're welcome to them.''

''It's perfect, but how did you happen to have so many?''

''I have a lot of odds and ends lying about that I'm trying to clear away. I found these while doing some unpacking today. Much of my kit is absolutely useless at the moment, but now and then it fills an unexpected need. It occurs often enough to justify the presence of so much rubbish.''

So two nights later I was in my Buick with three dozen empty sandbags, a new shovel, some rope, and a new trunk. It was smaller than the one I'd initially bought to rest in for the day, which was currently in Escott's basement. The new trunk was easier to manhandle from the car, and though cramped, it was large enough to hold a body, namely my own. Inside, still in the original feedsacks, was my home earth, which for reasons I did not understand, I was compelled to lie in during the day. The stuff gave me rest and strength and was as necessary to my survival as blood; I could no more question its importance to me than anyone else could question the need for air and water.

I passed through a sleeping little town, one of the many on the road that rolled up the sidewalks at night. The reversed image of the welcome sign was receding in my mirror when the black Lincoln reappeared, this time with its headlights off. They were about a quarter mile back, and if they'd been after anyone but me they would have been invisible in the dark.

That clinched it, they were following me. The idea that they may have had their own brief rest stop and then forgot to switch on their lights was quickly discounted. On a night as black as this, human eyes needed all the help they could get.

Then I wondered if they were like me. That particularly uneasy idea held my attention for several miles before I filed it away for later consideration. It was not impossible, just unlikely.

My original thought that they were members of one of Chicago's mobs seemed the best explanation. But previous experience with them was in the nature of shooting first and never questioning later, so why just follow me? I'd have been easy enough to overtake on this lonely section of road. A few seconds of parallel driving would be long enough to deliver a .45-caliber greeting from a well-oiled Thompson, and they'd think themselves rid of me. They'd already had the chance to perform such an unsocial action outside Indianapolis. If their game was only to follow, it was becoming annoying, because I don't enjoy such games.

I kept my speed steady for many more miles, searching my memory for a clue as to who in the gangs would know me, and only came up blank. Perhaps it was some remnant of the Paco mob, or maybe something to do with Escott and that business with Swafford. I was getting more curious by the second.

Another hill loomed ahead and I hoped the far side would prove suitable. I stepped on the gas to gain a little more distance and time and topped the crest with the Lincoln half a mile behind. That would give me plenty of time, if my brakes were any good.

On the other side of the hill, I skidded to a stop and killed the lights, left the motor running, and got out. Standing in front of one taillight and holding my hat over the other, I waited for them.

They came over the hill, their lights still off. My estimate of their common sense was less than flattering, but the lack of extra glare was fine with me; their faces were now visible.

The one on the left was a scrawny brown chicken of a man in his late fifties, wearing a hat with a brim too big for him. The driver seemed to be of average height, but looked larger compared to his companion. From the look of his pocked skin and wet eyes, he was hardly out of his teens.

Both men saw me at the same time, and both registered the same expression: wide-eyed terror. Had it not been so genuine I would have laughed; as it was I resisted the impulse to look behind me, instinctively knowing that I was the inspiration for their fear.

The kid had quick reactions, he hit the gas, and the Lincoln stormed past, gaining speed from the slant of the hill. I got back in my car and roared after them. Their headlights came on. The following game had been shot all to hell and the high speeds put an end to their stupidity. I left mine off— the starlit landscape was like day to me and I wanted to get close to them.

The older man was turned around in his seat, watching for my approach. I got a good look at his face, which seemed familiar, and then memorized their number plate. They were from New York. That opened up a whole new line of questions as I dropped my speed and settled in to follow them for a change.

The new speculations were as futile as the old—I could think of no one from New York who'd have a reason to be after me. Curiosity was giving way to frustration, with a dash of worry for taste. Their terrified reaction had not been lost on me. I'd seen it before in the faces of people who knew what I was, but that only took me back to Chicago again.

There was Escott, but I trusted him. Besides, these two bozos were too amateurish to be connected with me. The same thing applied to Bobbi. Selma Jenks and her large friend Sled came to mind, but first they'd have to break jail or send someone after me—nope, that was too screwy even for Miss Jenks. The only one left was a mob strong arm named Gordy, but it didn't fit with him, either. If he had a grudge on me, and he didn't, he'd handle it himself and much more efficiently.

The Lincoln's brake lights flickered, held, and then the big car came to a stop, bumping onto the shoulder of the road. I stopped as well and watched to see what they were doing.

The kid backed the car off the road and it vanished behind a thick strand of trees and brush. It was just the sort of hideout that state cops liked to use to spring out on unwary speeders. My two friends were going to sit there and wait for me to pass.

I was pretty fed up by now and pulled off the road as well, shutting down the motor. The silence of the country jammed my ears. I got out, not quite closing the door—the slam might have carried to the Lincoln. Keeping low, I quit my car and tiptoed up to theirs.

Their motor was off and neither seemed inclined to any fact-revealing conversation between themselves. While they waited for the approach of my car, I crouched over their right rear wheel and performed a small operation. After unscrewing the cap in their tire, I located a pebble and jammed it inside at just the right depth and was quite satisfied with the faint hiss of escaping air.

Then I vanished.

It was a useful knack, and on occasions like this it was also fun. I materialized right by the open driver's window, clamped my hands on the kid's arms so he couldn't move to start the car, and asked a reasonable question.

"Who are you guys?"

Sometimes the element of surprise is not a good tactic. If your quarry is too surprised, the reaction you get is not necessarily the one you want.

Close up, the kid looked younger than I thought; his face still had the lingering softness of baby fat. There was a layer of smooth fat all over his body that didn't suit his years or his sex, and he'd have to lay off the sweets or the problem would get worse with time. Between that and a colorful display of pimples in various stages of development and decay, I didn't think he was much past eighteen. I'd seen younger thugs, but this guy didn't fit the mold.

His partner looked the age I guessed, past fifty or so. His hat was off now, revealing a thick growth of greasy hair that was too black to be true. His face had two deep scores on the cheeks, which were repeated countless times on the dry brown skin of his throat. He made me think of Boris Karloff in *The Mummy*, as though all the water had been squeezed out.

Both men confirmed that they knew what I was, and their reactions were again identical: utter terror.

The kid began yelling and fighting to get away. His legs had gone stiff and he was making a laudable effort at trying to levitate through the roof of the car. If Satan himself had appeared at his elbow in a cloud of sulfur, the reaction could not have been more violent.

His friend's mouth was wide open in shock. As a side issue I noted the yellow teeth and a number of black fillings. He was making incoherent, panicky sounds, and his eyes were stabbing around the car interior, looking for something. He was searching for a weapon, as I found out when, in desperation, he tore off one shoe and began hammering at me with the heel. It was an ineffectual attack. Between the kid's struggles and my ducking, he kept missing. When he did connect, it was usually with the kid, and that set up a whole new series of howlings.

Loud noises at close quarters make me nervous, but I was game enough to try and last it out. I ended up joining the chorus, shouting at them to shut up. Nothing less than violence would bring that about, as I quickly deduced, and so suited action to thought. I freed one hand and punched out the old guy and his annoying shoe, and he slithered from sight somewhere under the dashboard. The kid freshened his own fight until I stuck a mild fist in his stomach and knocked the breath out of him. He doubled over, bumping his head on the steering wheel, and once again the country silence thankfully descended on us all.

While the kid worked to get air back in his lungs, I slipped the wallet from his coat and nosed through it. He was carrying thirty bucks and a New York driving license bearing the unlikely name of Matheus Webber. There was a small photo of two chubby people, who were probably his parents, a membership card to an athletic club, and a number of business cards from various New York bookstores. I shoved it all back in the leather folder and returned it to his pocket, then opened the door and dragged him out.

He was gasping for air and gray in the face, and I reasoned he must be a sporadic visitor to his club at best. Leaving him on the ground, I reached across the seat to the other guy and pulled him up. His wallet contained a hundred twenty bucks, and said he was James Braxton of New York and the owner of Braxton's Books in Manhattan. He still seemed familiar, though the name didn't jog anything in my memory.

Neither of them looked like gangsters.

Matheus was just getting his breath back and seemed likely to bolt, so I caught his collar and tie before he got his legs set and pulled him up against the Lincoln so that we were face-to-face. He stared, lips flapping, and nothing coming out.

"Okay, bub, why were you following me?"

He looked wall-eyed toward Braxton for some moral support but got none. His legs sagged and I had to straighten him up. I repeated my question until it finally penetrated, and then he only looked incredulous. He seemed to think I already knew why. This little act went on for several minutes; me asking variations of why and him blubbering and not giving out any answers. I probably wouldn't have liked them, anyway. He wasn't even attempting to lie, it might not have been in his nature. He must have been real cute when his mom caught him raiding the cookie jar.

As with Selma Jenks, I could force a way into his mind that would make him cooperative enough, but decided against it. There was no real harm done and I'd scared them far more than they had annoyed me. I'd try a more reasonable approach.

After saying the kid's name enough to get his attention, I eased my grip a little when I was sure he wouldn't try to run. He was as relaxed as he'd ever be with me, which wasn't much. I pulled out my cigarettes and offered him one.

He looked at it like it was a snake and barely shook his head. "I don't smoke."

I nodded agreeably. "It's a bad habit." He had some idea that I was an inhuman monster, so I lit a cigarette, because in my limited experience, inhuman monsters rarely smoke. I puffed and blew the smoke out downwind of his face, trying to look harmless. "I'm sorry I popped you and your friend, but things were getting out of hand, don't you think?"

He bobbed his head cautiously.

"Now, do you know me from somewhere? Do you know my name?"

Reluctantly, he nodded again.

"How do you know me?"

"Mr. Braxton told me."

"Fine, how does *he* know me?"

"I don't know."

"Why were you following me?"

"T-to see where you were going."

This was getting nowhere fast. "Could you be more specific?"

He had to think that one over, but I waited him out. "W-we were going to see where you went for the day."

"You mean where I was going to hole up?"

Another nod.

"Why?"

That one was too much for him and he tried to get away. I held him with one hand and advised him to calm down. After a minute he ran out of steam, his legs went like jelly again, and I let him sink down to the running board to rest.

I crouched to be at eye level with him. "You seem to know what I am. Do you?"

"Yes."

"Were you and your friend planning to make the world a little safer from vampires?" I should have been more diplomatic—his eyebrows were galloping into his hairline again.

"Please . . . don't . . . ." The kid was crying, actually crying, he was that scared. I felt sorry for him and a little embarrassed, and finally pulled out a handkerchief and gave it to him. He stared at it.

"Go on—it won't bite you."

He took it, suspicious of some kind of trick. When the trick failed to happen, he finally blew his nose.

I shook my head. "Van Helsing you're not."

He stiffened again. "You know about that?"

"What, *Dracula*? Yeah, reading it is one of the requirements for joining the union. Maybe you've heard of us, the International Brotherhood of Vampires. I'm with Chicago Local three eleven."

He stared. Well, *I* thought it was funny, but the kid was taking me seriously.

"Matheus—do they call you Matt?"

"No, they call me Matheus."

They would.

"All right, Matheus, I think you should listen to me very carefully so you can get this straight. You and your friend need to go back to New York and do business as usual. You're probably a very nice kid—you don't need to be chasing after vampires in the wilds of Indiana, you're not cut out for it. You got that?"

Now he was looking stubborn. Somewhere deep inside he had a backbone.

"Don't get me wrong, I think you've got a lot of guts to even be thinking of tracking me down. How did you latch on to me anyway?"

"The papers."

"What about them?"

"Your ad stopped."

This was a can of worms I hadn't expected. "Tell me about the ad."

"It stopped and we wanted to know why, so we called the papers and got your address."

"How did you know about it? What do you know about Maureen?"

"Nothing!"

"What does Braxton know?" But I was overanxious and the kid clammed up again. I counted ten and tried a calmer voice. "Did he know Maureen?"

"I think so, years ago."

"How long ago?"

"I don't know. Honest, I don't. But he knew you had been with her . . . that she had . . . had . . . that you might become . . . but we weren't sure."

My grip on him relaxed; the muscles felt like water. "Is Maureen alive?"

He shook his head. "No, she's like you."

"Is she alive?"

"I don't know!"

"Does Braxton know?"

"Uh-uh. He said he lost her trail, you were his only lead. When the ads stopped he thought you'd found her or that you'd died. . . ." The realization that he was talking to a dead man must have hit him all over again. He sat with his arms dangling, looking at me with helpless horror.

"How did you get on my trail?"

"Through the papers. We only got into town this afternoon, and spent the day looking for you. We got to your
hotel, but they wouldn't help us, even when we described
you, so we waited across the street for you to come out."

"So Braxton knew what I looked like?"

"Yes . . . but I thought you were a lot older."

The kid was right. I was thirty-six, but my condition and
diet made me look about twenty-two.

"We saw you putting the trunk in the car and thought you
were running away, but we weren't sure—not until you went to
the Stockyards, then we knew that you were . . . you had . . ."
He gulped the idea down. "We followed you, but when you got
on the road you didn't act like you were running, so we just
stayed back and followed."

"Biding your time until the dawn, huh? And then what? A
stake in the heart and garnish with garlic?"

He squirmed, utterly miserable.

"Well, you ought to feel uncomfortable, that's just about
the dirtiest trick I've heard of, and I've heard plenty. Have
you actually *thought* about what you were planning?"

He had not.

"Come on, Matheus, I'm really a nice guy once you know
me. I am not some kind of diabolical maniac; I even send
money home to my mother. Think of it as a medical condition. You wouldn't try to kill me if I had polio, would you?"

Seeing things from my point of view was a whole new
experience for him.

"Except for some physical and dietary restrictions, there's
really nothing bad with being a vampire."

He acted like I'd said a dirty word.

"Would you be more comfortable if I said Undead or would
you prefer something else? I know lots of substitutes, but
they're harder to pronounce." I waited for an answer and
tried again. "Come on, kid, if I could go back to being like
you I would, but I can't, so I'm just trying to make the best
of the situation. I'm not what you expected, am I?"

He shook his head grudgingly.

"Don't listen to him, Matheus!" It was the mummy, Braxton. He'd come awake and was struggling to pull himself
together. He lurched from the car, looking ridiculous as he
waved his shoe in one hand like a weapon. After a second

he realized a shoe was hardly appropriate, so he dropped it and pulled a big silver cross from his pants pocket.

I stood up, uncertain how to react at this point. Crosses don't affect me unless they're large, wooden, and used as a club on my head. My theory on this is that I'm not an evil creature; the use of a cross against a vampire is primarily an invention of the stage and Hollywood. Having the vampire cowering away from one makes for a good dramatic scene, but in reality, things are far different. If these guys were ignorant enough to rely on one for protection, it might be in my best interest to play along. On the other hand, Braxton might just be trying to test me.

He pushed himself and his cross between me and Matheus. I moved back quickly because he practically shoved the thing up my nose.

"Back, you demon!" he said, and quite dramatically at that. Matheus was impressed. I refrained from laughing and gave them some room.

"And how do you do?" I inquired politely.

"Did he hurt you, Matheus?"

"Well, no—"

"But he *was* trying to hypnotize you."

"He was?"

"I was?" I echoed.

It looked as though Braxton was just the sort of dedicated crazy I was occasionally compelled to interview when I'd been a reporter. Even at this early stage in our acquaintance, his manner was easily recognizable. I tried to recall if I'd once talked to him while on an assignment.

"Leave us and trouble us no more," he intoned solemnly.

"Who wrote your dialogue? Hamilton Deane?" I countered.

Matheus looked at me doubtfully. He knew who'd written the play, *Dracula*, but he still didn't quite know how to take a vampire with a sense of humor. It went right over Braxton's head, for he was too caught up in his Van Helsing imitation to pay attention to what I said.

"Leave us," he commanded.

"Listen, buster, *you* were the ones following me. I was minding my own business. I'll be a sport this time and let you go, as long as you run straight back home and stay there."

''No, we will follow you as long as necessary.''

That really wasn't the smartest thing for him to tell me. I sighed. ''Matheus, maybe you can talk some sense into him. If I was half as nasty as you seem to think, I could just as well kill you both as stand around all night. I haven't got the time to waste trying to convince you of my good character, either. Just stay out of my way or I'll kick both of your asses all the way back to Manhattan.'' I turned and walked until I was lost to them in the dark, then vanished and floated back to listen in on what they had to say.

It took a few minutes for their nerves to settle and to convince each other that they were all right. Once the question of health was out of the way, Matheus gulped a few times and asked, ''Was he really trying to hypnotize me?''

I could imagine Braxton nodding sagely.

''But it didn't seem like he was. He didn't say anything that sounded like it.''

''You wouldn't remember it if he did. It's like falling asleep, you don't know you've been asleep until you wake up.''

''Oh. What do we do now?''

''We wait him out. He has to come this way, and then we follow him.''

''But how can we be sure he won't just double back?''

''He has become a vampire, he *must* seek out his home earth. I know he comes from Cincinnati—''

How did he know that? I wondered.

''—and this is the road that will take him there the fastest. He said he had little time. For us time is on our side.''

He didn't know everything. He must have thought I'd changed only in the last day or so; he did not know I was merely augmenting my present supply of earth.

''Are you sure about this, Mr. Braxton? He could have killed us, like he said.''

Braxton had a blanket answer. ''Lies. He's only toying with us. They're very clever, these creatures, but you'll remember that he was the one to give ground before *us*.''

I could almost see him waving his cross and puffing out his chest. Whether I was playing with them or not depended on how much they bothered me. Amateurish and ill informed as they were, they could still prove to be very dangerous.

During my daytime oblivion I was completely vulnerable. My best chance of survival would be to lose them and hope they'd give up and go home. I had no desire to do them violence.

I left them and returned to my car, starting it up. They would hear the noise and be starting theirs as well. I drove slowly past, their white and defiant faces staring grimly back as I waved. Matheus was getting himself ready for the road race of his life.

It must have been a terrible letdown when their car swayed onto the road and with a lurch betrayed the presence of the flat tire.

I hit the gas and left them behind. It would take about ten minutes for Matheus to change the tire, probably a lot longer with Braxton helping him, and by that time I planned to have a healthy lead of fifteen miles or more.

▲ 4 ▼

LUCK WAS WITH me and I managed to avoid the notice of cops looking for speeders, arriving in Cincinnati with enough time to spare to find a place to stay. The best protection was with the herd, so I checked into one of the bigger and busier downtown hotels under a phony name. The Buick disappeared into a distant parking lot with a lot of other late-model cars.

A sleepy bellhop manhandled the trunk into a modest single with a bath. I dispatched him with a fair tip and hung out a sign to ward off the maid. My suit and body both felt rumpled from the long drive. I wanted a hot bath, a quick shave, and the inside of my trunk, and got them in short order.

Sunset seemed to come again a few seconds after I'd closed the lid. While in my earth there was no sense of time passing, but the day had gone by as usual, since I felt rested and alert. I was in fresh clothes, checked out, and in my car in record time. My goal was to be back in Chicago that same night, so I hurried now.

What was left of my grandfather's farm wasn't too far from the city, but owing to the twists of the road, it was still fairly isolated. Once I turned off the farm-market road and onto the weedy ruts that led to the house, the trees closed in, and it was like going back in time. The Buick was a noisy intruder into a simpler and slower age, so I cut the motor and walked the rest of the way with Escott's sandbags in one hand and the new shovel and some rope in the other.

The place hadn't changed since my last visit in August. It still looked forlorn and overgrown, but not completely neglected. My father came out occasionally to check on things. He kept the grass trimmed in the little graveyard where we'd been burying our own for the last seventy-five years. The house was boarded up. It would have looked sinister except for the neat paint job. Even the three-seater outhouse in back had gotten a coat against the winter. It was as though it had only been temporarily closed for the season and the family would return in the spring.

I went to the cemetery. The earth near the big oak tree was vaguely scarred from my last expedition for soil, but not so much that the casual eye would notice. As before, I cleared another large area of fallen leaves and began scooping an inch of topsoil off and into the bags. I could have dug deeper, but that would leave definite signs, and I had no desire to accidentally include earthworms in my booty.

Whether dirt specifically from the family cemetery was necessary for me to survive had been a question in my mind for quite a while. My prior researches indicated that all vampires must be in their graves by dawn, and had I truly died, my body would certainly be resting here with the other Flemings. I suppose any of the earth in the immediate vicinity would have been suitable, but there was no time for experiments. I had a traditional turn of mind, anyway.

As I worked, my mind was already on the road, retracing the route back to Chicago and deciding which places to stop for gas. I vaguely wondered if I would again be plagued by Matheus Webber and James Braxton. They were worrying, but there wasn't much I could do about them until I could get their names to Escott. Hopefully he might be able to trace them down in New York while he was there, then I might remember where I'd met Braxton—

The work and thought were interrupted by several heavy objects slamming against my body like cannonballs and knocking me flat.

Two hard things caught me full in the chest, and a third had cracked against my head. In the very brief time between impact and hitting the ground I decided they were large rocks and that somebody really had it in for me.

The last rock must have been the size of a brick, but I

hadn't been killed, or even concussed. There are undeniable advantages to being supernatural.

My body fell back and rolled. I glimpsed a whirl of leaves and branches that abruptly faded to gray and then to nothing. My body had taken things over again and I'd dematerialized from the shock of the sudden pain. No emergency called me back, so I remained disembodied and was glad of it. Floating upward until safely within the concealing branches of the oak, I slowly re-formed, arms and legs wrapped around one of the big limbs.

I was about thirty feet up, and once solid, had to endure a few bad moments of recovery. My head was the worst, I had to cling with my eyes squeezed tight until the dizziness passed. I *hate* heights.

While hiding in the tree and counting my blessings, developments were taking place below. Three foreshortened figures came into view and prowled uncertainly around my excavation. They were rough-looking men, each with a rock in one hand and a big stick in the other. Had I not vanished immediately they would have probably followed up with those clubs. The clubs were of wood and would have succeeded where rock had failed.

My headache rapidly subsided as I became interested in finding out who these guys were and why they'd attacked me out of the blue. Perhaps then I would work off the chagrin of being taken by surprise. They must have been hiding out the whole time I was digging, or else I'd have heard them sneaking up.

One of them cast around like a dog for a lost scent. "He musta rolled away fast after we hit 'em," he told the others. They agreed and made a swift search under the oak, then spread out among the grave markers.

"You sure we hit 'em?" asked one.

"Din' you keep your eyes open? We all hit 'em square. I know we did. Din' we, Bob?"

Bob grunted something affirmative and made a quick leap to look behind the big piece of carved granite over my grandfather's grave. It was the only possible hiding place, the rest of the stone markers being too small. They circled back to the sandbags and kicked at them curiously.

"What you suppose he was diggin' for, Rich?"

"How the hell should I know?" Rich was upset that I was missing. He looked at the oak tree, his eyes traveling up the trunk toward me. I kept still, knowing he couldn't see me in the darkness among the leaves. "Go check his car," he told Bob. "Mebee he got some stuff we can use."

Fugitives from a local Hooverville or tramps off of any of the trains that passed through the city, they'd been looking for someone to rob, and I'd been handy.

Bob was lumbering off to the car. The keys were still inside. I'd felt safe being back home, after all. Vanishing, I floated in Bob's direction, tracking the crunch his feet made on the gravel and old leaves. He was almost to the car when I re-formed in front of his startled face and gently knocked him out.

He was a gaunt, rawboned specimen and I'd have felt sorry for him had it not been for those well-aimed stones. Proving assault against them would be impossible, but I was, or at least I felt like, an outraged homeowner and they were trespassing.

I sandwiched Bob into one of the road ruts in front of the car, which gave me an idea: it was more of a childish impulse, but irresistible.

Rich and his pal separated, looking for my missing body and puzzling over the odd situation. It was easy to wait for a convenient moment and take the pal from behind. His unconscious body went next to Bob's in the adjoining rut. For an artistic effect, I folded their arms funeral style and decorated each with a large weed, as though it were a lily. When things were ready, I tooted the horn a couple times, turned on the headlights, then ducked into the cover of the trees.

Rich didn't delay investigating. He was complaining about the noise in a few short, coarse words, which trailed off when he saw his friends lying neatly in the ruts. He went on guard, held his stick at a threatening angle, and listened. It seemed a shame to disappoint him, so I threw a fist-sized stone at his legs. His yelp was more of surprise than pain, and he hopped to one side before twisting to face me.

I wasn't there anymore. By vanishing and shifting around I could move without being detected. In the darkness outside the glare of the headlights I was all but invisible by simply standing still. Re-forming a short toss behind him, I bounced another stone, this time off his butt. He had no appreciation for my marksmanship, though, and came charging at me with his stick. While he viciously assaulted the foliage, I moved back to the first hiding place and gave him another volley of rocks.

Not surprisingly, he got tired of this very quickly and bolted for the road, urged on by several parting shots. I couldn't let him leave without a personal good-bye and made a point to appear directly in his path. He had no time to stop and we connected solidly. He dropped, the breath knocked out of him, but he quickly recovered and took a swing at me with the stick. I went to a partially solid state and it passed right through, which was not what he expected. He stared at the stick, then at me, and tried again and failed. That was one too many and he ran away.

That didn't work, either.

I caught him at the front gate, swung him around, and pressed him face first against the bole of a tree, making sure he got well acquainted with the bark.

"Lemme go, I din' do nuthin'!"

He struggled, but I had him firmly pinned and he eventually stopped. There had been a lot more fight in little Selma Jenks.

"Okay, I'll do what you want!" This was indistinct, as his mouth was mashed into the bark.

I whipped him around. He knew he was in trouble as his feet left the earth. I held him up by his stinking clothes, with his toes swinging free in the air.

"How long you creeps been here?"

"C-couple days."

"How'd you find this place?"

"Mailbox—sign on it says it's safe here."

"You're gonna change that, understand? It ain't safe anymore."

"Yeah—whatever you want."

My next action was pure show-off, but it also served to drive home the point that I was more than capable of handling him. I forced him over double and snaked an arm around his midsection. He was too dumbfounded to vocalize a protest as his feet left the ground again and he was carried like a sack of flour along the road to the mailbox. There, he erad-

icated a symbol scratched on the post and substituted another
that meant "keep away" to any other bums that might happen
by.

"That okay?"

He wasn't getting any pats on the head from me. We locked
eyes and I gave him a few choice words of advice, nothing
as specific as those I shared with Selma, but along similar
lines. I last saw him pelting for Cleveland at a dead run. If
he kept up the pace he'd make it by morning.

His pals looked like they'd be out for some time, so I left
them and had a good look around the house and barn. The
barn was untouched, but the house had been broken into via
a back window. Through it I could see signs of recent and
very messy occupancy. This discovery inspired a lot of violent thoughts aimed at the two remaining bums. The only
thing to do would be to give the cops an anonymous call and
ask them to come out. They in turn would contact my father;
by that time the bums would be gone, which was probably
just as well. If Dad had come out for a visit alone, he might
have been the one assaulted, not me. That idea had set my
blood to boiling when I'd been talking to Rich, and now I
stalked back to revive his two friends.

A little shaking did the trick, and I gave them no chance
to run away. I had their full attention as I picked up the
discarded clubs. They were heavy and hard, like baseball
bats, but not so thick that I couldn't get my hands around
them. I held them out front, making sure my guests had a
good view.

"You boys get out and stay out, or I'll break your necks."
At that I snapped the clubs in two with a sharp movement.
The men were impressed, but didn't stay for an encore. If
anything, they moved even faster than their leader as they ran
for the road.

Satisfied, I threw the wood shards away and went back to
my unfinished work.

Like a lot of chores, the digging took longer than anticipated
and, coupled with the delay of dealing with the tramps, severely cut into my travel time. I could have probably made it
all the way to Chicago the same night, but not without a lot
of speeding. Allowing for state cops, unexpected flat tires,

washed-out bridges, and other hazards, I could still easily make it to Indianapolis with a comfortable margin of time.

With the last dusty bag tied up and stowed in the trunk, I drove back to town in search of a phone, turning one up at a gas station. While a kid in greasy overalls fed the tank, I made a call to the Cincinnati police. After giving them the name of another farming family on the same road, I extracted a promise from them to investigate and, if necessary, roust the tramps from the Fleming place. They were given the impression the intruders were still there because it would do no harm for them to be cautious. I gave them my dad's name and number so they could inform the owner, and hung up.

Having the time and inclination, I decided to indulge in some nostalgia and drive through my old neighborhood. I needed some reassurance that the haunts of my youth were still there, still in use by another generation of kids.

I wasn't going to visit my parents, only look at the house and drive on. Visiting them would have been too complicated and painful. I'd be expected to stay the night and stuff myself with food and there was no way I could fob them off with some light excuse. I could also be honest and tell them the truth about myself and hope they'd understand and accept it, but that was something I absolutely was not ready to try yet.

Dad had moved off the farm years ago to be closer to the store he owned and to give Mom her long-coveted indoor plumbing. Their neighborhood looked smaller and dowdier to my eyes now, but still homey. There was ample evidence that the radio had not yet destroyed the quality of family life as had been predicted. There were plenty of people lounging on their front porches, seeking a cool breeze from the darkness. Windows were open and shades were up, their softly lit squares revealing a minute glimpse into other lives. I observed each with the detached interest of a gallery patron.

The detachment evaporated the second I saw the black Lincoln parked in front of my parents' house. Now I was really angry. They could follow and harass me, but not my family. I braked and was out of the car and halfway up the walk before common sense took over and counseled caution. My sudden appearance at the front door might send Braxton into a fit of cross-waving hysterics, which was the last thing my mother needed.

Crossing the yard, I stationed myself in the bushes just under the open parlor window. Like most families, our friends usually ended up in the kitchen for their visits; strangers were shown to the more formal parlor. Mom was running to form, and through the gossamer curtains of the open window I could see them all, and my sensitive hearing picked up every word. Braxton and Webber had apparently only arrived and were just settling in for a talk. Braxton was doing most of it, the padded and polite kind of speech reserved for people that you want something from.

None of it impressed my father, for he dealt with salesmen every day.

"Mr. Braxton, you said you wanted to talk with us about Jack," he said, interrupting the flow of words.

"Indeed, yes, Mr. Fleming." Braxton's voice was smoother and more cultured than I'd thought possible, no longer strident with vanity or fear. It was that persuasive tone that kicked my memory into gear. "How long has it been since you last heard from him?"

"Why do you want to know?"

"At the moment that might be difficult to explain."

"He sent us a postcard just this week," said my mother.

"Did he mention anything unusual?"

"Like what?" asked Dad.

"An odd experience, perhaps?"

Mom was worried now. "Why do you ask? Has something happened to him? What is it?"

"Please, Mrs. Fleming, so far as we know he is all right and we are doing our best to see that he remains so."

Dad's temper was starting to flare. "Out with the story, Mr. Braxton."

"Of course, of course. Your son, unknown to himself, may have gotten into some trouble when he moved to Chicago."

"How so? What kind of trouble?"

"When he lived in New York he often wrote stories on the criminal element there for his paper. He had access to information sources that they would like to see eliminated, what we call informants and the like. Some of these criminals became very suspicious at his sudden departure and they are anxious to find out why he left. Matheus and I must talk with him about this and we must see him personally."

"His moving was hardly sudden," said Mom. "Besides, he moved nearly a month ago."

"Yes, unfortunately certain individuals from the underworld were arrested at the same time, and they are blaming him for their capture. Whether he was responsible or not makes little difference to them."

There was a pause as Mom and Dad exchanged worried looks.

"Then we have to warn him, send him a telegram or something," said Dad.

"No, you must *not* do that, such things can be intercepted. I know that from experience."

"What experience?"

"I work for the government; I must ask you to keep this meeting secret, of course."

"Government?" Mom echoed uncertainly.

"Here, my identification."

Dad looked at something Braxton passed to him. "You don't look like a G-man—neither of you," he added, to include Matheus, who was being very quiet about things.

Braxton chuckled easily. "None of us really do. For instance, young Webber here is one of our trainees. This is his first assignment, you know, so you see there is no real danger involved, but that does not lessen the importance of what we are doing. We must make contact with your son as soon as possible. We have to warn him about what is going on."

"We'll call him, then."

"I'm afraid he's no longer at the place he was living in. He moved out last night and we were only able to trace him part of the way here."

"He's coming home, then?" Dad was puzzled.

"Possibly, perhaps he learned of the trouble independently from us and he may try hiding out from them here."

"Or at the farm—no one would think to look for him there," Mom said helpfully. I groaned inside.

"Farm?"

Dad began explaining about the farm, with Braxton avidly listening, and I could see the next question coming a mile off. They didn't need to be nosing around my home earth and learning of my excavations. Before things could go further, I picked up one of the whitewashed stones that divided the lawn from the bushes and sent it crashing through the parlor window.

Mom screamed and I was sorry for that, but I wanted those bozos out of the house, where I could deal with them. Dad was roaring mad and the first one out the front door, with Braxton and Webber at his heels. But I wasn't hanging around, and bolted for the Lincoln. Opening the driver's door, I released the hand brake and pushed. It wasn't so dark that they couldn't see their car moving off by itself.

Matheus noticed, yelled, and gave chase. I had a good lead; he was out of shape and Braxton on the arthritic side. It was a good block's run before they caught up with the car. I ducked low, seeping into the backseat, and waited for them. They were both wheezing when they tore the doors open. There was no sign of Dad. They'd left him back in the yard looking in the bushes for the vandal.

"I'm sure I set the brake," Matheus insisted in reply to Braxton's irritated question.

"Well, start it up and let's get back there. I almost had him."

"But who broke the window?"

"I did," I said, leaning forward to clamp a hand over their mouths. For once the lack of an image in the rearview mirror had worked in my favor. They gave only a token struggle—I was strong and they were pretty winded after their dash to the car.

"I *told* you to go back to New York," I reminded them.

Braxton mumphed something loud and defiant. He squirmed and twisted, trying to get something from his pants pocket. I could guess he was after his cross again and shifted my hand until it was over his nose. He was already short of oxygen, in a few seconds he was weakly trying to tear free.

"You gonna behave?" I asked him.

He mewed desperately down in his throat and I eased off just enough so he could breathe.

I looked at Matheus, who was too scared to move. "Okay, kid, you drive to my directions, understand?"

He gurgled.

"You drive nice, or I'll break the geezer's neck."

Another gurgle. It sounded like an affirmative.

I let the kid go and he started the car without any argument.

He seemed used to taking orders. Our drive was not a cordial one, and out of necessity I was forced to keep both hands tight on Braxton—one over his mouth and the other encircling his wrists. After several miles I was feeling very cramped.

We drove northeast until I judged that the distance was enough to keep them busy, then had the kid stop. He was visibly trembling and Braxton was sweating bullets. The area was well clear of the city, dark and deserted. They must have concluded that I was going to kill them and leave the bodies in a roadside ditch. It was tempting, but only as a joke. Instead I pushed them out of the car, got behind the wheel, and turned the big machine back toward the city. They gave an angry and halfhearted chase, but were easily left behind in the exhaust fumes.

If they got lucky they might turn up a ride in Montgomery, but in the meantime I planned to head for Indianapolis.

I left their car parked across the street from a fire station and had a brisk walk back to my own. By this time the neighborhood had settled down. The lights were still on in my parents' house, but the rest were dark, their occupants sensibly asleep. Dad had nailed a board over the broken window. I rolled quietly away to look for another telephone.

Dad answered on the first ring and I blandly said hello.

"Jack!" He sounded excited.

"Is something wrong?" I asked innocently.

"I'll say there is." He gave me a slightly garbled account of what had happened earlier and wanted to know if I knew there were some gangsters after me.

"Wait a minute." I tried to sound skeptical. It wasn't hard. "How do you know these guys were G-men?"

"He had an identification card, it said he was with the FBI."

"Those can be printed up by the hundreds in any joke shop. What did they look like? Was it a little guy and a chubby kid with bad skin?"

"That's them."

"Dad, I hate to say it, but you've been had."

"What d'ya mean?"

"I did a story on those fish last year. They're a couple of con men. Because of me, the cops went after them, a lot of their victims turned up in court, and these guys got sent up. Did they try talking you into buying anything?''

''No, they wanted to know where you were, and then someone broke the window—''

''That was the third man in their team. They'll be coming back and trying to sell you some kind of phony U.S. government insurance. . . .''

I gave Dad an imaginative account of their criminal career, stating that Braxton was a dangerous crazy and that he and Webber indulged in some bizarre sexual practices. Then I held my breath to see if he believed it, because I'd always been a lousy liar.

Dad said a few well-chosen obscenities, but they were directed at his recent guests, not me.

''Watch out for them,'' I suggested enthusiastically. ''The little one's a real weasel when he's cornered. If they bother you again, just call the cops. Don't let them back in the house.''

''I won't, I just wish you'd called earlier. Why are you calling now?''

''I've been moving, I wanted to give you my new number.''

''They said you'd moved. Where are you?''

''I found a nice boardinghouse. If there's an emergency they'll get a message to me.'' I gave him Escott's phone number and told him to keep it to himself.

''What about the address?''

''I'll be getting a box at the post office, the landlord likes to steam things open.''

''That's illegal.''

''Yeah, but the rent's cheap and the food's good. How's Mom?''

He put her on the line and we exchanged reassurances and other bits of information. She thought I had a job at an ad agency and asked how it was going. I let her keep thinking it. Except for the Swafford case, my modest living expenses and the money I sent home to help them out had come from an inadvertent theft from a mobster and some engineered luck at a blackjack table. Neither of them would have won her approval.

I promised to call again in a day or two for further news and hung up, grinning ear to ear.

A few years ago I walked into a small bookstore in Manhattan. The window on the street was just large enough to display the painted legend: BRAXTON'S BOOKS, NEW & USED, and the inside sill held a few sun-faded samples of literature. In the last few weeks I'd seen a hundred hole-in-the-wall places like this; I liked them.

A bell over the door jingled as I entered. Dust motes hanging in the sunlight were stirred by the draft and I sneezed. By the time I straightened and wiped my nose he had appeared out of one of the alcoves formed by bookshelves.

"Good afternoon, sir, may I help you?"

He was shorter than me, with dark wrinkled skin like a dried apple. There was a suggestion of black shoe polish in his hair, but the world was full of people who didn't want to look their age.

"Got anything on folklore or the occult?"

"Yes, sir, in this first section." He indicated the area and watched with a pleasant smile as I went to look it over.

It was a fairly complete selection. There were copies of Summer's works on witchcraft and vampires, even Baring-Gould's book on werewolves, but nothing I hadn't already seen and read before. I checked the fiction section, drew a blank, and finished off with the occult shelves. They were also very complete, but only with the usual junk. I said thank you to the general air and started for the door.

"Perhaps," he said, stopping me, "if you're looking for something special I could be of help. I have other books in the back."

It was my day off, I was in no hurry. "Well, sure, if you don't mind."

"What are you looking for?"

Speaking the title always made me feel vaguely foolish. "A copy of *Varney, the Vampire* by Prest."

He knew what I was talking about, not surprising considering the contents of his well-stocked shelves. His brown eyes got brighter with interest. "*Or the Feast of Blood*," he said, completing the title. "Yes, that is a rare one. I have a copy, but it's part of my own collection and not for sale."

"Oh," I said, for want of something better.

"May I ask why you are interested in it?"

The real reason I couldn't talk about, so I had a fake one practiced and ready. "I'm working on a book, a survey of folklore, fact and fiction."

"That is a very wide field."

"Not when you're tracking down certain books."

He looked sympathetic. "I'd like to help, but it could only be in a limited way."

Strings of some kind? He'd find out real soon I wasn't rich.

"You'd have to read it here in the shop, that is if you want to. I value it too much to loan it out."

"I can understand that," I said gratefully. "Are you sure it wouldn't be too much trouble?"

"Not at all, but it would have to be during working hours."

"That would be fine, thank you."

He offered his hand. "I'm James Braxton."

"Jack Fleming."

"Come in the back, I'll show you where you may read."

"You have it right here?"

"Oh, yes. Yes." He threaded past ceiling-high shelves, leading me deep into the narrow shop. He switched on the light over a desk and chair and swept some account books to one side. The light revealed shelves crammed with a faded patchwork of book spines of every shape and age. It looked like a duplicate of the folklore section out front, but more so. Some of the volumes were very old, with odd titles, others were recent and by skeptical writers. One shelf held only copies of *Occult Review*. He was more than casually interested in the subject himself, and I wondered if he sincerely believed in it. If so, I'd have to watch my lip.

He knew exactly where his copy was located and pulled it out, placing it on the desk. "I hope you enjoy it," he said.

"Thank you, you're very generous to do this."

"I'm just in favor of expanding knowledge in a neglected area," he smiled.

"You have quite a collection."

The bell on the door out front rang, interrupting his reply. He excused himself with a rueful smile, and for the next few hours was too busy to return.

I'd already read the first chapter in another book, so I

skipped it and went through the second and third in short order. I was a fast reader, but did not plan to spend the rest of my life poring word by word through the book's more than two hundred chapters. In its original state, it had been published a chapter at a time for weekly consumption by the newly literate masses. A fast writer could keep himself employed for years with a popular series. In the previous century, the penny dreadfuls were just as popular as the current radio and movie serials were now.

I skimmed the pages, reading the brief descriptions given under the chapter titles, and touching on the dialogue whenever it popped up. The gist of it centered on the tribulations of the Bannerworth family as they nobly bore the attacks of Varney upon their daughter, Flora. A good family, but not too bright: if they'd simply moved away at the start they would have saved themselves a lot of trouble, but the plot dragged on regardless of such logic.

It was really better than I expected—at least at first, then the quality of the writing began to deteriorate along with the continuity. A cliff-hanger ending was never resolved and one of the Bannerworth brothers seemed to disappear completely from the story. When he did return, the author had forgotten his name. Whole sections written for no other purpose than to fill a word quota tried my patience and I skipped them altogether. I focused on the few scenes where the vampire appeared and had dialogue.

His blood requirements were only occasional, usually after he'd been killed and his body was carelessly left out in the moonlight, which revived him. The moonlight device had been lifted wholesale from Polidori's story and used shamelessly each time Varney was shot dead, or in one case, drowned. He had no trouble with running water, crosses, or garlic, not that anyone thought of using the latter two against him.

Eventually all the Bannerworths disappeared, to be replaced with a steady parade of beautiful young girls that he kept trying to marry, either in the hope their love would end his curse or because he was thirsty. Sometimes, the reason was a bit vague. He was usually kept from the nuptial feasts by an interfering old enemy, the man the bride truly loved, or the bride's suicide. He soon ran out of nubile prospects as well as European countries to ravage.

Tough, he was able to recover from mortal wounds with some lunar help, but he certainly lacked a talent for hypnotism. His victims always ended up screaming for help and interrupting his dinner. The one point I did find very interesting was that each time he was resurrected, he had to soon feed or die.

I shut the book with a slight headache and a sigh of relief just as Braxton was coming back.

"I was closing up for the day. . . . Surely you haven't finished it?"

"Not exactly." I explained my skimming method to him.

"Are you sure you got sufficient detail for your research? I thought you'd be here for several days, taking notes."

"I can hold it in my head long enough to jot the high points down later."

He registered mock disappointment. "And I'd been looking forward to some company. It is so rare for me to meet someone with a similar interest in the unusual."

"I couldn't help noticing your collection. . . ."

He was proud of it and this time able to talk. "Fortunately my business gives me an advantage over others. I often get advance notice of private collections going up for sale and can get first pick." He pulled out a volume, but didn't open it. "That's how I found this one. A friend of mine who arranges estate sales told me about it, and I made an early purchase ahead of the auction."

With a slight shock I deciphered the title; the script lettering was hard to read. "But I thought this was a fake, it has to be."

"As did I when I saw it, but here it is. It came from the library of a university professor. His relatives sealed up his house when he suddenly disappeared. The police thought he'd been kidnapped and perhaps murdered, but never found the body—the case is still open. His family waited seven years, had him declared dead, and settled his estate."

The story stunk like a barrel of very old fish. Braxton's friend must have taken him for plenty over that book. He had believed it, though, and expected me to as well. "What was his name?"

"I don't remember, this was years ago."

"Maybe he wrote it on the inside of the book."

"No, not *this* book."

"Mind if I flipped through it?"

He was uneasy. "I'd rather you didn't. The *Necronomicon* isn't just any book, you know. That does sound ridiculous in the broad light of day, I realize I must appear to be superstitious."

"Why did you buy it if it makes you uncomfortable?"

"I don't really know, perhaps it's the collector in me. I suppose I also wanted it kept somewhere safe, where it would not be used." He sucked in his lips and looked embarrassed.

He wanted to impress someone, anyone, and I was his latest effort. Projecting an air of mystery and implied danger concerning his possessions was his method, and it put my hackles up. I'd met people like him before; he was more subtle than most and probably had a small, handpicked circle of acolytes. I wondered where they held their weekly seance.

"Yes, I guess it could be misused," I commented neutrally.

He was relieved that I hadn't laughed, and re-placed the book. "Some of these others might help you in your research. I wouldn't mind you looking them over."

"Thank you very much, but I'm afraid most of them are outside my immediate study range."

"Are you researching vampires exclusively?"

"For this book, yes. They're popular now."

"They always have been. Hardly a week goes by that I don't have a customer asking for a copy of *Dracula*. Business was especially good last month, when the movie began showing. It would seem to be the last word on the subject."

I knew better but said nothing. "Yes, I'm trying to locate Stoker's sources. I don't have the British Museum available so I've been hitting every bookstore and library in the city."

"Why are you interested in his sources?"

"To see if there were any true accounts of vampirism in them."

"Do you believe in vampires?"

I didn't like the way he focused on me. "In a way . . . I've read about people like Elizabeth Bathory and others. There's always going to be a few oddballs running loose, but as for the *Dracula* kind of vampire, no, I don't believe in them." And I said it with perfect sincerity, but his intense, inquiring look made me uncomfortable.

"You don't believe in supernatural vampires?" he pursued.

"No."

"But what if they exist despite your disbelief?"

"They don't."

He smiled tightly.

"You believe in them?" I asked.

"I'm not sure." He gestured at all the books. "I've read them, all of them, and there *is* a lot of evidence. Most of it is quite absurd, of course, but once sifted through, some of it refuses to be dismissed. I like to keep an open mind."

"To each his own," I said meaninglessly, trying to think of a polite way to end the conversation. Someday I might want to come back, though that possibility was not looking very attractive at the moment.

His expression was still disturbing. "But tell me, Mr. Fleming, and with all truth, what would it mean if there are such things? What would it mean to you?"

"I'd have to think that one over."

"I already have. I've thought a lot about it. We have this bright world of daylight, predictable and comfortable to us. Normal. But what do we do when something happens that simply does not fit into that world and makes us conscious of another world altogether, existing and blending closely with our own? A world we can but glimpse and then dismiss as a fantasy, a world we cannot sanely accept, for that would doom our complacent security. Its citizens are beautiful monsters, to be feared or laughed at as at a dream. But if their reality were to be proved to you, how would you react? You can deny it or accept the truth. One keeps your illusion of your world safe and the other . . . well, your hand might hesitate tonight before it turns out the light. How can you slumber in peace when you cannot see what the darkness conceals? Our eyes blink against it, our ears hear things that *might* be moving, our skin shivers and anticipates crawling things beneath the covers. Within that dark, which is as sunlight to them, they watch and bide their time until sleep takes you; they sense it as we sense the heat and cold. They approach, marking you, stealing your heart's essence to strengthen their own Undead bodies, and when the dawn comes they're gone . . . and one more part of your soul is gone with them.''

It was past time to leave. The man knew too much and yet too little. He was perceptive enough to know there were other reasons besides a bogus book to inspire my research. Maybe he hoped I would confide in him, show him the marks on my throat and ask for help. That was out. I was not under any restraining hypnotic suggestion from Maureen, but I did have a share of common sense. Even if I told him the truth about vampires, it would do no good. He was the wrong sort to unlearn all the nonsense he had sitting on his shelves, such truth would endanger his illusions just as he said.

He read my face correctly and knew he'd gone too far too soon. Cultivating acolytes takes time. ''I'm sorry, I do ramble on a bit.''

''That's all right. It was very interesting, but I have to be going. Thank you very much for letting me read the book. I really appreciate it.''

''Not at all,'' he replied, shaking hands. ''I hope you'll come again?''

''Sure,'' I lied.

Social conventions sometimes come in handy. We smiled, said the usual things, performed the expected rituals, and pretended all was right in the world. It was for me as soon as I stepped out into the brisk March dusk to walk home. Braxton's outlook on reality was enough to throw anyone off center. If nothing else, he personified my own fears of vampirism and made me realize how groundless they were. Compared to Maureen, Braxton was far more frightening.

The relationship Maureen and I shared was hardly consistent with the popular image of vampire and victim. Our lovemaking was astonishingly joyous and normal, and if at its climax she drew a little blood from me what did it matter as long as we both enjoyed it? Maybe she wasn't a typical vampire, maybe there were others just as dangerous as Stoker's creation. I did not know.

I never mentioned Braxton to Maureen; I didn't want her to know about my fears, especially now that they'd been dispelled. She needed my love and support, not my insecurities. After a very short time, the incident faded from my memory.

5

AGAIN TAKING REFUGE in a large, anonymous hotel under a
different name, I stopped for the day in Indianapolis. My car
was left several blocks away in another hotel's garage. Not
the best kind of subterfuge, but I was hoping Braxton was
not that good a detective. My hopes panned out or I was
lucky again; the next night I was back in the familiar and
relative sanity of Chicago. My first stop was Bobbi's place.

I waved at the night clerk as usual, he nodded back, turned
to a pillar near his desk, and resumed talking to it. This sort
of behavior makes me curious, so I walked over to see what
made the pillar such a fascinating conversationalist. Leaning
against it, just out of my line of sight, was the house dick,
Phil. He was a medium-sized, slightly tubby man in an old
derby and a loose collar. He didn't look like much, but Bobbi
said he could take care of himself and knew where to go for
help if he needed it.

He saw me and nodded. "Morning, Fleming. You up early
or out late?"

I shook his calluses. "I'm always out late. How's business?"

"Slow, but there's the weekend coming up."

That was when he made most of his tips. As long as the
trysting couples were quiet about it, he was conveniently blind
and deaf; disturb the other guests and the offenders were out
on their ears.

"Good luck, then. Listen, could you do me a favor?"

"Depends." His face was as carefully blank as the lobby's marble floor.

"There's been a couple of guys following me. . . ." I gave him an accurate description of Braxton and Webber and an inaccurate account of their activities. "They've already pestered my folks and I figure they might try bothering Miss Smythe next."

"They can try." The only thing Phil liked better than bribes was kicking pests around.

"I'd appreciate it if you kept your eyes open." I stuck my hand out in farewell and we shook again briefly. He pocketed the sawbuck I slipped him with the discreet manner that made him so popular with the other hotel patrons.

"I will do that," he promised. The only thing Phil liked better than bribes and kicking pests around was to be bribed to kick pests around. "Please tender my regards to Miss Smythe."

Phil and the clerk resumed their discussion, which had to do with the merits of various betting parlors in the city, and I completed my journey to the elevator. The operator put up a good imitation of being awake and he took me up to Bobbi's floor.

"She's got guests tonight," he told me.

"Anyone I know?"

He shrugged and opened the doors. "They look the fancy type to me."

That could mean anything. I stepped out and immediately picked up the loud thrum of conversation down the hall. Bobbi had mentioned her plans for a little party a few days ago. Her idea of a little party meant inviting only half the city, not all of it.

The door swung open at my knock and a dangerous-looking female barred the way in. She sucked in a lungful of smoke from a skinny black cigar and let it blow out her nostrils to corrode the air. "Well, speak of the devil."

Not knowing how to respond to that one, I waited for her to stand aside, only she didn't, and hung on to the doorknob to look me over.

She had well-powdered white skin stretched over her bones, and dark eyes, which were made larger and darker by a liberal use of makeup. Her hair was jet black, shaped like a helmet with thick, severely cut bangs that just covered the eyebrows. The rest was leveled hard against her jawline. If any single hair dared to rebel, it had been rigorously dealt with by a dose of lacquer.

She wore something box shaped and bright purple, with green sequins edging a deep neckline that didn't suit her long face. The talons she affected were another bad choice, as they accentuated the developing witchiness of her fingers. They were painted the same color as her wide mouth: a deep maroon. I put her down as a case that was determined to look a young and sophisticated twenty no matter what her actual age. As far as I could tell under the war paint, she'd just edged her way over forty.

She'd finished assessing me as well, took a step backward, and swept her hand in a gesture to indicate I could pass. We locked eyes for a second and she smiled. It was no more than a thinning of the lips, but it expressed her contempt as plainly as if she'd spit in my face.

Then Bobbi said my name, threw her body against mine, and we forgot about everything else for a few moments.

"You should have called." Her mouth was very close to my ear and I enjoyed the tickling of her breath. "I didn't know when you'd be back."

"I like surprising you."

"It *is* easier to catch them out that way," the woman said agreeably.

Bobbi pulled back a little, but kept her arms around me. "Jack, this is Marza Chevreaux. She's my accompanist."

I had wondered what she was. "How do you do?"

"Not as well as you, dear boy," she drawled sweetly, and held out her hand, forcing me to relinquish my hold on Bobbi in order to take it. It wasn't a fair exchange; her fingers lay briefly and limply in my palm and then recoiled to be better occupied at playing with the chain of her long necklace. She smiled again, took a step backward, pivoted on the same movement, and left us.

I hoped she was out of earshot and opened my mouth, but Bobbi beat me to it.

"You don't have to say it, I already know."

"I never saw her at the club."

"Slick didn't like her."

"Fancy that."

"She really is a good accompanist, once you get past all
her dramatics. We're a good team and I got the station to
agree to have her play when I sing."

"She said 'speak of the devil'; should my ears be burn-
ing?"

"A couple of the girls were wondering who I was dating,
and I can't help but talk about you. Because of Slick, Marza
doesn't think much of the men in my life, but she'll come
around once she gets to know you."

"Do you have some less discriminating guests in the meantime?"

"Sure, come in and meet them."

"What's this about again?"

"Just a little pre-broadcast party, then afterward we'll have
a post-broadcast party."

"I didn't know you were so social."

"Neither did I, but getting away from the club was like
getting out of jail. I just want to celebrate." Then she kissed
me again, linked an arm in mine, and pulled me into the
living room with all the noise.

It wasn't as large a group as I thought, but they made up
for it in volume. A half dozen were in the immediate vicinity,
with several brands of cigarettes and perfumes, none of it too
breathable, so I only indulged when it was necessary to talk.

Marza Chevreaux had taken up a station at the piano, but
was clearly not about to play it. Her purpose must have been
to prevent others from doing so. She clutched a drink and
stared with glassy eyes at an intense-looking man crouched
on the floor next to her. He wore thick glasses and had short
skin-colored hair on the sides and long dark hair on top. It
looked too much like a toupee to be one, so it had to be his
own. He was making short, waving movements with his hands
as he tried to prove a point of some kind to Marza.

"That's Madison Pruitt," Bobbi whispered. "Marza
brought him along because he irritates everyone."

"He looks more than capable of it. Why is he so irritat-
ing?"

"Because if you give him half a chance he'll try to get you
to join the Communist party. He's as bad as the Jehovah's
Witnesses."

"You're kidding me, nobody could—" I hauled up short, staring at the mountainous back of a man on the sofa. "What's he doing here?"

"Are you angry?"

I thought it over. "Actually, no, just curious."

She was relieved. "He's my friend, Jack. I wanted him here. You don't have to talk to him, he'll understand."

"That wouldn't be polite. Besides, this place isn't that big and he's a hard man to duck."

"You going to be nice?" She was half-joking, half-serious. I felt like kissing her and saw no reason not to and followed through.

"I'll be nice," I promised, and walked over to the sofa.

He was taking up most of it, a big man with hard muscle under the tailored lines of his evening clothes. With short-cropped blond hair and a grim set to his lips, he wasn't the sort you invite to liven up a social occasion. His eyes were slightly sleepy from the drink in his hand until he looked up at me. They visibly sharpened, went on guard, then relaxed into a pseudo-dullness. I knew that to be one of his defenses, that dull look. People expected a big man like him to be stupid. He let them think what they liked and consequently learned more about them than they cared.

I put my hand out. "Hello, Gordy."

He registered a flicker of surprise, slowly stood, and shook hands. He was beyond trying to prove himself with a crushing grasp and gave me a firm, careful grip.

"Fleming," he returned. "Bobbi said you might turn up."

"Yeah."

"She says you're taking good care of her."

I wasn't sure how he meant that. Bobbi wasn't dependent on me financially, so he must have been referring to our emotional relationship. He was too polite where Bobbi was concerned to make cheap remarks on our sex life.

"She's a wonderful girl."

"Glad you know that."

"And if I didn't?"

"I'd sic Marza on you."

It was my turn for surprise. I hadn't expected him to make a joke. I glanced over to the piano and saw he was serious, after all. Marza was glaring at us, and from her expression, all she needed were some snakes for hair to turn us to stone.

"No, thanks." I hooked a chair so we could sit and be eye to eye. Standing with him was uncomfortable. I wasn't used to looking up at people, and Gordy was tall enough to give Paul Bunyan a stiff neck. "How are things at the club?"

He shrugged and settled into the sofa. "Had to put up with a raid last week."

"The casino?"

"It looks good for City Hall in the papers, but they should hold off until just before election, like they usually do. They grabbed all my slot machines and chopped up the tables. Take a few weeks to get new ones, but by that time the heat will be off. The club's still open, lot of the regulars still ask after Bobbi."

"You think she'll go back?"

"Not after all that mess with Slick. Can't blame her."

"Nope."

"You working?"

"Sort of."

"Need a job?"

"What kind?"

"What kind you need?"

I shook my head and smiled. "Thanks."

"About that mess with Slick—"

"No hard feelings, Gordy."

"Yeah?"

"Yeah."

"I mean, sorry if I hurt you. I was just doing a job."

"You didn't hurt me."

"I didn't? How come?"

"You already know that."

He took a long pull on his drink, studying me. " 'Sfunny, you don't look any different from a hundred other guys off the street."

"If I did, I wouldn't survive long. People notice when you're different."

"Hell, you don't have to tell me that."

"You always been big?"

"Ma said I weighed thirteen pounds when I was born. Damn near killed her. You wanna drink?"

"No, thanks."

Again the long study. "You eat anything?"

"Not eat."

"So that stuff's true, that you only drink—"

"Yeah, that part's true."

"What about Bobbi? Doesn't that hurt her?"

"If it did, I'd stop seeing her. Why not ask her yourself?"

"Nah, I couldn't do that."

"If you're worried, just look at her, she's healthy."

He looked. She was in a corner talking and laughing with a white-haired man with a beard. "She's not under some kind of spell or something?"

I made an effort to match his serious face. "None."

He digested this. "Okay. I just wanted to make sure about a few things."

"On the other hand, I could be lying."

His head went back and forth in a slight wobble, his version of laughter. "Hell, kid, you ain't no liar."

Bobbi introduced me to some names and faces, and a couple of the voices that went with them were familiar because I'd heard them on the radio. We made the rounds, and then it was my turn to do some steering.

"What gives?" she asked when I took a determined grip on her arm.

"You'll find out."

The only unoccupied place was the bathroom, not the most romantic setting, but it was private.

"Alone at last," I sighed.

"At least until the next customer comes—there's a lot of booze flowing out there."

"Too bad. I wanted to see you for a minute without an audience."

"Oh, so what do you think?" Hands on hips, she did a slow turn. She was in her best color, which was no color; something white and clinging, probably silk.

I shrugged. "It's all right, but the hem's too long."

She made a playful swat at my stomach. "Stinker, it's perfect and you know it."

"Only because you're in it." Then we took up where we left off when I first came in.

After a few minutes she came up for air. "Say, you *did* miss me."

"Very much," I muttered, nosing around in her hair. Her head tilted back and my lips brushed against the large vein of her throat. I ran my tongue over the two small wounds there, taking in the slight salt taste of her skin and feeling the strong pulse beneath.

Then the damn phone rang and made us both jump because it was so close.

"Hell, what's that doing in here?" I complained.

"Better in here than the bedroom. Hello?"

It was someone from the radio station working late. They hashed out a minor scheduling problem and hung up.

"Why the long face?" she asked.

I curled my upper lip back and made a mock growling sound.

"Oh," she said with vast understanding, and cuddled back into my arms.

"When can you get rid of your friends?" I lisped.

"As soon as the booze runs out, which shouldn't be too long with that crowd. Why wait? You can nibble on me in here."

"That's like going straight to the dessert and skipping the rest of the banquet. I want us to take some time and enjoy everything."

This disconcerted her a bit, and a blush fanned over her cheeks. "Dammit, sometimes I feel like a schoolgirl with you."

"Isn't it great?"

On this occasion, Bobbi proved to be a terrible hostess and ran out of drinkable alcohol before the guests had run out of party enthusiasm. But her guests were resourceful: one of the girls suggested removing to a nearby bar that she thought was still open and led an exodus for it. Bobbi and I promised to be along and somehow forgot about it the moment the last person was gone.

Her white dress was certainly beautiful, but since I'd arrived, the major thought on my mind had been how to get it off her. The fastenings were located on the left side instead of in the back, but she slipped away before my inquisitive fingers could accomplish anything.

"Help me search the place," she said from the kitchen.

"For what?"

"In case someone got left behind. That happened to me once, and it's damned embarrassing."

We searched the place and then later, much later, in a sleepy voice she said, "Welcome home."

"Thanks."

"I mean it. Move in with me."

"Move in?"

"I want you around all the time."

"What would the neighbors think?"

"Whatever they like, I don't care."

"Bobbi, I don't want to say no—"

"But that's your answer."

"It has to be."

"Why?"

"Because of what I am."

"Because you have to be up to your eyeballs in some cemetery by dawn, right?"

"Something like that. I'd be very dull company during the day. I just don't want you to see me like that. You don't let me see you in curlers."

"Listen, if I can get used to your not breathing—"

"This is different, it's different for me. What I've been through, what I've become—I'm still trying to get used to it. I don't know how else to explain why. This is nothing against you."

"I know. You've had a lot of things happen to you all at once."

"I need some time."

She sighed. "Then don't worry about it. If it's no, it's no."

"You can be pretty damn terrific."

"Yeah, and I just realized what sort of commotion would happen if someone like the maid happened to find you while she was dusting. Having a coffin lying around with a body in it might upset the hotel staff."

I laughed. "Good grief, I don't use a *coffin*."

"I thought all vampires did."

"Maybe they do, but not me—I have a more modern

steamer trunk. It's smaller, just as light proof, and a lot less conspicuous.''

''Very clever.''

''I have to lay low for a while, anyway.''

''What's wrong? Is it Gordy?''

''No, nothing like that.''

We lay comfortably tangled together in the dark, and I told her about my trip and in particular about Braxton and Webber. ''They can travel during the day, so they're probably in Chicago by now and looking around. I just want you to watch out for them, or for anyone asking after me.''

''You're the one who needs to watch out if they're trying to kill you.''

''They won't. I can lose myself in a city this big.''

''Forever?''

''Until I can figure out what to do about them or until they run out of money.''

''Look, I can call up Gordy. He and some of the boys can throw a scare into them—''

''Bobbi, my sweet, they are determined to track down a hideous, bloodthirsty vampire; a demonic creature of the night. Do you think they'll be intimidated by a couple of gangsters with guns and brass knuckles?''

''Who said anything about intimidation? Gordy can just have their legs broken.''

''I can do that myself,'' I said dryly. ''Just promise me you'll be careful. They may try to save you from my evil clutches.''

''But I like being clutched by you.''

''I doubt if they could understand that.''

''Got any idea what to do about them?''

''I don't know, I'd like to talk it over with Charles first and see what he thinks.''

''I'm glad you mentioned him. He called today, but I'd forgotten all about it because of the party. He wanted you to drop by when you got back, no matter how late.''

''Even this late?''

''He said if the lights were on to come in.''

''I hate to leave you. . . .''

''Oh, pooh, you'll have to go sooner or later, so come on.

I'm hungry now, anyway.'' She rustled her way out from the sheets, and I obediently followed her to the kitchen.

What with our reluctant good-byes and some unexpected early traffic, it was close to six before I got to Escott's. My rear-view mirror was clear all the way over, which was encouraging, and when I arrived, there were welcoming lights in the windows. He must have heard me pull up, for the door opened before I knocked and a cloud of stale pipe smoke and white dust billowed out along with his greeting.

''I finally got your message. Sorry I'm so late.''

''Not at all. Do come in.'' He was dressed uncharacteristically in some ancient paint-spattered overalls and his hair was full of plaster dust. ''Please excuse my appearance, I started the job today and it turned out to be more involved than I thought.'' He ushered me into the parlor.

''What are you doing?''

''At the moment, taking a well-deserved break. It seems the previous owners subdivided all the bedrooms so they could accommodate more customers at one time. I've been upstairs knocking down a wall.''

''You've been at it all night?''

''It's a very stubborn wall, if I may anthropomorphize it.''

''When do you sleep?''

''Hardly ever,'' he said in an indifferent tone.

''What'd you want to see me for?''

''This. I'm not in a position to judge. It will be for you to decide what to do.'' Before I could ask what he was talking about, he reached for a folded newspaper and pointed to a circled item in the public notices. My fingers grew cold as I read it.

Jack, will you please call me. I want to talk to you about Maureen.

There was no name, only a phone and room number. I stared at the symbols on the page as though they could tell me more.

''Sorry about the shock, old man,'' he was saying. ''I knew you would want to know about this as soon as possible, but I couldn't really give any details to Miss Smythe.''

I read the ad again, not believing it, but none of the wording had changed. "How long has it been running?"

"It started the day after you left."

Then I stopped being stunned and things cleared up for me. "That old bastard . . ."

"I beg your pardon?"

"Braxton must have planted it to try and trap me."

"Who is Braxton?"

"Someone else you can check up on when you go to New York. He knew Maureen, or at least I think he did." I settled back and told him the story of the last three nights of my life. "The kid said they began looking for me when they noticed my ad was gone. This is probably just bait to flush me out."

"I think not. I took the liberty of tracking down the number. It belongs to a small but respectable hotel near the Loop. When I made inquiries, I was told to go to room twenty-three, occupied by a Miss Gaylen Dumont. She arrived two days ago from New York; a semi-invalid, she takes her meals in her room and is regarded as a very quiet, trouble-free guest. The name suggests that she is a relative of Maureen Dumont."

"Gaylen?" I repeated blankly. "I wouldn't know, Maureen never talked about her family."

"People who don't generally have a good reason. In the simple cause of common sense, I counsel you to be cautious about this."

"Hell, yes, I'll be cautious. Did you learn anything else?"

"She is in her seventies, listens to dance music on the radio, and doesn't like fried foods."

"How did you—"

"It is amazing how much one can learn from a hotel's staff when the right questions are applied in the right manner. Have you any reason to think that Braxton might be connected with this woman?"

"If he knew Maureen, he might know this Gaylen. I just don't know."

"This could be bad timing or coincidence, but it will be safer if you assume it is not. You removed your ad and some people noticed."

"Yeah, but not the one that mattered." The paper twitched

in my hands. "I'm checking on this first thing tomorrow night. Want to come along?"

"I was leaving for New York tomorrow, or rather today, but I can postpone the trip if you wish."

"No, I couldn't ask you to do that. I guess I can handle one old lady."

Escott looked out the front window. "Jack, it's getting lighter. If you've no other place to stay, perhaps we should move you in now."

"Jeez, I forgot."

My second trunk went into the basement next to the first, and between us we emptied the car of thirty-six bags of earth, piling them neatly in a corner. The faint gray of dawn was just beginning to hurt my eyes when we finished. Escott dusted his hands off.

"I'll bid you good morning now, I still have some cleaning up to do."

"It won't disturb me," I assured him.

"No, I daresay it would not. Pleasant dreams." He climbed the basement steps and shut the door.

As long as I had my soil around me I was past the point of being able to dream. All the speculations tumbling through my brain would have only given me nightmares, anyway. There were some compensations to my condition, I thought as I wearily lowered the lid of my trunk to hide for another day.

6

ABOUT THIRTEEN HOURS later I emerged from the basement, drawn by the swish-and-crinkle sound of pages being turned. Escott was in the parlor, half-buried in a drift of newsprint.

"I thought you'd be on a train by now," I said, dropping into a leather chair next to his radio.

He gave out with a slight shrug. "I seem to be acquiring your habits. I was up late and overslept."

"The whole day?"

"Most of it. Knocking down walls is a very exhausting exercise. This afternoon was too late to make a good start, and by then my curiosity about Gaylen Dumont had grown considerably. If she has any useful information it could save me much trouble. I'd like to meet her, but if you would rather go alone, please don't hesitate to say so. I shall be more than happy to wait here for your return."

"Nothing doing, I could use the moral support."

He looked relieved, but covered it by picking up his cold pipe and fiddling with it. "I'll do my best."

The papers weren't thrown about haphazardly, but shuffled into stacks on the sofa and floor. A neat pile was on one end of the table, each refolded so that it was open to the personal column. I flipped through them, and each had the same ad he'd shown me the night before.

"They are all the papers that you had used," he pointed out. "Either she knew which ones or she is remarkably thorough."

"I'll find out."

His phone was clinging to a dingy wall in the kitchen, which he hadn't gotten around to repainting yet. With one of the papers in hand, I carefully dialed the number. A professional voice answered, identifying the West Star Hotel and asked if it could help me. I asked for room twenty-three and heard clicking sounds.

After five rings a woman said hello. Her voice jarred me to the core because it was Maureen's voice. I bit my tongue and counted to five until I could respond normally.

"I'm calling about the ad. I think I'm the Jack you want to talk to."

There was a pause at the other end and I heard a long, soft sigh being released. "Jack," she finally said. "Could you prove that somehow? I've had two crank calls already."

It wasn't Maureen. The voice and inflection were very similar, but this one had the reedy quality of age in it. "How can I do that?"

"If you could just tell me the color of Maureen's eyes—"

"Blue, sky blue, with dark hair."

This time there was an intake of breath. "I am so glad to hear from you at last, Jack. My name is Gaylen Dumont and I would like very much to meet you."

"Where is Maureen? Do you know?"

It was as though she hadn't heard me. "I am so very glad you called, but it's difficult for me to talk over the phone. Could you come over?"

There was no other answer but yes. I got her address and promised to be there within half an hour. She thanked me and hung up. I stared at the earpiece and wondered suspiciously what her game was.

"She wasn't too talkative," I told Escott.

"Some people don't like to use the phone."

I was more inclined to think some people don't like to deliver bad news on the phone. Maybe I could have stayed on longer and tried to get more information. I was vulnerable to making mistakes because of my emotional involvement and was very glad Escott was coming. He might help me to think straight. As we drove over, half-formed thoughts and questions and alternatives to what I should have said were running through my mind like insane mice.

The West Star Hotel was nothing to write home about; neither old or new, flashy or drab, there were hundreds like it all over. We parked, went in past the front desk and elevator, and walked straight up the stairs to the right room. I hesitated before knocking.

Escott noticed my nerves. "Steady on," he said under his breath.

I nodded once, shook my shoulders up, and tapped on the door. No immediate answer came from within. I knocked again and heard faint movements now: a shuffling, a muted thump, the knob turned, and the wood panel squeaked open.

The voice was softer and less reedy than it was on the phone. "Jack?"

I swallowed. "Yes, I'm Jack Fleming."

The small shadowy figure in the dark dress stepped away, turned slowly, and retreated into the room. Her heart and lungs were laboring. She was either very excited, very ill, or both. I stepped forward and Escott followed quietly, taking his hat off with a smooth and automatic movement and nudging me to do the same.

We took in her plain impersonal room with a quick glance. The window was open only a crack, and the air well tainted with the smell of soap and strong liniment. A radio on a table crackled out the news of the day. She hobbled to it, using a cane for balance, and turned it off, then sat down with obvious relief.

"I'm so glad you could come over to talk," she said. "I did so want to meet you, and it is difficult for me to get around."

A suitcase stood at the foot of the bed and beyond that a stiff and ugly-looking wheelchair. She noted where my eyes went.

"That's for my bad days. They come more and more often, especially when it's damp. I have arthritis in my legs and it gives me a lot of trouble."

"Miss Dumont, this is my friend, Charles Escott."

She extended a frail, yellow hand. "How do you do?"

Escott took it and said something polite, making a little bow that only the English can do without looking self-conscious.

She smiled, pleased at the gesture. "I'm glad to meet you,

both of you, but you must call me Gaylen, everybody does. Pull those chairs a little closer to the light so we may have a good look at each other.''

We did as she said and sat down. Maureen's eyes looked back at me, but the dark hair and brows had faded and gone white. The angle of her jaw was the same, and there were a hundred other similarities too subtle for immediate definition. Her face was scored with wrinkles, the skin puffy and gone shapeless with age—a face like and unlike Maureen's. It was an agony to look at it.

She was smiling. ''I can hardly believe you're here. I hardly dared hope you would see my notice, especially after yours stopped. I was afraid you'd moved again.''

I explained how Escott had pointed it out to me.

''How very fortunate. You see, it was only a few days ago that I saw it. I live in upstate New York, pretty much by myself, and don't read the papers often. My housekeeper had a stack of them for her chores, though, and I saw one opened to the right page, and Maureen's name caught my eye. I remembered she once knew someone named Jack years ago, and I had to find out. I called the paper and they said you'd moved to Chicago. By then I'd found some of her letters to me and I knew you were the right person, so I came out.''

''Gaylen, do you know where she is?''

She bowed her head. ''I'm sorry, I am so dreadfully sorry to disappoint you.''

Everything inside me twisted sharply. ''Is she dead?''

''I don't know,'' she whispered. ''I haven't heard from her for nearly five years.''

The twisting got tighter. ''When did you last see her? What did she say?''

''I didn't see her, she called me. I don't know from where. She said she was going to be gone on a long trip and not to worry if she didn't write for a while.''

I shut my eyes for a moment. When I opened them, I was able to speak quietly, lucidly. ''Gaylen, tell me the whole story, tell me everything you know.''

''I'm not sure that I know very much. I only wanted to see someone else who knew her, who could remember her with me. I'd hoped you may have seen her in the last five years.''

I felt sorry for both of us. "You have the same name. How are you related to her?"

She seemed surprised. "I thought you knew. Surely she mentioned me?"

"She never talked about her past."

"How very unlike her. . . . Are you certain? Well, I am her sister—her *younger* sister, Jack."

"Younger," I echoed back softly.

"I'm seventy-two, Maureen seventy-six—did she tell you nothing?"

Her look made me acutely uncomfortable. "No, I'm afraid not."

She shook her head. "You poor young man, you must be starved for information. I'll try my best, but I hope you'll be as frank with me."

"How so?"

"When I told you her age, you were startled, but not incredulous. You are aware of her—her unusual state?" Her eyes went from me to Escott inquiringly.

Escott cleared his throat. "Please feel free to speak openly about your sister. Jack has made me acquainted with the facts. *All* the facts."

She regarded him soberly, pursing her lips. "Your accent, you're from England?"

He nodded once.

Gaylen's eyes were lighter in color than Maureen's. Now they faded to pale gray as she thought things over and made up her mind. "If it's all right with Jack . . . but some of my questions might be too personal."

"Questions?" I said. "No, Charles, stay, it's all right. What questions?"

She hesitated, struggling with something difficult within. She finally took a deep breath and said: "How close were you to Maureen?"

"We were in love."

"Then why did you separate?"

"It wasn't my choice, believe me. She left me a note . . . she said she had to leave because some people were after her. She would be back when it was safe."

"What people?"

"I don't know."

"And that was five years ago. Were you in school?"

"No, I was working for the—" I stopped and we looked at each other. Her expression was kindly and concerned, but I was in sudden doubt about how much I should confide in her.

She saw it and leaned forward. One of her small bony hands closed over mine, light and cool. "Jack, I'm old enough now to understand these things, and I hope wise enough to accept them. You can tell me, you loved each other. . . . Were you lovers?"

The words got stuck in my throat so I nodded.

She smiled. "Then I'm glad that she found some happiness. Could you tell me why you stopped the ad? Had you given up or was there another reason?"

"It's been so long. If there had been word, a single word from her, I'd have waited forever, but there was nothing. I had to get out of New York to try and start over, so I came here." I stopped, wanting to get up and pace. She patiently waited me out. "Well, I met new people and have new friends. I thought it was time to let the past go. If Maureen's alive, if she wants to find me, I left word at my old paper; they'd send her here."

"You don't think she's alive?"

"I don't know."

"Jack, I must ask you just one more question: you were lovers . . . did she *change* you?"

That was one I didn't want to answer, but my long silence was an answer regardless.

"If she did . . . well . . . it's all right. She was my *sister*. When it happened to her I still loved her; she was different, but not in any way that really mattered."

"Your older sister," I prompted, wanting to shift the subject around.

"Yes, it's hardly fair for me to ask all the questions. I should tell you some things as well. Go over to that table, bring me the picture on it."

I picked up an old-fashioned hinged frame for photos. It was ornate silver and just a little tarnished. I gave it to her and she opened it lovingly.

"You see?" She smiled and pointed at the soft, distant images on either side of the hinges. "I was just seventeen when we sat for these, and very nervous. I was afraid of shaking too much and ruining it, but it turned out very nice, after all. I'm on the left and this is Maureen on the right.''

I knew her instantly. Her hair was different, piled high with a cluster of small curls over her forehead. She wore a high collar, and pinned to it was a gold-and-ivory cameo that I remembered her wearing. Her pose and expression were stiff, but it was Maureen, her face identical to the likeness in my memory. Escott leaned over for a look.

''Maureen was twenty-one. As you can see at the bottom, those were taken in the year 1881. Oh, but we were pretty girls back then, all the boys were after us.''

''Did she marry?'' Escott asked.

''No. Neither of us. We were destined to be spinsters. Sometimes it works out that way. You don't plan on it, it just happens. Our dear parents passed on and we were alone; we couldn't bear the idea of becoming separated by a marriage. Life just went on and we were busy with charity work and the church and the literary club and the sewing circle. There seemed so much for us to do back then and the years slipped by so fast, but then it all changed.

''She met him at one of the literary club meetings. They'd got to talking about some terribly popular book that had just come out, though I couldn't name it now if I tried. His name was Jonathan Barrett, and we had all teased him a little because of Elizabeth Barrett Browning, you know. He was very nice about it and so handsome and all the girls were silly about him, but it was Maureen that he talked to at each and every meeting. She was in her thirties then and he in his twenties, and I tried to tell her he was too young, but she didn't care. He was so charming and proper I couldn't dislike him or be jealous of her, and so he often stopped by our house in the evenings.

''You can probably see the rest, but at the time I did not. Our lives were changing and I didn't see it at all. Maureen was so happy then and I was glad for her and I suppose these days no one would be too terribly shocked at what happened.

''Now back then, ladies were properly courted. They had chaperons and other difficulties, it's a wonder anyone ever got married with all the manners, requirements, and formalities. Only 'fast' girls would think of meeting a man alone, and of course if you went beyond that you were no longer considered fit for decent society. But she was in love with him. I suppose I was, too, a bit . . . sometimes a look would flash from his eyes and that made me quake all over. If it had been me instead of Maureen I would have done the same thing as she, and we would have been lovers as they were.''

I was not surprised at this news, but it was remarkably painful to hear.

''They saw each other for several years. He often had to be away on business—investments or something, he said— and in all that time he never mentioned marriage. Our friends speculated about it and I did, too—at least to Maureen—but she told me not to push her into things and forbade me to speak of it to Jonathan. Not to push her—this went on for eleven years, if you can believe it. Eleven years of courtship, or so I thought at the time.

''He only came at night. We'd visit, the three of us, then he would bid us good night and leave. Maureen and I would lock the doors, turn down the gas, and go up to our rooms. I suppose they waited until I was asleep, and then somehow he would come to her.

''I must have been completely blind at the time or it was my sheer innocence. Not once did I ever guess what went on, and it did go on for many years. It might still be going on.''

''What do you mean?''

''If she were still alive . . . still breathing, that is. It was 1904—they say things were quieter back then, but it wasn't so, things were just as noisy in the streets as they are today. Wagons made such a rattle and rumble, especially on the paving bricks. People shouted, children played, perhaps if there had been a little less noise that day she would still be with me, who knows?

''We were just crossing the street, it was nearly Christmas, there were a lot of people around us, other shoppers. I remember a band playing on the corner to collect money for the poor. It was cold and we were wondering how the players could keep warm if they never marched around. We laughed and skipped along in step to the drum. What a sight we must have been; two spinsters in their forties acting so silly. We heard only the music, nothing else. Then Maureen turned her

head to look up the street and suddenly pushed me. She
pushed very hard, my shoes slipped on some dirty ice, and I
was almost flying away from her. There was a rumble that
drowned out the band and a bell was ringing and I was thrown
up against a mass of people on the sidewalk. I was stunned
and couldn't move; they said I struck my head when I fell.
Some men carried me into a store, I fainted, and was then
taken to a hospital.

"She saw it coming, but there wasn't enough time for her
to do anything but push me out of the way. They said she
couldn't have felt much, that it was very quick. I like to
believe it did not hurt her. It was a firewagon and the horses
were running at full speed.

"I woke up in the hospital ward. I thought I'd die when
they told me she'd been killed. Jonathan came by that night
and tried to comfort me, but I was so wrapped up in my own
grief that I didn't notice his, or his lack of it. The funeral
was held the day I left the hospital, but he didn't come, and
I was very angry with him. He'd known her for eleven years
and did not come to see her buried. I was alone, utterly
shattered and alone.

"He came back again after a few days. It was a very difficult interview between us and he asked me some strange
questions. He was talking about living after death, whether I
would consider such a thing as a reality. He wanted to know
if I wanted to see Maureen again. Then he looked at me—
just looked—and it did not seem so absurd or horrible anymore. He told me I should be happy because Maureen was
really all right. I was shaking my head and smiling; it was
like dreaming, but he said he could prove it. He opened the
door and Maureen walked in.

"She wore a new dress . . . it was blue, just like her eyes,
and she was young, a girl again, and so pretty. . . ." Gayl-
en's head drooped, she looked very tired. She pulled a bit of
lace and muslin from her sleeve and dabbed her eyes. "I'm
sorry to get like this, it just all came back to me again."

"Can I get you anything? Some water?"

"No, I'm fine, I want to finish. They talked to me most of
the night and I learned a great deal about things I'd thought
impossible. But they were right there in front of me—Maureen

had been changed by Jonathan and had returned from the grave because of it.

"They were going to go away; she said she could not be with me anymore, it was hardly something our friends could understand, and of course she didn't want any of them knowing about her. She had wanted to see me again, she couldn't bear the thought of me grieving for her. It was so hard, almost cruel to have her back and then lose her again. She wrote me often, from many places, and she mentioned meeting you and how happy she was. I thought perhaps you knew more than I did about where she went. I'd hoped so hard. . . ."

"I am sorry." The words were inadequate, but they were all I had to give her.

She took my hand again. "That's all right, there's nothing we can do about it. At least for her sake—if you don't mind— perhaps we may be friends."

"Of course."

"What happened to Barrett?" asked Escott.

She looked at him, her face blank for a moment. He'd been keeping very still throughout the whole story and she must have forgotten his presence. "He was with Maureen at first, and then I suppose they drifted apart. I asked—but she said she didn't want to talk about it—she acted unhappy and I didn't want to pry."

"So you did see her occasionally?"

"Yes, but not very often."

"I see," he said neutrally.

She turned back to me. "Jack, would you be able to confide in me?"

I started to act puzzled, but she waved me down with a gentle gesture.

"It's all right. I think you know I've already guessed. It was from the first . . . you have the same look about you as Jonathan; it's some quality that I've never been able to define."

"I do?"

"Perhaps you are yet unaware of it. How long have you—"

"Just after I moved here," I said quickly. It was damn hard for me to acknowledge the truth to myself, much less a near-stranger.

"You poor man, was it an accident?"

"No, I was—" But I couldn't tell her. It was an ugly story and I couldn't tell her the truth of how I'd died.

Escott broke in. "Jack doesn't like to speak about it, it was rather unpleasant at the time. The doctors diagnosed it as food poisoning. He remembers being ill, passing out, and then waking up in the hospital morgue. It was quite sudden."

I gave him a quick, grateful glance. He looked concerned, but with a touch of blandness. He was an excellent liar.

"It must have been horrible for you."

"Not really, just a surprise." It had indeed been a surprise, so I wasn't exactly lying. "Maureen told me pretty much what to expect and what to do if it happened."

"And your family?"

"They know nothing about this. They think I'm still alive—in the conventional sense."

"Yes, that's good. At least you're not completely cut off as Maureen was; you can still visit them. It may be hard for you in the future when they begin to notice you don't age."

"I'll let the future take care of itself."

She turned her eye on Escott. "And you, Charles, how did you come to know about Jack?"

"I happened to notice that he did not reflect in polished surfaces and became curious to make his acquaintance."

"But you don't care what he is?"

"Not really. I find the condition of vampirism to be a fascinating study, but not something to fear. Knowledge is an excellent cure for fear. On the other hand, Jack is the only vampire I know. If this genus of the human race is at all representative of the majority, then there might well be a few of whom we should be wary."

"You sound like a very exceptional individual."

He made a depreciative little shrug.

"Gaylen, I asked Charles along to meet you because he wants to help us find Maureen."

"After all this time?" She was very doubtful.

"I can make no promises, ma'am, but if you could provide me with enough solid facts about Maureen and perhaps the loan of this photograph—"

"But I don't understand. How can you?"

"I am a private agent, an investigator. I shall be leaving for New York tomorrow on business, and as long as I'm there I'm going to look into the matter of her disappearance."

"To New York? Tomorrow? You mean you're all prepared?"

"Yes, I've planned on this for some time. In fact, I was to leave today, but decided to stay to meet you. Your notice appearing when it did was very fortunate. Any information you give me about Maureen could be helpful."

"I don't see how. After all this time do you really think there's any hope?"

"We shan't know until I try."

"When do you plan to return?"

"In two or three days, sooner if I should be lucky."

"That seems a very short time."

"Not when one is digging through official records and documents."

"He knows his job," I added.

She took her eyes from Escott, visibly changing mental gears. "Of course I'll help in any way I can."

"For a start, what do you know about a man named Braxton?" he asked.

"Who?"

"James Braxton," he repeated. "He owns a bookstore in Manhattan."

"I've never heard of him."

A stray thought occurred to me. "You said you had some crank calls; could you tell us about them?"

"Why do you want to know?"

"Just tell us."

My insistence was not what she wanted to hear, and I felt frozen out for a moment. There was also a quality about her, a kind of authority that made me very much aware of our age difference. She swallowed it and decided to answer.

"The first call was a girl. She said she was Maureen and she didn't like people talking about her, then she giggled and hung up. The second was from some man who wanted to know more about the notice. He called yesterday with a lot of questions that were not his business, and I finally told him as much. He never said who he was and I didn't want someone like that bothering me."

"Maybe that was him," I said to Escott.

"It would seem likely," he agreed.

"Who? Are you talking about this Braxton?" she asked.

"Yes."

"Who is he?"

"A self-styled vampire hunter."

Her expression went from curiosity to complete horror and her heart rate shot up accordingly. *"What?"*

I smiled. "Please don't worry about it, he couldn't find his a—his head with both hands."

"But if he knows about you, if he's after you—"

I took her hand and made reassuring noises until she was calm enough to listen, then told her a little about Braxton and his acolyte, Webber. In the end, she was still upset, but mastering it.

"There's really nothing for you to worry about," I said. "They don't know where I'm living now, and in a city this big they never will, unless it's by accident."

"But he read my notice and connected it with you—he knows where I am and could be watching this hotel. He could already know you're here and be waiting outside."

"There's an idea," I admitted. "But I've been keeping my eyes open. If I spot them, I can lose them."

"But if they find you during the day . . ."

"They won't, I promise. I'm in a safe place, really. I am much more worried about them bothering you."

"But what will you do about them?"

I shrugged and shook my head. Since coming back I hadn't had much time to think about it, and there had been no real chance to talk strategy out with Escott.

"Can't you do something to make them go away?" she pleaded.

Her concern for my safety was touching and embarrassing in its strength. She'd just found someone she could link to a pleasant past and was in danger, at least in her mind, of losing him. She would worry, no matter how much I reassured her. I regretted letting her in on the story, but she was better off knowing about Braxton; at least now she would be on guard.

Escott pulled out a small notebook and pencil. "And now,

Gaylen, if you can put up with a few questions about your sister . . .''

She blinked at him, distracted out of her worry. "Oh, yes, certainly."

It didn't take long. He gleaned a phone number and a couple of addresses from her memory, none of them familiar to me.

"I only wish I could be of more help," she said.

He gave her his best professional smile. "I'm sure this will be of great help, though I can make no optimistic promises."

"I understand."

"We have imposed upon you long enough, though, and must be going ourselves."

"Will you let me know if you find out anything?"

"Are you going to be in town when I return?"

"Yes, I shall be here awhile; it's a change for me. Jack, have you a number I can reach you at?"

"Um, yes, just a second." I scribbled down Bobbi's number. "You can leave a message for me at this one."

"And will you let me know what happens with this Braxton fellow?"

"As soon as I know myself."

Her eyes were shining. "Thank you. Both of you."

7

WE LEFT HER, neither of us saying much of anything. Escott was mulling things over in his head, and I was too drained and disappointed to want to talk right away, but not so tired that I didn't check the mirror now and then. There were plenty of headlights to fill it, but none of them belonged to a black Lincoln.

It was past Escott's suppertime, so I drove at his direction to a small German cafe a few blocks off the Loop. He gave his order in German, hardly glancing at the menu chalked on a blackboard above the cashier. We found a booth and settled in to wait for the arrival of his food.

"Thanks for the poisoning story. I was about to say it was a car wreck."

"Not at all," he said, absently aligning a saltshaker up with the checked pattern on the tablecloth. "An accident would have been acceptable, but she might decide to look up any records on it. There's the same problem with hospital records, but they can be more difficult to obtain."

"You don't think she'd check up on me, do you? She doesn't seem the type."

"Hardly, but if one must lie, it should be a simple one and difficult to disprove."

"What'd you think of her?"

"An interesting woman; she told a very pretty story. She seemed too good to be true."

"You didn't like her?"

"Emotions are the enemy of clear thought; my appraisals have nothing to do with personal affections."

"I'll put it this way, then: what bothered you about her?"

The pepper joined the salt on the checkered pattern. "She seemed terribly old."

"She *is* seventy-two."

"I speak of her state of mind. You can be seventy-two or ninety-two and still feel young inside."

"People are different."

"Mmm. Well, call it my natural caution at work. You were cautious as well. Why did you give her Miss Smythe's telephone number and not my own?"

I shrugged. "I didn't really think about it at the time. You're going to be gone for a while and I'm over at Bobbi's a lot."

"And perhaps you're worried that Braxton might trick or force my number from Gaylen and trace it down."

I frowned agreement. "There's that. I've got the house detective looking out for him, though, so Bobbi should be all right. The geezer's a little cracked, but I don't see him getting violent with an old lady."

"No doubt, but violence can emerge from the most unexpected sources. I can recall an exceptionally sordid case of two children knifing their grandmother to death to obtain her pet cat."

Escott's food arrived and delayed conversation for a while. Between the smell of the steaming dishes and his story, my stomach began to churn.

"I saw a drugstore on the corner and need to get some stuff," I said. "Be back in a few minutes."

He nodded, his attention focused on carving up his meal.

My shopping expedition left me with some mouth gargle, shoe polish, new handkerchiefs, and a handful of change for the phone. I folded into the booth and got the operator.

This time my mom answered, and for the next few minutes bent my ear as she reported the latest domestic crisis. Webber and Braxton had shown up at the house early the next morning, but unfortunately for them my brother Thom had dropped by for breakfast. The last three generations of Fleming males have been on the large side, and so he and Dad had no trouble throwing the troublemakers out. The yelling and language woke up any late-sleeping neighbors, but they were more than compensated by the show.

That same day the cops came, and at first Mom thought Braxton had called them, but they had different business altogether. Someone from the Grunner farm had reported vagrants on our old place, but the Grunners maintained total ignorance about the call. However, there had been a break-in as reported.

"Your father is fit to be tied over this, I can tell you," she concluded after giving me a full inventory of the damage.

"Is he fixing it, then?"

"Well, certainly, but it will take him awhile, and then there's no guarantee that the place will be left alone."

"Oh, yes, there is."

"What do you mean?"

"I mean, what would it cost Dad to install some real indoor plumbing?"

When we'd still been living there, Mom had known the figure down to the penny, but now she wasn't so sure. "What does it matter now, anyway?"

"Because if he puts some in he can rent the place out. That way it's occupied and you two have some extra income every month."

"You want a bunch of strangers running all over our old house?"

She'd never been so affectionate about the place when we'd been living there. "Better a bunch of strangers paying you rent than some tramps tearing it all up."

"Well . . ."

"Try to find out how much and I'll put up the money—"

"But you can't afford to—"

"I can now. I have a very understanding boss who pays bonuses for good work."

"In these hard times? He must be one of the Carnegies."

"Just about. Will you do it?"

She would, and when I hung up it was with a little more confidence in their future.

My personal future included immediate plans to visit Bobbi. I dialed her next and asked if she were receiving callers.

"That's a funny way of putting it," she said.

"I'm feeling old-fashioned tonight."

"Oh yeah? Well, come on over. I'm rehearsing, but I think we can squeeze you in."

I was disappointed, but kept it out of my voice. "You've got company?"

"Uh-huh."

"Marza?"

"Yes, that's it." Her phrasing indicated she was being overheard.

"Maybe I should stay away."

"No . . ."

"You mean if you can stand it so can I."

She laughed. "Sure, that sounds right."

"Okay, but if she threatens my life I reserve the right to withdraw to a safe distance."

She laughed again in agreement and we said good-bye.

Escott was in deep conversation with a stout bearded man wearing a white apron when I returned. They seemed to be talking about food from their gestures. They were using German and I only knew a couple of words. The man made some kind of point, Escott conceded, and the man looked pleased and left.

"What's all that about?"

"Against my better judgment, Herr Braungardt has tempted me into dessert, a torte of his own invention. This may take some time, I don't wish to tie you up."

"How long could it take to eat a dessert?"

"Long enough for him to try and persuade you to have a sample. I can find my own way home. Don't worry."

"If you need help, I'll be at Bobbi's." Grinning, I left him to his overstuffed fate.

I found a place that sold flowers and bought a handful of the least wilted-looking roses. They were cradled in my arm when I stepped off the elevator onto Bobbi's floor. The operator didn't have to tell me she had company this time, I could hear the piano and her voice clearly enough, despite the walls and solid door.

I thought to wait outside until the song was finished, but she cut off in mid-note. There was a murmured consultation, then the music began again. Marza's voice was hardly recognizable, and when she spoke to Bobbi her tones were soft and affectionate and heavily sprinkled with endearments.

"You've got to hold the note just a bit longer, baby. Count one, two, three, then we both start the next phrase. . . ."

I knocked and a second later Bobbi answered.

She just looked at the flowers, and her face lit up in a smile that sent me to the moon and back. She accepted them gracefully, her hands lingering on mine. "Any special reason?" she asked.

"I felt sentimental."

"Do I do that to you?"

"Among a lot of other things."

She took my hand and led me inside. Marza was at the piano, just lighting a thin black cigar. Her posture was straight and stiff and she was wearing another V-necked disaster, this time in yellow. It was quite a contrast to the pink satin lounging pajamas that Bobbi had clinging to her rounded figure. Marza glanced once in my direction without making eye contact, then pretended to study the sheet music before her.

On the sofa sprawled her Communist friend, Madison Pruitt. He looked up doubtfully, having seen my face once, but unable to attach a name to it. He was holding a tabloid, apparently interested in a murder investigation that the police weren't conducting to the satisfaction of the paper's editor.

"Madison, you remember Jack Fleming from last night?" prompted Bobbi.

"Certainly," he replied, still uncertain. At the party he'd been too involved spouting politics to Marza to notice our introductions. I regretted that the present circumstances were not similar, and didn't relish the prospect of conversing with a zealot.

"I think we should take a break," said Marza, not looking up from her music. "My concentration's all broken. Some coffee, Bobbi?"

Bobbi took the broad hint and I offered to help, so we had some semi-privacy in the kitchen. It was cramped, but organized; she worked on the coffee, and I ended up scrounging for something to put the roses in. I found a container that looked like a vase and loaded it with water.

"Here, put a little sugar in the bottom, they'll last longer. What's so funny?"

"Marza. I have to laugh at her or sock her one."

"I don't blame you, she can be a little trying at times."

"A little? That's like saying Lake Michigan's a little wet."

She stifled her own smile, and then we said hello to each other until the coffee was ready.

"Time to get the cups," she murmured.

"Couldn't we do this for a few more hours?"

"The coffee'll get cold."

"I don't want any."

"Yes, I suppose you want something else."

"Bobbi, you're psychic."

"Nope, I've got eyes. You're showing."

I snapped my mouth shut, trying the gauge the length of my canines with my tongue. Bobbi snickered and pulled out a tray, cups, and saucers. I carried it all in while she got the coffeepot.

Marza was next to Pruitt on the sofa and looked up. "What did you two do, go to Brazil for the beans?"

"No, just to Jamaica," Bobbi answered smoothly, filling the cups.

Marza approached her coffee delicately, tested one drop on her tongue, and decided to wait for it to cool. In contrast, Pruitt just grabbed his cup, leaving his saucer on the tray. I supposed he considered saucers to be an unnecessary bourgeois luxury.

"Your flowers, Bobbi, where are they?" Marza asked.

"Forgot 'em. I'll be right back." She slipped into the kitchen, but didn't come right back. Instead she was opening a cupboard, clattering a plate, and making other vague sounds.

"Flowers, such a thoughtful gift," Marza said sweetly. "You did know that Bobbi is allergic to some of them, or didn't you?"

"A lot of people are," I said evenly, and smiled with my mouth closed. I was speaking normally, but taking no chances on revealing the length of my teeth.

"Waste of money," said Pruitt, his nose still in the tabloid. "They die in a day or two and then you're left with rotting plants and no money. *People* are fighting and dying, you know."

"So you've told us, Madison," she said. "I don't notice you joining them, though."

"My fight is right here, trying to bring the truth to—"

"Cookies?" said Bobbi, just a shade too loud. She put the roses on the piano and offered the plate of cookies to Pruitt. It was a skilled move on her part—he had to choose between the plate, his coffee, or the paper. A hard decision for him, but the food won out and he dropped the paper. He was further distracted from his train of thought as he tried to figure out how to help himself to a cookie with both hands occupied holding the plate and his cup.

"You're not joining us?" Marza asked me as she wall-eyed Pruitt's juggling act. If he dropped anything it would be on her.

"No, thank you."

"Watching your weight, I suppose."

"No, I have allergies."

Pruitt finally gave the plate to Marza, then grabbed some cookies from it. They didn't last long and disappeared all at once into his wide mouth.

"You'll have to excuse Madison, he was raised in such a large family that he had to compete with his siblings for food, and learned to eat quickly in order to gain any nourishment."

"You know I'm an only child, Marza," he mumbled around the mass of crumbs in his mouth.

"Oh, I must have forgotten."

Pruitt nodded, content to correct her.

"What do you do for a living, Mr. Fleming?" she asked.

I couldn't say I was an unemployed reporter doing part-time jobs for a private investigator and opted for the next best thing. "I'm a writer."

"Oh? What do you write?"

"This and that."

"Fascinating."

"Need a writer," said Pruitt. He cleared his mouth with a gulp of coffee. "We need people good with words, articles for magazines, slogans—can you do that?"

"I'm sure anyone who knows even a little about the alphabet can help your cause, Madison," she said.

"Great. You think you could help out, Fleming?"

I could see how he was able to get along with Marza, since

he was totally oblivious to her sarcasm. I was beginning to like him for it. " 'Fraid I don't have the time."

"For some things in life you have to take the time. People have to wake up from their easy living and realize they must join with their brothers to battle for the very future of man on earth."

"H. G. Wells."

"Huh?"

"That sounds like his *War of the Worlds*."

"Who's that again?" He pulled out a little book and scribbled it all down. "What else has he written?"

"Lots of things. They'll be in the library." I wondered how many English courses he'd skipped in school to go to political rallies.

"Madison can't go there," said Marza. "They won't let him in."

Pruitt got a look on his face that would have done justice to a New Testament martyr.

"Why not?"

"Because there is no true freedom of speech in this country. The people here think there is because their capitalistic lords say so, but that isn't really true."

"Why not?" I tried again, this time with Marza.

"The library didn't happen to have a copy of some book he wanted. There was no English translation available and they weren't planning to order one. Madison protested by setting fire to some newspapers in the reading room, and they had him arrested."

"I had to bring to their attention that censorship to one is censorship to all."

"His father paid the fine, but the library still won't let him back in again."

"Censorship." He shook his tabloid. "This story is a prime example. A man speaks his mind in a so-called public place, and then the police arrest him because his political views disagree with the established order."

"They arrested him because he shot at a heckler," I said.

"That's what the paper *wants* you to think. That 'heckler' was really an assassin for Roosevelt's Secret Service. He'd been sent to silence a voice of freedom for the masses and only got what he deserved."

My mouth sagged a little. Pruitt got the satisfied look of one who had scored a real point. A half dozen counterarguments popped into my head, but the best course was to say nothing. There was absolutely no point having a battle of wits with someone who was unarmed.

Bobbi put her cup down and suggested more rehearsal. It was gratefully accepted and the ladies returned to the piano. Madison stretched his legs out, crossed his arms, and yawned loud and long. The volume was sufficient for yodeling and the size of his mouth—a quantity of crumbs were still trapped in his molars—was an inspiration to well drillers everywhere. He wound up his musical solo and shut his eyes. From the not-so-subtle movements of his jaw, he seemed to be rooting out the last remnants of cookie with his tongue. I settled back in my chair to listen and wondered what the hell Marza saw in him, not that she was any social bargain herself.

Her true worth, as Bobbi had said, was as an accompanist. Her hands went solidly over the keyboard with expert ease, though she had to hold them at a low angle to keep her long nails from clicking against the ivory.

They did a warm-up on scales, and then Marza began one of the songs Bobbi would sing for the broadcast. It was a rich slow number and made a good showpiece for her voice, which was excellent. I sighed and let the sound wash over me, soothing and exciting at the same time. Perhaps later in the soft darkness of her room I would ask her to sing again.

They finished and held a consultation over it and I cast around for something to read, my eye catching on a fresh copy of *Live Alone and Like It* on the end table. I flipped through, noticing it was a gift to Bobbi from Marza. It would be. I was just starting to read a chapter with the unbelievable title: 'The Pleasures of a Single Bed,' when the room got unnaturally quiet.

Pruitt was staring at some point behind me, mouth and eyes looking as if he'd borrowed them from a dead fish. Marza and Bobbi were also frozen and doing a reasonable imitation of gaffed sea life. My back was to the door, and with a sinking heart, I turned to see what inspired the tableau.

Advancing slowly from the wide-open door, with large silver crosses clutched in their hands were James Braxton and

Matheus Webber. Both of them looked determined, but very nervous.

What made the bottom of my stomach drop out was the revolver Braxton held stiffly in his other clenched fist. His finger was right on the trigger, and I didn't know how much pressure it would take for the thing to go off. If the damned idiot forgot himself . . .

I stood up cautiously, my hands out and down and my eyes fixed on Braxton's. His were little pinpoints in a sea of white, gleaming with fearful triumph. Mine must have been just as wide, but without the triumph, only the fear. Unless that gun had wooden bullets, I had no concern for my own life, but anything else was another matter. If he shot at me, the bullet would pass right through, going on to Bobbi and Marza, who were right in the fool's line of fire.

From somewhere I heard myself speaking, pleading, "Please don't do anything, Braxton. These people are innocent, please don't shoot."

The seams on his brown face twitched a little, but I couldn't read him. I didn't dare try any kind of hypnotic suggestion—the least mistake on my part could kill Bobbi.

"I'll do what you want, just don't shoot," I told him. "These people . . . they're . . . they're not like me, I swear they're not. They know nothing about this."

"That remains to be seen, you leech," he said. He punctuated this by a wave of his cross and took a step forward. I flinched and fell back, but also stepped to one side. Bobbi and Marza were still out of sight behind me. Maybe they were marginally clear, but only if Braxton were a good shot.

Matheus was as keyed up as the rest of us, but he looked around and tapped Braxton's shoulder. "Mr. Braxton, look—they had coffee."

His eyes snapped to the tray and cups. "Is that true? Did you have coffee?"

Only Bobbi understood the significance of his question. "Yes, we did, and cookies, too. Didn't we Madison?"

Pruitt's head bobbed several times.

I heard Marza shift next to Bobbi. "That's right, we all had coffee and cookies." She spoke slowly, as though to an idiot child. In this case she wasn't too far off the mark.

Braxton shook his cross at me. "But not him."

I repeated my flinching act and moved another step to the side. "Braxton, they know nothing at all. You have no reason to involve them—"

"Shut up."

He had the gun and I still couldn't see Bobbi, so I shut up.

"You two—sit on the couch. Now!"

Bobbi and Marza made haste to join Pruitt. Good.

"What are you going to do?" Bobbi asked.

Braxton smiled at me. "I'm going to wait. We're all going to wait for morning."

"But why? What do you want?" demanded Marza.

He ignored her and stared at me grimly. Bobbi knew very well what such a wait meant, but hid it. The three of them fell silent, their stares divided between me, Braxton, and the gun.

"What kind of bullets, Braxton?" I asked.

"The best kind. They were expensive, but I judged them worth the cost."

"Silver?" I mouthed the word, not wanting the others to hear.

He smirked.

Bobbi moaned and her head swayed. "Oh, God, I'm going to be sick." Marza put a protective arm around her.

"What do we do, Mr. Braxton?" Matheus was bug eyed at Bobbi's white face.

"What?"

"I'm going to be sick." She gulped air and jerked to her feet.

"Follow her," he told the kid. "The rest of you stay where you are."

Bobbi ran to the bedroom with Matheus close behind, but she shut him out when she reached the bath and slammed the door in his face. He was still very much the kid and hardly had the gumption to go inside after her. Through the walls I heard her coughing, then the rush of water when she flushed the toilet. She took her time at it and Braxton started to fidget.

"Look," I tried again, "we don't need to be here."

"Quiet and keep your eyes down."

"What do you want?" asked Marza. A large chunk of her veneer had come off in the past few minutes. She looked much more real to me now.

Braxton pretended not to hear and called to Matheus. "If she's done, get her out."

The water was still running. Matheus knocked gingerly on the door. "Uh . . . miss . . . uh . . . you all right?"

Bobbi mumbled a no and turned on a sink faucet.

"You have to come out now." She didn't answer. He appeared at the bedroom door, shrugged helplessly at Braxton, and went back again.

"I'll go get her," said Marza.

"No." Braxton was not about to let the situation get any more out of hand.

"How did you find me?" I asked, distracting him.

"What? Oh, it was the old lady. I knew you would go see her eventually, so we waited at her hotel and followed you from there. This time we were more careful about it."

"Smart, real smart."

He made a little formal nod of acknowledgment like an actor in a play. He must have cast himself as Edward Van Sloan to my Lugosi. The only things missing were the accents and evening clothes.

"Miss? You've got to come out." Matheus sounded a little more impatient now, and that gave him confidence. "I mean it, come out of there."

The water cut off and the knob rattled. "Don't rush me, big shot," she growled. She pushed unsteadily past Matheus and stood in the doorway. The tableau hadn't changed. She took a step toward me.

I shook my head minutely. "You look done in, Miss Smythe, you'd better sit down."

She nodded, figuring out the reason behind my sudden formality. She had no wish to have Braxton breathing all over her neck looking for telltale holes. Things were safe for the moment; her lounging pajamas had a high Oriental collar. She glided back to the sofa, glaring at him.

"You mugs have no right barging into my home. My neighbors are bound to hear all this and call the cops."

He waved her down. "I have every good reason behind my actions, however strange they may appear to you. If you do not yet understand my mission, I promise you that you soon will, and when you do, you shall approve of what I am doing."

"It's the police state," said Pruitt, gaining a revelation from God knows where. "Who are you with, the Secret Service?"

"Secret Service?" said Matheus, looking blank. He was standing next to Braxton now, keeping me covered with his cross.

"Yes, the Secret Service, you fascist."

Marza spoke through her teeth, which were exactly on edge. "Madison, this is no time for politics, so shut up."

"I'm telling you—*ouch*!"

"I said shut up."

"Who's a fascist?"

"Matheus—"

"But he called me—"

"Everyone *quiet*!" Braxton must have felt the situation physically slipping out of control. He was already sweating from the strain and certainly not used to it. He'd never last until morning the way things were heading.

"Braxton, please listen."

He liked the pleading tone in my voice and considered my request like a magnanimous ruler. "All right, what is it?"

"What Miss Smythe said was true, this is no place to settle things. There's a hotel detective downstairs—"

"*You* think there is, leech."

So they had slipped by Phil somehow. It was time to change tack. "I can't help what I am, I've tried to tell you that."

He shook his head. "And I am sorry for you. I think I know what kind of hell you face each night. . . . I will end it for you."

Good God, he thinks he's doing me a favor. "No, not here, please, at least for the sake of the ladies."

"We will remain here. You seem to care for these people. I do not wish to use them as hostages for your behavior, but I see no other way."

He sounded very certain of his hold over me. He was either stupid or had an extra ace up his sleeve he hadn't yet shown. I was inclined to think he was stupid. He was badly underestimating my will to survive and believed crosses and silver to be a strong check. The only thing actually holding me back was trying to come up with a way of safely disarming him without revealing my true nature to Marza or Pruitt.

I glanced at Bobbi to see how she was doing. Perched stiffly on the edge of the sofa, her whole posture was tense, natural enough under the circumstances, but something in her manner struck me as odd. Her left arm lay across her knees, the right hand resting on the left. The long sleeves of the pajamas were pushed up to the elbows. Her eyes caught mine and her mouth twitched in an almost-smile and she winked, her eyes dropping to her hands. Her right index finger was tapping once a second against the crystal of her watch.

I got it, or thought I did.

"Matheus," I said, sounding reproachful. "I asked you to talk with him. I was pretty reasonable about it all. Remember, I could have hurt you then, but I didn't. Does that fit in with the things he's been saying about me?"

"It was a trick," he said. He spoke with the haughty conviction of a convert. "Besides, you left us stranded and stole the car."

"I left it at a fire station, for cryin' out loud. You two were bothering my family, I had to do something."

"We were trying to warn them about you."

"How would you feel if I did the same to your folks? Do they know what you're doing? What do they think of this quest you and Braxton are on? Do they approve?"

That one hit a sensitive spot and the kid went all red, right up to the ears. "They wouldn't understand."

"So you haven't told them. Maybe you should. Write a letter: 'Dear Mom, tonight Braxton and I held four people at gunpoint—' "

"Enough!" Braxton was actually stamping his feet. "Matheus, I warned you how he would twist things. He's one of the devil's own and will try and confuse you."

"Not me, Braxton, you've already done that. You don't want the kid to think for himself. You might lose your only hold on him."

"Shut up."

"I figure he's really smarter than you, but you don't want him to find that out."

"Shut up!"

I am not overly brave, and baiting a nutcase holding a gun is not something to do for fun, but it is a hell of an attention getter. Everyone was gaping at me, each with expressions varying from rage to puzzlement to worry, and one in particular of intense concentration. The last and most welcome face belonged to Phil, the hotel dick. He had just walked in the still-open door and was trying to sneak up on Braxton. In this hotel he never got much practice at being quiet, so it was costing him some effort. I opened my big mouth again to cover any creaking floorboards.

"Yeah, I guess the truth hurts. It must be nice to have someone around to agree with you all the time, or do you pay him money for it? There's not enough of that stuff in the world to make me want to put up with your kind of bull—"

Then Phil lunged, both hands grabbing Braxton's arm and dragging it down. Marza and Pruitt screamed as the gun went off and thunder and smoke filled the room. A furrow appeared in the floor near my left foot, and I foolishly jumped back from it.

There was a good fifty-pound difference between them, and Braxton's light frame didn't stand a chance. He went down like a tackling dummy, his knobby joints knocking hard against the floor. Phil was on top and his extra weight had pushed all the fight out of the little guy. A second later Phil was in possession of the gun and getting to his feet.

He dusted his knees absently, and glared all around. "Someone want to explain things to me, or do I really want to know?"

Matheus began to edge toward the door, but Bobbi spotted him. "Hold it right there, buster."

He held it right there and looked to Braxton for help, but his mentor was too busy getting his breath back and nursing his new bruises. Phil went to the door and checked the hall, keeping the gun out of sight.

"Nuthin' to worry about, folks, just a party trick. Sorry about the noise." He waved an apology at someone and shut the door.

"What *is* this all about?" demanded Marza, her voice shaking.

"They're just a couple of mugs from my shady past," I said. "The geezer here is a con man that I once did a story on. It blew his game to hell and he's looking to get back at me. The kid is just his latest trainee. The last I heard, it was an insurance scam. Looks like he's switched to religion. What are you doing these days, Braxton, swindling old ladies for church funds?''

Braxton flushed, jerkily stood up, and shoved his cross at me. I ducked back so it missed my nose. ''Away, you demon.'' Somehow, he'd sounded a lot more convincing on that lonely road in the country.

''He's crazy,'' concluded Pruitt.

''For once, I'll agree with you,'' said Marza.

The cross jerked again and I stepped away from it.

''Braxton?'' Phil made certain he could see the gun. ''Sit down and shut up.''

''But you don't know who or what this man is—''

''As long as he's not waving guns at the tenants, I don't give a damn, so clam up. What do you want I should do with 'em, Miss Smythe?''

Bobbi looked at me. I shrugged. ''Call the cops?''

Pruitt suddenly found his feet. ''I think I'll go home now, it's awfully late.'' He grabbed his hat and hurried out.

Marza stared after him. ''Why, that no-good—how does he expect me to get home?''

''Oh, Marza,'' Bobbi groaned.

''What's with him?'' asked Phil.

''He's crazy,'' said Matheus.

''So coming from you that means something?''

''He called me a fascist—''

''Shut up, kid,'' Bobbi told him. He looked hurt. ''Jack, I don't think the cops could do much for us.''

''They could take his gun away and lock him up if we pressed charges, but that'd mean court appearances, the paper—you don't need any bad publicity before your broadcast.''

''Yeah. But what do *we* do with them? I could call Gordy.''

''Don't tempt me. Phil, have you got some place you can stash these two?''

''Depends for how long.''

''An hour?''

He nodded. ''If you give me a hand.''

''Sure.''

We wrestled Braxton into the hall and took the service stairs down to the basement instead of using the elevator because the operator liked to talk. It was an interesting parade:

I had Braxton's arms twisted behind his back and Phil was keeping the kid in line with the borrowed gun.

In the basement, Phil directed us to a broom closet that was made to order. Brooms must have been at a premium in the building, because the place was like a bank vault. Two of the walls were part of the cement foundation and the third was solid brick. It was about ten feet long and only four feet wide. We pushed them in with the mops and buckets and Phil locked it up.

"They gonna be able to breathe in there?" I asked.

Phil studied the blank face of the door for a while, then nudged it with one toe. "There's a pretty good gap at the bottom. If they get desperate, they can stick their noses down there."

We heard a thump and dull clang from within. Someone had tripped over a bucket. Matheus hit the door a few times and yelled to be let out.

We climbed upstairs. "Sure it won't be too noisy?"

"I'll make certain no one bothers them."

"Thanks. I'll go see if Bobbi's all right and work out what to do with them."

"I'll be in the lobby."

Four floors later I was back in Bobbi's apartment. She was just giving Marza a drink, then ran over to me, her arms open. We held on to each other, not speaking for a long while. Marza finished her glass, put it on a table, and stood.

"No more rehearsal tonight. I'm calling a cab."

Bobbi whispered, "She was really shook, can you take her home? Would you mind?"

When she looked at me like that I wouldn't mind walking over hot coals, or even taking Marza home. "If you'll be okay."

"I'll be fine. Marza . . ."

She got in my car and said nothing for the next ten minutes except to give directions. We stopped in front of her apartment building and I waited to see if she wanted me to walk her in or not.

"We're here," I said when she didn't move.

She stopped boring a hole in the windshield and tried it

with me. I was getting another once-over, and the reappraisal was even more critical. "Why were they after you?"

"I told you."

"The truth this time."

I shook my head.

"Are you with the gangs?"

"No. This is some old business that followed me from New York. The guy is crazy, you saw that."

"Yes, I saw that. So what was it about? Why come after you with a couple of crosses? Why call you those names?"

"I said the guy's nuts. Can you account for all the stuff Pruitt lets out?"

"Madison's preoccupied with politics and being paranoid, so what is your friend preoccupied with?"

"With trying to blow my head off."

"And what happens to Bobbi when he comes back?"

"They're after me, not her.'

"They were holding all of us. Do you think he won't try again?"

"He won't get the chance. I'm going to have a little talk with him tonight and straighten things out. Bobbi will be okay. I promise."

"I hope you mean that. I don't want her hurt. Not by them or you, you know what I mean? She's a beautiful girl and that's attracted the wrong kind of men to her in the past. Did she tell you what the last one was like and what happened to him?"

"I know all about it," I said truthfully.

"Good, because that's what I want to see her free from. You have no right to bring it all back."

She had some guts. If I'd really been like Slick Morelli, she was courting some broken teeth. "I don't plan to. I'm on your side."

She was anything but convinced, but there was no way I could prove my sincerity except to go back and deal with the problem. She gave me a "we'll see" shrug and got out. I waited until she was inside and drove a beeline back to Bobbi.

She unlocked the door after hearing my voice. "I thought you'd never get back."

"Same here."

"Thanks for taking her, Jack."

She was hugging me again. It was becoming a habit, a very nice one. Then it was time for my reaction and I couldn't stop it. My arms moved on their own, wrapping around her and lifting her from the floor. I held her hard, as much for warmth as for comfort. I was cold from the inside out and shaking all over.

"Jack? What is it? What's wrong?"

It was a long time before I had the strength of will to release her. I was damned near to crying. "That idiot . . . I was afraid he'd kill you."

Her light fingers stroked my brows and lids. "But he didn't. Everything's okay. He wasn't even aiming at me."

"He didn't have to, the bullets would have gone right through me. His silver is no more use against me than any other metal."

"You mean the bullets—"

"They're metal. The silver makes no difference. He's gotten vampires mixed up with other folklore."

"His cross held you back, though," she said in a small voice.

"That was acting." I looked around. She'd been cleaning up. The coffee service was gone and there was a throw rug covering the bullet furrow in the floor. On the table was Braxton's cross. He'd dropped it in the tussle with Phil. I carefully closed my hand over it and held it up for her to see. "There, nothing happens and it's made of silver."

"But why not?"

"I guess it's because God doesn't work the way Braxton thinks he should." I opened my hand and let her regard what lay in it. "I'm not evil, Bobbi. I have no fear of this, but I was afraid of losing you and can only thank God you're safe."

She came into my arms again and this time we did not let go.

I carried her to bed and tucked her in, which she thoroughly enjoyed. She was always a little sleepy afterward, regardless of how little I took from her. I sat next to her on top of the spread and kissed a few spots that had been missed earlier and made her giggle.

"Damn, you're good."

"So are you."

"Do you have to go?"

"There's some unfinished business downstairs. Say, how did Phil know to come up here, anyway?"

"You forgot about that phone I keep in the bathroom."

"Then your getting sick—"

"Hey, you think you're the only one who can act if you have to?"

Her door was locked and I left it that way, slipping quietly through into the hall and taking the stairs to the lobby. Phil was behind his pillar, talking odds with the night clerk again. He saw me and nodded, then led the way down to the basement.

I planned to have him baby-sit Matheus while I had a private talk with Braxton. It wasn't something to look forward to, but I'd decided to try hypnosis on him. The man was stubborn and would be on guard, though. I was certain I could break through, but afraid of hurting him, of hurting his mind. The last man I'd done it to . . . well, the circumstances were different now, things were controlled, and I was emotionally calm. I had no wish to hurt Braxton, only to find out his connection with Maureen and then make him go home.

Plans are just fine when they work out, but this one would have to wait. The closet door was hanging open and the two hunters were gone. Phil stooped to examine the lock, holding a match to the inside of the door. He shook his head in mild exasperation.

"The old goat musta had skeleton keys. Who'da thought it?"

"I should have."

Braxton had underestimated me and I'd stupidly returned the favor. The man most certainly planned to kill me, and to do so he might have to break into almost any kind of building. He was sure to be outside to track me home when I left. The keys would jingle, the lock giving way to them, and then his shadow would fall across my trunk. . . .

"Can you keep an eye on four tonight—make sure Miss Smythe stays okay without disturbing her?"

"I can do that. What about you?"

"I'm going to get lost."

"Sounds like a good idea. I'll show you the back door."

8

HE LET ME out in a wide alley where delivery trucks trundled through during the day with their loads of food and linens. Things were comfortably deserted now, but I still felt like a shooting gallery target, and vanished as soon as Phil locked up.

I didn't know this area particularly well and being in a non-corporeal form only added to the disorientation. My sense of solid objects, even the push of the wind was heightened and extended, but since I couldn't see, it was hard to gauge distance. When moving, I had to rely on memory.

The alley entrance to the street was fifty feet to the left, with a row of garbage cans just before it, but the wind was throwing my direction off and to the right. Compensating, I drifted past the cans like smoke that wasn't there, then found the corner of the building. Left, right, or straight? Right. Move away from the hotel and car, float softly down the sidewalk, gain some space, and look around.

An alcove opened in my path, which meant a doorway. I entered the building and solidified in a closed pawnshop. The street looked clear; they might have returned to their own hotel for fresh strategy, but I couldn't count on that. They might also have my car staked out, so it would have to stay put. It was getting late for me and playing car chase with them might take too much time—was there anything in the car that would lead them to Escott's? The papers inside were in my name, with my old hotel as an address. No one there knew Escott except by sight. The dealer could be traced, but that would lead them to the hotel again. I could relax. If they did break into the car all they'd find was a dead end, along with some mouth gargle, shoe polish, and handkerchiefs.

All the same, having to leave my car behind was a disgusting situation. Braxton would have a lot to answer for the next time I saw him.

I took some bearings, disappeared again, and didn't re-form until several city blocks were behind me. I checked the view, found it clear, and started walking.

Maybe I could have scoured the area until I found them, but there was no guarantee that Braxton didn't have a second gun on hand. If he used it the racket would bring all sorts of trouble. I shook the thought out of my head. One thing at a time, one day, or rather night, at a time. I was tired, the sunrise was coming, and I still had to make sure they weren't following me to Escott's.

I eventually seeped inside his back door and listened. The place had its own little creaks and pops, each loud in my straining ears. There were also small scratchings and a rhythmic gnawing sound; mice in the basement. Overall, it was a good normal silence, but it meant I was alone in the house. Where the hell was Escott?

My answer was propped against the saltshaker on the table.

JACK,

ALL THINGS CONSIDERED, I DECIDED TO TAKE A NIGHT TRAIN TO N.Y. AND CLEAR UP THIS BUSINESS. MY OVER-SEAS SHIPMENT SHOULD ARRIVE TOMORROW AT 7:45 P.M. PLEASE CALL ME WHEN IT COMES. I'LL BE STAYING AT THE ST. GEORGE HOTEL.

ESCOTT

On my own again. Great.

There wasn't enough time to call a cab and find a hotel to hide in, I'd have to hope Braxton hadn't had Escott followed from the restaurant. And then there was Gaylen—had he bothered her? I speculated briefly and irrationally if she had put him onto me, but shook that thought off as well. She'd been far too concerned for my welfare; no one was that good an actress. My troubles were my own; no one else could be blamed for them and no one else could clear them up. But that was tomorrow's problem.

Escott had given me the run of the house. I went up to the top floor, floating carefully over a patch of undisturbed plaster dust so as not to leave footprints. A small door at the end of the topmost hall led to yet another stairway, a short one that served the attic. There was dust everywhere and a number of interesting artifacts left by previous generations of owners. It looked suitable, but I still did not feel really safe.

I ghosted over to the one window at the far end. It faced another window in the next building just across the narrow alley. I gulped, tried not to think of the drop, and vanished, feeling a dull tug all over as I passed out of Escott's house to the one next door.

The attic was similar to the one I'd left: full of dust and domestic junk, but I felt much more secure. The place was occupied below, but I was more willing to chance spending the day here. It would be better to be found by Escott's neighbors than by Braxton, though from the condition of things they hadn't been up here in years and it was likely to remain so.

I went back to Escott's, retrieved a single bag of earth from the basement, and borrowed a blanket and pillow. The invisible nets that went out around me when I vanished, the ones that allowed me to retain my clothes and such, were sufficient to take in my light burdens. I floated directly up through the many floors to the attic again and moved next door, leaving no trace of my passage for inquisitive eyes.

Somewhere outside, the sun was creeping to the horizon, but the one window was deep in the shadow of the roof overhang and opaque with grime. The light would not be too bad. I had certain powers, but very strict limitations as well, and sunlight was one of them. It blinded the eyes and stiffened the limbs, and then the numbness beginning in my feet would travel slowly to the head until it mercifully brought unconsciousness. Being subjected to the unpleasant inertia of dying only happened if I fought to stay awake after dawn, or if I was without my earth. Since my change I'd tried staying up only once voluntarily as an experiment. It was not something I ever wanted to repeat.

Spreading the blanket, not for comfort, but to protect my clothes, I stretched out behind some old boxes, the pillow resting firmly over my face to block the light. The earth was in the crook of my arm and reminded me of the stuffed toy rabbit my oldest sister Liz had given me thirty years ago. They were her specialty. She'd made them for her own children and all the nieces and nephews of our big family. She was a sweet woman.

And then I surrendered all thought and became very still.

The pillow slid from my face as I sat up and listened. A car rumbled by down below, interrupting the neighborhood kids in their game of street tag. Another day had slipped past and they were playing all the harder at its end before their mothers called them in to supper, bath, and bed. The air was dry with the smell of dust and coming up from the kitchen was the odor of boiled cabbage and fried fish. I wondered if the kids would survive to adulthood on such a diet. I had, but maybe I'd been tougher.

My own diet was of concern for me tonight. The relationship Bobbi and I shared was an emotional one, after all. The small amount of blood she provided was for the purpose of lovemaking, and not to satisfy my nutritional needs. More blood than she could spare was required for that. Later on I'd have to visit the Stockyards, but my trips there were less frequent than they were before we met—only once every three or four nights, rather than once every other night.

Gathering up the bedding, I sieved across the alley to Escott's attic and sank down through the floors to the kitchen. It was a neat trick; if Escott ever went back to the stage we could make a fortune with a magic act. The only drawback was that I'd never be available for the matinees.

I worked the phone and Bobbi's welcome voice said hello and I said hello back and we each made sure the other was healthy.

"Phil told me you were going to lay low for a while," she said.

"Just until I can locate those bozos. I didn't have the time last night."

"You won't have to look far. Phil called and said they're parked down the street in a black Ford."

"Is he sure about that?"

"Fairly sure, and so am I. I took a gander out the window a minute ago and there's a car there now that's new to the usual scenery. Phil thinks they're waiting for you to come back for your own."

"Good conclusion. I'm just surprised that Braxton thinks I need it."

"What do you mean?"

"Considering his expertise, he's more likely to suspect me of traveling around as a bat or a wolf."

She giggled. "They might miss a bat, but a wolf's kinda noticeable out on the sidewalk."

"Maybe I should reeducate him. What do you think?"

"I think I'm going to take a cab to the studio."

"I'm sorry, I know I promised—"

"Oh, don't be a sap, this is an emergency. Oops, I just remembered, some woman named Gaylen called a minute ago. You running around on me?"

"Never. What'd she want?"

"For you to come by and see her tonight. Who is she?"

"It's something I'm working on with Charles. He's out of town, so I gave her your number for daytime calls."

"Wish you'd told me."

"We were kind of busy. . . . Did she say anything else?"

"Nope. You going to tune in and listen to me?"

"I'll be at the studio. I wouldn't miss it for the world."

"But what if Braxton follows me there?"

"Don't worry, I'll have taken care of him by then."

"But what if you miss him?"

"I said don't worry. You aren't going there alone, are you?"

"No, Marza's coming with me."

"Then God help Braxton if I do miss him."

"Oh, *Jack*." She was exasperated. "The man *is* trying to kill you."

"He won't. I'm only trying to keep him from hurting others."

"And I don't give a damn about others"—she cut off a moment and collected herself—"I'm worried about *you*."

"And about that broadcast, too. All this mess came at a bad time for you. Try to calm down and think about how great you'll be tonight. You don't have to worry about me, you know I'll be fine." I put a lot of confidence in my tone and it worked. We said a few things and she gave me directions to the studio twice and I told her to break a leg. It was a phrase picked up from Escott and apparently applied to all performers because she was glad to hear it.

I hung up and dialed Gaylen. She was upset because Braxton had been calling her, and now she wanted to see me. The little bastard was becoming a real nuisance.

"I'm pretty tied up tonight. . . ." I was also reluctant to face another emotion-laden talk with her.

"Not even for a little while? Please?"

A supernatural softy, that's me. Besides, she might have some useful news. "It may take me awhile to get there, and I can't stay long."

"I understand, I'd really appreciate it."

The schedule would be tight. Bobbi's broadcast was at ten and I was stuck in the house until quarter to eight, or at least until Escott's delivery came. In between I had to have a heart-to-heart with Braxton, and then go hold Gaylen's hand. If things went right I could go home with Bobbi, enjoy the party she was throwing, and still have time to visit the Stockyards.

It looked like a busy night ahead, and I wanted to get on with it; the waiting chafed at me like starched underwear. I filled in some of the time by cleaning up and changing clothes, but with that out of the way, the minutes dragged. At five to eight I was annoyed, and at a quarter after I was ready to strangle the driver.

Twenty after the hour a truck finally rolled into the street, stopped two doors down, and backed up. The guy inside squinted at house numbers. I went outside and he asked if I were Mr. Escott. To save him confusion I said yes, unintentionally puzzling any neighbors taking in air on their front steps. We gave them a good show and lugged several crates off the truck and into the narrow hall. He didn't say much, which suited me, and I signed Escott's name to the sheet on his clipboard. He gave me a receipt and drove off.

There was one last obligation and I was free. The operator

put a call through to Escott's hotel, and then asked their operator to connect me to Escott.

"I'm sorry, sir, but Mr. Escott is not here."

"Then I'll leave a message for him."

"I'm sorry, but he has checked out."

"What?"

"Yes, sir, earlier today. He left Kingsburg as his forwarding address."

Now, why the hell was he running upstate to a little backwater like Kingsburg? Gaylen hadn't mentioned the name. He was probably returning something to one of the many blackmail victims on that list. "Did he leave any messages for a Jack Fleming?"

"No, sir. No messages at all."

I hung up and pessimistically wondered what was wrong.

My visit with Gaylen was going to be brief, so I told the cabby to wait. He rolled an eye at the meter and agreeably turned me down, having been stiffed once too many in the past.

She was waiting at her door and I apologized for being so long.

"I'm just glad that you could come by." She eased painfully into her chair.

Nothing had significantly changed since yesterday, except for some watercolor paints scattered on a table with some brushes and a glass of gray water. A wrinkled sheet of paper taped to a board was drying next to it all. I expressed some interest, which warmed her.

"It's only a hobby, just to pass the time," she demurred, but held it up for inspection. The light gleamed off some damp patches. There was no model in the room of the pink, blue, and yellow flowers on the paper, so it had come out of her own head. As in most amateur efforts, it was noticeably flat, but the colors looked nice, so I complimented her and knew from her reaction that she would someday make a gift of it to me.

"Sorry I got held up, but I really don't have a lot of time," I explained.

She took it without visible disappointment, because something else was on her mind. "That Braxton man tried to get in to talk with me. I had to have the manager throw him out."

"That's good. I'm very sorry you were bothered."

"Then he started calling. I kept hanging up until I finally decided to talk and tell him to go away."

"What'd he say?"

"All kinds of things. He was very excited and asked if you had hurt me, and practically begged for the chance to talk to me face-to-face. My legs were aching and made me a bit short with him. I said it was the phone or nothing. He asked if I knew what you were and what kind of danger I was in, and what did I know about Maureen, and if I would help, and a lot of other nonsense. I told him he was a very silly and stupid man and never to bother me again, or I'd get the police on him. After that he stopped calling."

"Good for you."

"But he still frightens me; not for myself, but for you."

"I'm safe enough. Anyway, the next time I see him, I'll talk him into going back to New York."

Her expression was sharp. "But how can you do that? What will you do?"

"Only talk to him, I won't hurt him. Please, Gaylen, don't worry about it."

Her eyes dropped and she looked away. "What will you do?"

Had I been breathing I would have sighed. "Remember telling me about Jonathan Barrett and how he talked to you just before Maureen came back? That's how I'll talk to Braxton."

"And you'll ask him about Maureen?"

"Yes."

She was quiet a moment, thinking.

"I'll let you know what he says. Charles says even negative information is better than none at all."

"What about him? Has he left yet?"

"He left sometime last night. I guess he was in a hurry to get on with things."

"But you haven't heard anything from him?"

"Not directly. I tried calling him, but he's gone to a little town called Kingsburg. . . . Does that ring any bells with you?"

She went still and thought, her heart racing. "I'm not sure. I think I once got a letter from Maureen from there, but memories fade—I don't know."

"It could be some other errand as well. He'll let us know."

"Yes, please, I want to know everything." But there was a hollow note to her voice, something else was bothering her.

"What is it?" I asked gently.

She made a brief gesture with her blue-veined hands. "This is hardly the time. . . . I wish . . . ."

I stayed quiet. She would either talk or not, with or without my encouragement.

Her eyes had changed color. The blue had faded and now they were light gray. Maureen had been the same way when she was upset over something. "Oh, Jack, how can I put it in words? How can I ask you?"

"Ask what?"

"You can see how it is for me. I'm not well and it seems that with each passing day it grows worse; not just my legs, but other things. It's so awful to be like this, to feel so weak and helpless all the time."

I waited her out, for the moment unsure.

"And I haven't seen Maureen in so long. What if I never see her again? That *could* happen, I am so afraid it will."

What she wanted was right in front of me now, and I didn't want to look. She saw the answer in my face long before she could word the question.

"Oh, please, Jack, you can't deny me in this!"

I wanted to get up and put some space between us, but her eyes held me, eyes full of anguish and asking for something I would not be able to give her.

"I'm sorry."

"But why not?"

I had no answer. That was the really hard part. I had no answer, no real excuse—and she must have known it. "Because I can't. You don't know what you're asking."

"But I do. I'm asking for a chance to live. I'm asking for a body that doesn't hurt all the time. Is it so much to want to be young and healthy again?"

"I'm sorry." I had to turn away and pace or blow up. Her eyes followed me up and down the small room until I stopped in front of the window to stare out at nothing. "You don't know what it's like. I'd give anything to go back, to walk in the sun again, to eat food, feel real heat and cold, to feel my heart beating. I have no stability. I can't go back to my family and will never have one of my own. Worst of all, Maureen's gone.''

''And yet she changed you. If the life you have is so awful, why did she do that?''

''Because the kind of love we had would have made it all bearable. There was no guarantee that I even would change, but it was a hope we shared. At the very least we would have been together for as long as I was . . . alive. But something happened and she had to leave.''

''And if she ever comes back, you'll still be here. I don't have that luxury. She *was* going to change me, she promised me that in our last talk. You are all of her left to me. All I ask is for you to fulfill a promise she could not keep.''

''Why didn't she do it earlier?''

''I don't know.'' Her eyes held mine steadily, still pleading, then dropped to her lap. ''I don't know.''

She knew and Maureen knew. I didn't and would have to go by my own instincts. A lot of emotions were getting in my way, and I wasn't sure if I was right to say no, or reading things into her manner that weren't there. I could do as she asked, the chances were very great it wouldn't work, but everything in me recoiled away from taking that step.

''I'm truly sorry, but it's impossible. I can't.''

''No, please don't leave yet.'' She stopped my move for the door. ''Please . . . will you at least just think about it?''

If I said yes, she would know it for a lie. I crossed the room, hat in hand, head down.

''Jack?''

I paused, my back to her. ''I'm sorry. If there's anything else you need, you can call me. But not this.'' Then I walked out, my guts gone cold and twisting like snakes.

The cab dropped me within sight of a two-year-old Ford parked across the street from Bobbi's hotel. Gaylen's voice still lingered in my head, pleading. None of my reasons to refuse seemed very good now, but even after discarding them all, I was not going to do it. Something was bothering me; I wanted advice, or at least to have someone tell me I was right. Escott might be back in a day or two; I'd talk it over with him. Or maybe not.

Hands in pockets, I made myself small behind a telephone pole and tried to see the driver of the Ford. From this angle, he wasn't too visible. He was slouched down in the seat, it could have been either Braxton or Webber. They worked as a team; why was only one on watch? On the remote chance that there was a third member on their hunt, I copied the license-plate number in my notebook for Escott to check. The plates were local. They might have rented it, wanting something less conspicuous than the big Lincoln.

The Ford was parked in with a line of other cars. If Bobbi hadn't tipped me, I'd never have noticed it or the man inside. The rest of the street looked clean. No one was loitering in any doorways, it seemed safe enough to approach. I strolled along the sidewalk, breasted the open passenger window, leaned over, and said hello.

The man inside turned a slow, unfriendly eyeball on me. He wasn't Braxton or Webber and looked bored to death. I landed on my feet and asked if he had a light, hauling out my face-saving cigarettes.

He considered the request with indifference, then pawed around the car for some matches. It took some hunting before he found them; the seat was littered with sandwich wrappings, unidentified paperwork, crumpled cigarette packs, and smoked-out butts. I offered him one from my pack and he took it.

"Been here long?"

"What's it to you?" He lit his cigarette on the same match that fired mine, his long fingers shielding the flame from the faint night breeze. He was a good-looking specimen, with a straight nose, cleft chin, and curly blond hair. Up on a movie screen he might have stopped a few feminine hearts. I pegged him to be a college type, but he was too old and had seen enough to have a cynical cast to his expression.

"You're making the hotel dick nervous."

"I should if I'm doing his job for him. He send you or are you from Mrs. Blatski?"

"What's the difference?"

"He sent you then." He blew smoke lazily out the window.

"What if I am from Mrs. Blatski?"

"No skin off my nose. She has a right to hire someone as long as they leave me alone—or are you the guy she's sleeping with?" He eyed me with a shade more interest.

"You a dick?"

"Got it in one, bright eyes."

I pushed away from the Ford in disgust. Not Braxton or any connection to him, just a keyhole peeper trying to get the goods on his client's wife. Three steps later a crazy thought occurred and I was back at the window again.

"Charles, is that you?"

He gave me an odd look and I deserved it. A second and more detailed check on his face was enough confirmation that he wasn't Escott got up in disguise. The eyes were the wrong color, brown instead of gray, and his ears were the wrong shape, flat on top, not arched.

"What's your problem?" he asked, squinting.

"Thought you were someone else."

"Yeah? Who?"

"Eleanor Roosevelt. I was gonna ask for an autograph."

"Hey, wait up."

I waited up. He got out of the car slowly, stretching the kinks from his legs and back. He was average in height and build, but it wasn't padding that filled out the lines of his suit. He didn't look belligerent, so I wanted to see what he wanted. He came around to the front of the car without any wasted movement and rested his backside against the fender.

"Yeah?" I said.

"Nothing much, you just look familiar to me."

"I got a common face."

"Naw, really, you from around here?"

"Maybe. What's your game, anyway?"

"Minding other people's business."

"That can be dangerous."

"Nah. Like this job, nothing to it but following some old bitch around to see what kind of flies she attracts. She's filthy rich and all that dirt attracts plenty."

I nodded. "And you think I'm one of them?"

"It don't hurt to ask. Sometimes you can do a fella a good turn, keep him outta the courts, then maybe he feels like doing me a good turn."

A shakedown artist to boot. Well, it's a big nasty world and you can meet all kinds if you stand still long enough. "You got the wrong man this time, ace."

"Malcolm," he said, holding out a hand.

My manners weren't quite bad enough to refuse, so we shook briefly and unpleasantly. He had a business card palmed and passed it on to me.

"Just in case you need a troubleshooter." He smiled, tapped the brim of his hat, and went back around to the driver's side. "You never know." He slid behind the wheel, still smiling, his lips pressed together into a hard, dark line. He had dimples.

I barely smiled back in the same way, but without dimples, and took a walk. Creeps make me nervous and I felt sorry for Mrs. Blatski, whoever she was.

Oozing through the back door, I found my way to the lobby, kept out of view of the front windows, and got Phil's attention by waving at the night clerk. He crossed over casually.

"How'd you get in? The back's locked."

"Better check it, then. Any sign of Braxton?"

"He ain't in the car?"

"I had a look. It's some private dick on a divorce case."

"Then I ain't seen him."

"I guess that's all right, as long as they leave Miss Smythe alone."

"It doesn't mean they stopped lookin' for you, though."

"Yeah, but I'm being careful." We went to the back door, which I had unlocked once inside. Phil let me out and locked it again.

After five minutes of studying the street I tentatively decided that my Buick was unobserved. I was back to feeling paranoid again and went as far as checking it for trip wires and sticks of dynamite. Bombs were an unlikely tool for Braxton, but then why take chances?

The car was okay and even started up smoothly. There was little time left to get to the broadcast, but the god of traffic signals was with me and I breezed through the streets as quickly as the other cars would allow. Bobbi had left instructions with the staff about me, and as soon as I was identified, a brass-buttoned usher gave me an aisle seat with the rest of the studio audience.

The room was smaller than I'd expected, roughly divided between audience and performers, with only slightly more space given over to the latter. There was a glassed-in control booth to one side filled with too many people who didn't seem to be doing much of anything at the moment. Bobbi was on the stage, looking outwardly calm. She was seated with a half dozen other people on folding chairs, all of them dressed to the nines, which didn't make a whole lot of sense for a radio show. Across from them a small band was tuning up, and in between, seated at a baby grand, was Marza Chevreaux, flipping through some sheet music.

I caught Bobbi's eye and gave her a smile and a thumbs-up signal. She smiled back, her face breaking composure to light up with excitement. She was in her element and loving it.

A little guy with slicked-back hair and an oversized bow tie stepped up to a microphone the size of a pineapple. Someone in the booth gave him the go-ahead, he signed to the band, and they started up the fanfare of the show. For a minute I thought the little guy was Eddie Cantor, but his voice was different as was his style of cracking jokes. A studio worker in an open vest and rolled-up shirtsleeves held up big cards printed with instructions telling us when to clap or laugh. The audience liked the comedian, though, and hardly needed the prompting.

A deep-voiced announcer stepped in to warn us against the dangers of inferior tires, then the band came up again, and Bobbi was given a flowery introduction. She was standing and ready at the mike. Marza got her signal from a guy in the booth, and they swung into a fast-paced novelty number. It was one of those oddball songs that gets popular for a few weeks and then you never hear of it again, about a guy who was like a train and the singer was determined to catch him. Off to one side, a sound-effects man came in on cue with the appropriate whistles and bells. Before I knew it I was applauding with the rest of the audience and Bobbi was taking her bows. She'd gone over in a big way and they wanted more.

When the noise died down the comedian joined her, and

they read from a script a few jokes about trains the song had missed. The tire man came on after them with his stern voice of doom, and that was when someone poked me in the ribs from behind.

Braxton had turned up another gun and was hunched over me with it concealed in a folded newspaper.

"Stand up and walk into the hall," he told me quietly.

He was damned right that I'd do what he wanted. We were in a vulnerable crowd, and all I wanted was to get him alone outside for just two seconds. Showing resignation, I got up slowly and preceded him. The usher opened the door, his attention on the stage. He must have really liked tire ads.

The hall was empty except for Matheus, who was clutching his cross and looking ready to spook off. Braxton had done quite a job on him.

"I give," I said. "How'd you find me this time?"

Braxton was smug. "We didn't have to. We've been waiting. Last night you said Miss Smythe was going to be in a broadcast. I merely called around to find out which station and when. There was a risk you wouldn't show, but it all worked out."

If he expected me to pat him on the back for smarts, he'd have a long wait. "Okay, now what? You gonna bump me off ten feet away from a hundred witnesses? The wall between isn't that soundproof."

He hadn't picked up on the fact that I wasn't as afraid of him and his silver bullets as I'd been last night. The gun moved a degree or two left. "In there, and slowly." He indicated a washroom across the hall.

"That'll be some headline," I grumbled, " 'Journalist Found Dead in Men's Room; Police Suspect Lone Ranger.' Matheus, you better stay out here, this could be messy."

"Shut up."

"Have some heart, Braxton, you don't want the kid to see this. Save him some nightmares."

The elevator opened at the far end of the hall and a man in a long overcoat got out. He noticed our group, looked at his watch, and walked away, turning a corner. He was just part of the background to me, but he made Braxton nervous. He was suddenly aware of the openness of the hall and didn't like it.

"Move," he hissed. *"Now."*

I looked past him to Matheus. Our eyes locked for an instant. It was long enough. "Stay out here, kid."

His expression did not change, nor did his posture, but I knew I'd reached him. He stood very still.

Braxton saw this exchange and his eyebrows went up, adding more lines to his dry, scored forehead. The gun wavered as he tried to decide whether to snap the kid out of my suggestion or shoot me outright. I saved him the trouble; when he came a half step closer and tried to urge me backward, I shifted my weight as though to comply and turned it into a lunge. It was faster, literally faster, than he could see and much faster than he could react.

The gun was now in my pocket, and he was staring at his empty hand as unhappy as any kid whose toy had been taken away. He looked up at me and thought he saw the grim reaper and made an abortive attempt to run, but I grabbed two fistfuls of his clothes and swung him around against the wall. His mouth opened and sound started to come out, but I smothered it with one hand.

Far down the hall I heard approaching footsteps. It was too public here, so I adopted his plan and dragged him to the men's room. The door swung shut and I rammed a foot against its lower edge to keep people out.

He was trying to struggle, his body bucking ineffectually against my hold. He was finally getting a clear idea of just how strong a vampire can be at night, with all his powers.

"Hold still or I'll break your neck," I said, and perhaps I meant it. He subsided, his eyes squeezed shut. From the pressure of his jaw, he was trying to hold his chin down. I was hungry, but not that hungry. It'd be a cold day in hell before I'd touch his blood.

His breath was labored, the moist air from his nose blowing out hard over my knuckles, and his heart raced fit to break. He needed to be calmer and so did I. Emotions, the kind of violent ones he stirred up in me, would only do him harm. I sucked in a deep lungful of air and let it out slowly, counting to ten. Outside someone walked past, the same steps that had chased us in here. They paused slightly, then went on, fading.

His eyes turned briefly on me, then squeezed shut again.

He had an idea of what I was trying to do and was on guard.
It might be too difficult to break through to him without doing
permanent harm. I shifted my grip and his eyes instinctively
opened.

"Braxton, I won't hurt you, just listen to me."

He made a protesting sound deep in his throat. My hand
relaxed enough over his mouth so he could speak.

"Unclean leach—"

"Listen to me."

"Damned, you're—"

"Braxton."

"—damned to—"

"Listen to me."

His muscles went slack, his lungs changing rhythm slightly.
I'd gotten to him, but had to ease up.

"That's it, just calm down, I only want to talk."

He looked up in a kind of despair, like a drowning man
whose strength has gone and knows you won't make it to him
in time.

"Everything's all right. . . ."

I didn't understand how it worked any more than I understood the mechanics of vanishing at will, but I had the ability
and now the need. My conscience was kicking up, but beyond moving to another state or killing him, there seemed no
other practical way of getting rid of him.

"Everything's fine, we're just going to talk. . . ."

Without any more fuss, he slipped under my control. I
relaxed and opened my cramped hands. His eyes were glassy
rather than vacant.

"Braxton?"

"Yes?" It was the quiet voice this time, the reasonable
one he'd used at my parents' house.

"Where is Maureen Dumont?"

"I don't know."

I was disappointed, but not surprised. "When did you meet
her?"

"Years ago, long time."

"When? What year?"

"I was twenty-five or -six." He struggled to remember.
"I opened the store in 1908, she would come and buy books
and talk. She was so beautiful. . . ." His voice was softer

with the memory. "She would talk with me. I dreamed about her. She was so beautiful."

What had he been like back then? The brittle body might have once been wiry, the seamed face once smooth. There had been a firm chin and dark eyes and skin; yes, to a woman he might have been handsome back then.

"Were you her lover?" I had to keep from touching him or he'd shake off the trance. Jealousy was foaming up inside; I couldn't touch him or lose control of myself.

"I loved her. She was so—"

"Were you her lover?" Stay steady.

His eyes were wide, blind, searching inward for an answer. "I . . . don't know."

"What do you mean? How can you not know?"

"I was, in my dreams. I loved her at night in my dreams. She would kiss me." One of his hands stole up to his neck. "She would kiss me. God, oh my God . . ."

I turned away. I never meant to hear this. "Stop."

He became quiet, waiting and unaware while I mastered myself. There was no point in hating him, no point in condemning Maureen; not for something that had happened nearly thirty years ago. She'd loved Barrett and Braxton and then me. Were there others? Had she indeed loved me?

"Braxton . . . did you take . . . did you ever kiss her in the same way?"

"No."

It was something.

"She wouldn't let me."

Oh, Maureen. Yes, it was something. He hadn't been that important to her. She'd been lonely and needed someone to hold and touch, if only in his dreams. That was it and that was all.

"When did you last see her?"

"Which time?"

I made a guess. "The first?"

"A year after we met. She never said good-bye; the dreams just stopped, I forgot them. But she came back."

"When?"

"Twenty years later? Twenty-two? One night she walked into the shop. I knew her instantly and I remembered it all. She hadn't changed, not aged a single day, but I—she didn't know me, not until I said her name. I was frightened, I knew what she was, what she had done to me and what I would become unless—'' He relived his fear quietly, the only outward sign of the inner turmoil was the sweat that broke out on his face. His heart was racing.

"Unless what?"

"I wouldn't be like her, feeding on the living, sucking men's souls from them. If I killed her first, then I would be free. I could die free of her curse. I began to hunt her."

"When? What year?"

"In 1931."

So this was the man. She'd run from him, leaving me standing in an empty room, a scribbled good-bye note in one hand and the life draining from my eyes. Five years of hurt, doubt, anger, and fear because this foolish man thought she wanted his soul instead of the warmth of his body when he was young.

"Did you find her?"

"No, but I found out about you. I knew what she'd done to you, but if I tried to help, you wouldn't have believed me. Your only hope was the same as mine—to kill her—but then you died first and now you're one of them. I'm sorry I couldn't have saved you."

It was pointless trying to explain it to him. Whether Maureen lived or died didn't matter; we'd exchanged blood, and hoped. She'd loved me, and had expressed it by giving me a chance for a life beyond life so we would always be together. But then something had gone wrong.

"Do you know what happened to her? Do you know where she is?"

"No."

"Are you the only one? Are there others hunting her?"

"Matheus, he believed me, he knows."

"Who else?"

"I don't . . . the old woman, she must know."

"Gaylen? The old woman here?"

"Yes. She knows something, she knew back then—"

"What do you mean?"

Something bumped against the door.

"I asked, but she wouldn't—"

Bump. ''Hey, open up.'' A vaguely familiar voice, but not Matheus.

''—tell me. She wanted—''

''Come on out, Fleming.''

''—life to live—''

''The kid says you're in there.''

''Cheated. She was sick—''

''Who was? Of what?'' The other voice was distracting, and I was losing the thread of Braxton's talk.

''—strong . . . frightening. I *told* her my story, but it was you she—''

''Fleming, it's now or I scrag the kid.''

What the hell? I yanked the door. He was in a long coat, which changed him enough from the last time, so from a distance he was unrecognizable when he stepped off the elevator, looked at his watch, and walked away. A long coat, which was all wrong because it was only mid-September and still mild. But he wore it because that made it easy to walk into a building with a sawed-off shotgun concealed under it. He shouldn't have been here, he was supposed to be in a parked Ford waiting for Mrs. Blatski.

He grinned at my surprise, his dimples nice and deep, and without any more expression or warning he pulled first one trigger, then the other, emptying both barrels into the open doorway.

▲
9
▼

I WAS ON the tile floor. It smelled of soap, cordite, burned fiber, and blood.

The impact of the blast had thrown me back against a washbasin, which altered the angle of fall and twisted me facedown. The agony of the shot passing through my body left me stunned as few things could. I fought to hold on to sanity and solidity. It was several long seconds before my shivering, jerking limbs recovered enough control to stand.

The door still hung open, and the air was thick with blue smoke. Ten seconds to find my feet, five more to stagger to the hall, but it was long enough. Malcolm was gone.

So was Braxton. He was on his back and not moving. The shot had all but cut his slight body in two. His blood flooded the black-and-white tiles. His face was calm and dreamy. Death had come so fast there'd been no time to react.

Matheus was on his side in the hall, one hand still clutching his cross. A smear of blood was over his right eye and a crimson thread flowed from it into his hair. Still alive.

The studio door opened. There was no time to explain, I vanished before anyone saw me, and sank down through the floors, hoping to reach the ground ahead of Malcolm. A few people were standing in the main lobby of the building. I took the risk of re-forming, but no one noticed; they were looking out the front doors. I pushed past and went outside. No Ford in sight, but there was a man running away, his long coat flapping. My legs gobbled up his fifty-yard lead and I hauled him up short and spun him around.

Watery eyes, a three-day beard, no chin, stinking of booze and sweat, he wore Malcolm's coat or one just like it.

"Easy, Captain!" he wheezed.

"Where is he? Where's the blond man?"

"Did what he said, was it good? I get another two bits if it's good. Was it good?"

"What'd he tell you to do?"

"Wait on the stairs 'n run, Captain. Lizzen fer the bang 'n run. Good joke, huh? Was it good?"

It was good, it bought Malcolm enough time to get out another way while I chased down the wino. I ran back to the lobby. The doorman was the first official-looking type, so I collared him, said there'd been an accident at the studio and to call an ambulance, then raced upstairs to look for Malcolm. It was a poor chance at best, he'd be gone by now.

The studio hall was in a mess. Men were peering into the washroom, and a small knot had formed around Matheus. Some woman was crying and another man was holding her. The stage was empty except for the chairs and piano. Crossing the divider between it and the audience, I was stopped by the man in shirtsleeves. He gaped at my shredded clothes.

"Sorry, you have to stay out."

"I'm with Bobbi Smythe, she was on tonight."

"She'll be backstage, but—"

The backstage door opened to a hall full of people all looking at me, questions on their troubled faces.

"Where's Bobbi Smythe?" I asked no one in particular.

"I think she left," a woman suggested.

"When?"

"She was here just a minute ago," someone else said.

There was another set of washrooms down the hall. I opened up the ladies' and called for Bobbi and Marza. No one answered.

"They must have taken the back elevator," the woman told me.

That was down the hall and around the corner, with more people in the way.

"What the hell happened?"

"I heard an explosion."

"Was it a bomb?"

"Nah, Big Al must be back an' havin' a party."

"Musta been a gun—Johnny said someone got shot."

"Goddamned drunks, screwing up the show."

I ignored their speculations and punched at the elevator button. This time I couldn't sink through the floors without getting unwanted attention, besides, the operator might have seen something.

He had, and told me about it on the way down.

"Yeah, the blond, a real bombshell—she stood out from that group like fireworks."

"What floor?"

"They got off on ground a few minutes ago."

"They?"

"She had some harpy with her. Seemed anxious to leave, and a couple of others, too. What's goin' on? What happened to you?"

We made the ground floor and I left him guessing. The back hall was empty, so I went around front. There was a cop in the lobby by now, asking questions. I waited until he was in the elevator and scanned faces. No Bobbi, but the doorman was still there.

"Hey, did a blond in a red dress go out? She was with a black-haired woman in green."

"Haven't seen 'em."

"If you do, ask 'em to wait."

"Cops say everyone has to wait, nobody gets out now."

I went through the ground floor, again checking the washrooms, but with no luck. They should have left by way of the front; it was a busier street and more likely to have cabs, but then they shouldn't have gone at all. If she'd heard a man had been shot, Bobbi would have been on the scene to make sure it wasn't me. Marza must have dragged her out to protect her. Damn Marza, anyway.

The rear exit was ajar and unguarded—so much for the cops' instructions. It opened to another street busy with cars and nothing else. I called her name, but no one answered.

After wasting a lot of time, I finally wised up and drove back to Bobbi's hotel. It would be the place for them to go since it was closer than Marza's. Before I reached the elevator, Phil flagged me down.

"What happened to you?" he asked, staring at the hole in my clothes where the shell had gone through.

"Fight." I was in a hurry to get past him.

"Some kid brought this in a minute ago." He gave me a large envelope with my name printed on it.

"Has Miss Smythe come in?"

"Her friend did, she's—"

I broke away. The elevator crawled up to the fourth floor. Without knocking I went in. Marza was on the sofa and jerked to her feet. Her lacquered hair was messed up and her eyes were blazing fire.

"Who were they?" she demanded.

"Where's Bobbi?"

Her body was shaking inside the green frame of her dress. *"Who were they?"* If looks could kill, I'd be on a slab next to Braxton. She started for me, her hands reaching. One of her inch-long talons had broken, but there were still nine more left and aimed at my face. I dropped the envelope, caught her arms in time, and held her at a safe distance. She kicked and struggled until she ran out of breath, then her knees gave out and she sank to the floor, trying not to sob from frustration.

"What happened?" I asked. Somehow her raw display kept me cold and thinking.

"They *took* her," she spat. "Who were they?"

"When?"

"When we left the studio. He said to come here and wait for you."

Oh, God. "A blond man, long coat?"

"Who was he? He had a gun—"

"Anyone else? Was he alone?"

"The woman with the knife." She gulped air, still shaking and her head sagged. Near her was the dropped envelope and its meaning suddenly blossomed in my mind. I grabbed it up.

It was flat on the edges and slightly thicker in the middle and whatever was inside rustled against the paper. I tore one end off with stiff, clumsy fingers and the contents spilled out.

Marza went dead silent, not even breathing. Her hand shot out and caught a last tendril of the cascade of platinum silk before it sifted to the floor.

Neither of us could move, each staring with numb shock

at the bright, soft nest between us. Marza swayed, her eyes flat from the faint coming on. I got her to the sofa, then went to the liquor cabinet and poured a straight triple from the first bottle I grabbed and made her drink it. She choked and pawed me away, but I made her drink it all.

"God, I *hate* that stuff." Her breath smelled of rum.

The dullness had left her eyes and she looked as though she might be useful again. I felt the shock hitting me now as I looked again at the pile of shining hair. A small piece of paper was lodged in the tangle. My guts were ice as I fished it out.

Sit tight or we'll give the whore more than just a haircut.

That was all. Marza whipped it from me and read. She was trembling, but trying to hold in the panic.

"Why? What do they *want*?"

There was nothing sane I could tell her. The fragments of Braxton's last words gave me an answer, but I was repelled by it.

Ring.

Marza flinched and stared at the phone as if it were a bomb.

I picked it up and waited.

"Jack? Marza?" It was *her* voice, breathless, strained.

"Bobbi!"

Marza stiffened and rushed in, trying to pull the phone from me.

"Oh, Jack, they're—"

And that was all, except for a muffled noise in the background and the final click of disconnection. Marza glared at me, for all the good it did her. I felt just as angry and helpless. We waited, but the thing didn't ring again.

"What do they want?" she repeated.

I shook my head and went to the bedroom to get away from her questions. Bobbi's rose scent hung lightly in the air. A couple of dresses tried on for the broadcast and then rejected were flung on the bed. The closet was open. I fumbled out of my tattered coat and shirt. Since I started coming over so often, she insisted I leave some spare clothes in with hers.

I pulled on a fresh shirt, my fingers working mechanically, as I tried not to think.

Marza was where I left her on the sofa, head in hands. "Why won't you tell me anything?"

"You know as much as I do, even more. I've seen the man in the coat, his name is Malcolm, said he was a private eye. He shot and killed Braxton tonight."

She swallowed. "And the other? That woman?"

"What'd she look like?"

"I don't know."

"Yes, you do, you said she had a knife. What else?"

. "About my age, bony all over, and hungry. Her eyes . . . she looked crazy. The man grabbed Bobbi and the woman put that knife to her throat, and they went out. He said to come here and wait for you."

"Was that all he said?"

She nodded.

Someone knocked at the door. Our heads swiveled and she went bolt upright. They knocked again. I signaled to her to stay put and looked out the peephole. It was Madison Pruitt. He saw my eye and waved and I opened the door a crack.

"Oh, Fleming, hello." He moved to come in, but I didn't stand aside. "Something wrong? Is the party still on? The broadcast stopped in the middle of—"

"Sorry, the party's off, Bobbi got sick at the last minute—"

Marza was at my shoulder. "No, let him in. Please."

I didn't exactly want to, but she looked like she needed him and pulled him inside. She wrapped her arms around him. He didn't understand what was going on, but instinctively offered what comfort he could.

"What's happened? Was there an accident?"

"Come on, I'll explain." I shut the door and made explanations. "There's going to be more people coming over soon, you'll have to get rid of them."

"But what can we do?" Marza asked.

"Just what I said. This guy's trying to make us nervous so we lose our heads. We do that and we lose Bobbi."

"And the police?"

"No. We don't dare."

The phone rang again. I picked it up before the bell had died.

"It's me, Jackie boy. Malcolm—you remember."

He got no answer.

"You gotta behave or I might get mad. Did you read my note?"

"Yes."

"And you heard her on the phone?"

"Yes."

"Good. Now you know we mean business. Your girlfriend got her ears lowered a little this time, but that's all—no real harm done. You do what we want and she gets to keep 'em."

"What do you want?"

"Nothing you can't handle, Jackie."

"What?"

"You gotta pencil?"

I wrote out the address he gave me.

"You come straight here and no cops. Just you or you'll never be able to find her again. Leave the other bitch where she is, out of trouble."

"I'll come."

"No smart ideas, either. We know all about you. That's why I aced the squirt, just to let you know. You see, I can't really hurt you, but the people around you is something else. No tricks. When you walk to the door you make noise and stay in sight, 'cause if you don't, your girl won't be using mirrors, either, but for a different reason. You got ten minutes to get here before she goes into surgery." He laughed, the line clicked, and my ear was pressed to dead air.

Marza's nails dug into my arm. "What do they mean? Where is she?"

"They want me, not her."

"But why?"

I memorized the address and tore the sheet from my notebook, folding it around Malcolm's business card. I scribbled Escott's name and the name of his hotel on the outside and gave it to her.

"This is a friend who can help us, but he's in New York. Call this hotel, they might be able to locate him. Say it's an emergency, life and death, but don't tell the truth to anyone but him. If he calls, give him the story, but no cops or Bobbi's dead. You got that?"

She nodded.

"He's got an English accent. In the meantime stay off the phone and keep the door shut."

"Yes, but—"

But I had bolted out the door, car key in hand and murder on my mind.

The address led to a warehouse that was a mountain of dingy red bricks and old wood held together by crumbling mortar and rusty nails. The street was deserted, the other nearby structures hollow and silent except for the rats. It was a good spot to kill someone. The river was only ten feet from the back entrance, and a body could easily be slipped unnoticed into the oily water on a black night.

The building was three stories tall, and a faint light shone in one of the top windows, outlining Malcolm's head and shoulders. He took his hat off and waved it. There was nothing else to do but go inside and see the setup. They knew what I was and what my capabilities were, but Malcolm was supremely confident, and that meant a bad situation for Bobbi. I glared at the grinning, waving figure, then tore open the warehouse door and left it on the walk.

The stink of wet rotted wood, oil, and exhaust filled the place. The exhaust was new and had come from Malcolm's Ford, the engine was still hot and ticking. Next to it was a paneled truck backed up against a loading bay, and beyond that, a freight elevator. Somewhere a motor whined into reluctant life, and the elevator descended from the top floor. It leveled and stopped. The doors opened horizontally like a set of teeth.

"Hey, it's the death of the party," said Malcolm, still grinning.

"Where is she?"

"I'll take you to her, Jackie boy." He gestured and I stepped onto the split, cracked boards, and he sent us grinding upward, to the top floor. He wrenched the doors open and motioned me to follow, feeling safe enough to turn his back on me as we crossed a hundred feet of empty storeroom. The dirty windows overlooking the street and river had been tilted open in an attempt to make a cross breeze, but the place was still stuffy. We approached a line of doors against the far wall; three on the right, four on the left, in the center an

arched opening to a stairwell. Light seeped from under two
closed doors in the line. He went to the one next to the outside wall and opened it.

A bare bulb hanging from a plain wire and socket disclosed
a small bare room. Broken glass was all over the floor, and
empty panes framed the sky and some buildings across the
river. In years long past, someone had had a nice view. Malcolm followed me in to stand by the windows. He looked out
and down, waved once, then turned to me.

"Where is she?"

"One thing at a time." He pointed at something on the
floor. It was a flat parcel of folded brown paper. "You check
that out first."

There was no reason to refuse; he had a purpose to his
games and I had to play. I picked it up. It was very light and
the paper came apart easily. Bobbi's red silk dress slithered
into my hands.

I started for him and he took an involuntary step back,
then recovered. "Don't do it, not 'til you see—"

My hands closed on his throat.

"See what, you shit?"

His eyes rolled toward the window and I followed their
path.

The river was night black and smooth, stray lights caught
in the surface barely moving. Below the window was a con-
crete loading pier with metal rings set in it. A length of rope
was tied to one, and the other end went to an old flat-bottomed
boat floating some thirty feet out. The woman Marza described crouched in the boat, leaning over its near side with
her hand in the water. She was looking anxiously up at us.

"Let . . . go . . . now," he gasped out urgently, and his
distorted tone suddenly convinced me. I released him and
backed away so that we were clearly separated.

The woman in the boat took her hand out of the water and
pulled on another piece of rope as though for an anchor, but
instead a head broke the surface. It shook and shuddered,
water streaming only from the nose, because the mouth was
taped shut. Her eyes were bulging with utter terror.

Oh, my God.

Malcolm coughed, recovering. "And don't run down for
her. She's tied like a mummy and weighted. The second you

walk away from this window Norma lets the rope go, and down she sinks. You'd never get to her in time, not with your problem about crossing water.''

I could cross water if I had to, but it was slow going. I'd never get to her in time. Never. I swung back on him, but he read my purpose and didn't look directly at me.

''No fish-eye, Jackie, I gotta stay in sight from now on. Norma has her orders, and if she thinks something's wrong with me, the girl is dead. You understand that? I gotta stay in her sight.''

Numbly, I looked down, straight into Bobbi's eyes. They locked helplessly on mine, pleading. I called to her, not sure she could hear me. Her expression didn't change.

''Good,'' he murmured. ''Real good.'' He took the dress from me, folding and rolling it into a ball. ''I don't blame you. She's a classy twist. Nice, like I always wanted to get for myself. She needed a lot of help getting out of this. I had to hold her down while Norma did the honors. I like 'em to fight, y'know? That always gets me going. A body like that must feel good under you, huh?''

''Shut up!''

He abruptly stepped away from the window. Norma pushed Bobbi under. I grabbed for him, but he dodged.

''Say you're sorry.''

''I'm sorry! Damn it, come back! *I'm sorry!*''

He eased back. Norma brought her up again. Bobbi's eyes flickered groggily, and her head lolled.

''Again, like you mean it.''

''I'm sorry,'' I whispered sincerely, but it was to Bobbi.

''You promise to behave?''

I nodded. Tried to swallow. Couldn't.

His smile returned. ''That's real good.''

''What do you want?''

''Like I said, nothing you can't handle.'' In a louder voice aimed at the next room over he called, ''It's all right, you can come now.''

A door scraped open, a rubbing, grating sound crawled over the floor, and she rolled into sight. The harsh yellow light did funny things to colors and Gaylen's blue eyes had faded to a pale, cold gray. She was in her wheelchair with the rubber-tipped cane across her knees. She looked up, frowning. Malcolm turned to face the window, giving us a kind of privacy. Neither of us spoke, each holding still like actors at the end of a play before the lights go out and the curtain falls.

At last she drew in a breath and spoke. "I didn't want to do it this way. I really didn't, but you wouldn't understand, you—"

"You asked this of Maureen?"

Her answer was plain. There'd been fire in Marza's eyes, but Gaylen's held acid. Sometime long ago they had argued it all out, and Maureen had realized the truth and run. Her note said, *Some people are after me because of what I am*. . . . Turned another way, the meaning changed. It was not Braxton she had feared with his cross and silver bullets, it was her sister. Five years ago she'd left to protect me. Had she stayed it would have been me down there with Norma, and Maureen standing where I was now.

"I begged her. It was just one little thing, and I would have left her alone forever had she wished. I *asked* you, and is it so much? All you can tell me are the shortcomings. They're *nothing* to what I'm going through now. This body is old and crippled and I hate it! I want to live!"

"You have to die for that—if it works."

"What's death compared to the pain I feel whenever I move? And as for it working, it must! Maureen changed and I'm her sister, I *know* it would change me."

"What about Braxton?"

"I tried to explain to him and he was too pigheaded with his talk of contamination and souls to listen."

"He was never a danger to either of us."

"Never?"

"I was taking care of the problem when this . . . Braxton was a nuisance, but he didn't deserve to die."

"He did if I wanted to make you understand how serious I am. It could have been *anyone* else—someone walking next to you on the street, your detective friend—anyone. Time and circumstances made him a convenient target." She let that sink in.

My hands clenched and I longed for the luxury of closing them around her neck.

"But that's past and finished. I want you to think about the girl. You've seen her and you know there are no safe alternatives but one, and what I'm asking for is not so terrible.''

I turned away as though thinking. I had no choice but to agree, but she expected reluctance and was getting it. "You don't know what you're asking."

But she'd heard that one before and had the same answer ready. "I *do* know, and I'm not asking now. Do what I want and the girl goes free. You already know what happens otherwise."

"You'd let them do that?"

"Yes."

My eyes were on Bobbi's face. "Will you free her unharmed?"

"Yes."

"All right."

She gave a sigh, very much like the one that came over the lines when I'd first called. "Good, then come here."

"Let her go first."

"No."

I glanced over my shoulder at Malcolm.

She shook her head. "No. He is to watch. If he thinks anything is wrong, he will take steps."

"Steps?"

"Whatever he thinks is necessary." She gave him her cane.

I looked at him. He was watching me, but not smiling as before, and I liked it a lot less.

"Come over here," she repeated. She extended her left arm, wrist up, blue veins bulging slightly beneath the thin crinkled skin. "Now. Do it now."

At least I'd be spared the intimate contact with her throat. To save Bobbi I would have done even that, but the thought of touching her in this way was sickening, and it showed on my face. She waited, though, until I moved a few reluctant steps closer. Her eyes took in every movement, as did Malcolm's. It was worse than being naked.

"Now, Jack," she whispered.

But the body was not cooperating. True, I had not yet fed; the hunger was there, but not the will. It would be many more days of fasting before I could overcome the physical revulsion with physical need.

My mouth came within an inch of the crepe-textured flesh,

smelling faintly of some kind of soap and with a smear of
paint on the upturned wrist. She painted pictures.

"Now."

Pictures of flowers. What had Pruitt said about flowers?
Roses for Bobbi, fading now, and I had to do this or Bobbi—

"Now."

Damn her. With cattle in the Stockyards it was simple feeding, a necessary chore. With Bobbi it was the only means left
to express physical love. With Gaylen it was obscene and hu-
miliating, and blinding white fury was the result. Most of my
concentration was on holding in the rage or the old woman would
find herself and her chair crashing through one of the walls.

She refused to meet my eyes, staring at her bared arm
instead.

"Look at me," I said.

"No."

"Look at me."

"Malcolm . . ."

His step behind me.

Bobbi. My eyes dropped.

"Wait, Malcolm."

He paused, then moved back.

Damn her. God *damn* her to hell.

Then anger tipped things and my canines emerged the necessary length and cut hard through her skin, tearing silently.
It hurt and her arm jerked, but her free hand came down and
she forced it to be still again. I swallowed her thin, bitter
blood and tried not to choke. I thought of cattle and tried to
pretend it was no more than a routine feeding, something my
mind could handle to keep from retching, because if I stopped
now I could not do this again and Bobbi . . .

The worst of it was that blood was blood, and my body
began to accept it. Never mind the source, that didn't matter.
This was food, all food and usable. Hot strength flowed down
and through and I held on more firmly. She wanted me to
take her blood, then so be it. Tonight I could and would take
it all, and then I'd deal with Malcolm. I'd open his mind up
like a tin can and not care what mess I made of it as long as
he freed Bobbi.

"That's enough." Her teeth were set from the pain because I was not being careful with her.

No, now I make my own choice.

"Stop."

I'll drain you dry until there's not enough blood in you to keep your brain conscious and your head droops—

"I said enough."

—and your heart stops because there's nothing left to pump and everything winds down to a final stillness and all that's left is a hundred pounds of carcass and a bad memory—

"Malcolm . . ." Her voice was weaker, frightened.

—and I lift my head in time to see it coming as a blur, but he's already into the swing and it's too late to react. The thing hits me square and hard and sends my skull spinning into the light, and I fall—fall—and hit something hard—and lie still—

The yellow bulb burned my eyes; I was faceup on the boards, with the two of them staring down at me to see if I were alive. That's hard to do, since there's no pumping of lungs or beating heart.

Malcolm set aside the cane he used to crack my skull, waved out the window with his hat, and knelt closer.

"Jesus, look at his eyes."

"Yes, they get that color during feeding. It fades."

And when we make love, so Bobbi and I leave the lights out . . . Light—the damned thing was boring right through me.

"If he's dead—"

"He can't be. You said they were tough, that there's only one way for them." He passed a hand over my eyes. His pink fingertips brushed the lashes and I blinked. He looked relieved. "It's all right, he's just stunned. What went wrong?"

"Never mind. Are they coming?"

"Yeah, but I think Norma needs some help."

"She can handle it." She was wrapping a handkerchief around her arm to stop the flow. Her face was white and her hands shook. I'd been very close but could do nothing more. The room spun sickeningly with the light bulb in the center and I couldn't move. It was different from being hit with a stone, I wasn't vanishing to heal. Something about my nature and the nature of wood prevented it, but I knew I'd recover soon and the feeding would help. A few more minutes . . .

Malcolm grabbed my ankles and dragged me from the room. My arms fanned out uselessly over my head; I was unable to control them or anything else. He had struck with killing strength, leaving me helpless.

Grunting and straining, he got me through the door and around a corner into the stairwell. We were on the top floor, but there was still one last flight leading up to the roof. He struggled hard with my weight until the length of my body was stretched halfway up. My head hung off the angle of the step, turning the room upside down for me. My knuckles brushed the landing.

I tried to move and got only the smallest quivering along the muscles for all the effort. Not yet, perhaps in a few more minutes, but not yet.

"Hurry," she said. She had wheeled her chair into the landing, set the brake, and Malcolm helped her out. He was as solicitous as any boy scout helping an old lady across the street. She shuffled close to me and stiffly sat on one of the steps below my head. With icy misery, I realized what was coming.

Her breathing was hoarse and labored. I'd taken a lot of blood from her, after all. Now she was going to take it back. This was the exchange she had to have. It had been very necessary for Malcolm to hit me and keep me quiet or I would not have been able to stand it.

She hovered close with something in her hand, but kept it just out of view. She turned my head away and I was staring at Malcolm. His eyes were peeled back with excited interest and he struggled to control his nervous laughter.

A tugging at my throat, a sharp sting, and then a strangled gag escaped me as she cut into the artery. I'd been placed head down so that gravity would speed the flow. Warm and wet, it trickled past my chin onto my face, filled a crevice in the corner of my mouth, overflowed, and skirted my eye and into my hair, tickling my ear and finally dripping onto the stairstep.

She drew a steadying breath and lowered her mouth to the open wound.

I didn't know how much it might take to secure the change she wanted, perhaps only a single mouthful was sufficient. She kept her lips hard on my neck, swallow after swallow, drinking quickly to keep up with the flow until it was too much for her and she had to stop. She was still alive and a living human unused to it cannot handle large quantities of blood, physically or mentally. She leaned back against the wall, eyes shut as she caught her breath.

Malcolm stepped forward and helped her back to her chair. "Can I—"

"No, later. I'll do for you later. I promise. Take me to the truck, I must rest."

"I thought—"

"Yes, you're right. Finish it."

The flow from my neck slowed and stopped. She must have used some wooden instrument to cut me—a sharp piece of ebony, perhaps. The pain in my head was subsiding, but not as fast as I wanted. Controlled movement was still a moment or two away. My arms were working a little, enough for the muscles to contract. It was a start. . . .

Malcolm's upside-down image was smiling at me; it grinned, it giggled. A long pole was in his hands, one chiseled end protected by a sharp metal tip to keep the point on the wood from splintering.

Panic roared up and took over. I tried to vanish and felt only a flicker of response brush over the nerves. The shock of the wooden cane had been too much. I needed more time and had none. My hands came up in a feeble effort to push away the tip of the pole. There was no strength in them. I was absolutely, utterly—oh, God . . . no . . .

With all his weight behind it, he rammed the thing into my chest and blood shot up and out. My body shook and bucked as if with seizure, hands clawed, legs kicked. A terrible suffocating weight settled on me, crushing and smothering out the life.

He pushed once more and the shattering, engulfing agony negated all thought and effort as a dying animal's shrieks filled the building; ugly, frightening screams that shook the walls and went on and on until there was no more air for the lungs to push out. The mouth hung uselessly open, and the last echoes hammered down the stairs and were finally lost in the darkness below.

10

FIRE.
BLACK FIRE.

Black fire you can't see or hear or smell, only feel, and by then it's too late. It's caught hold and is consuming everything.

Searing black fire that fills the chest from the inside out, until it should explode from the heat and end things forever, but doesn't. The silent body lies inert, enduring and somehow still conscious. Death is too far away for sanity to remain.

Gaylen's chair wheels grinding over the flooring, Malcolm's steps fading . . . crunch, bump, and they were in the elevator. The door was pulled shut and they began to descend. He would load her into the truck and they would go somewhere else. Somewhere . . . Bobbi . . . They'd pulled her out—their voices said as much in the distance. . . .

Move. Move *something*.

Bobbi had seen their faces, they couldn't afford to let her go. Gaylen would never take that chance.

But she had promised. She had—

Did a finger twitch? Or was that imagination?

My hands had only found movement at the end, when the wood stake plunged into me. The right one found direction, clawing to pull it out, and the left had convulsively torn through part of the steps. It was still there; damp river air curled around my fingers.

Doors slammed shut. The motors started, gears shifted, and they rumbled into the street.

Try to move.

Nothing. The body was still and dead, the brain was just taking a little longer. The cold was creeping slowly up my legs—cold and then numbness, something familiar and unpleasant. It was what had happened when I tried to stay awake past sunrise to see what it was like. I fought the numbness and clung to the pain. If I gave in and let the sleep take me now I would never wake up again.

Move.

Nothing.

Nothing at all for an infinity.

Alone in the dark with the pain and the cold and the fear for Bobbi. Would it be quick for her? Would they let her go?

Foolish thought.

Numbness from feet to knees. In a few hours it would reach my burst heart and smother the black fire raging there.

A soft crunch, conducted up through the stairs. It repeated and resolved; grit trapped between shoe soles and the flooring. Probably Malcolm returning at last to get rid of the body. I hadn't heard the truck coming back; must have blacked out for a while. I thought unhappily of the dirty river water closing over my head.

Scrape, scrunch. Pause. Not Malcolm, he wouldn't be so cautious. A tramp, then. He was in for a nasty surprise when he got to the top landing.

Numbness from knees to waist. Death was taking me an inch at a time and moving faster than I'd thought. Soon the ice and nothingness would flow over my brain. . . .

Move, damn it, *move*.

Someone breathing softly, listening at the foot of the landing below me, heart pounding, anticipating possible danger from above. Maybe he'd spotted my left hand poking through the underside of the steps and was having second thoughts about coming the rest of the way.

The first thin tendrils of cold streamed into my vitals like a dusting of snow off a glacier.

Heart thundering now, lungs taking short drafts of air, and

then a long one as he came up the last flight and stopped because now he could see me. I heard in his voice some fraction of the agony that was holding me so helpless.

"Jack . . . Oh, my God . . . Oh, my dear God . . ."

I tried to speak, tried to move, but the slightest flicker of an eyelid was too much. The thing piercing my chest held me frozen. I could not tell him that some part of me was still alive.

Then Escott's hand closed around the stake.

God, yes, pull it out.

He pulled once, twice, then stopped because the gurgling sob that came out of me startled him. Coming back to life was almost as bad as dying. The third tug did the job, and it scraped between the ribs, shook the breastbone, and finally came free. Blood welled up coldly in the wound, quenching the fire there, and the body shuddered as the numbness retreated a little.

His hands went under my arms and he eased me from the stairs until my body was level, slowing the downward flow of blood I couldn't afford to lose. My eyes were open now.

He looked worse than I felt, with his paper white face and new lines formed by the horror of what had been done to me and what he had had to do. I'd read a lot of nonsense about vampires, but there was truth to the stories about those killed; when the end came, it came violently and loud, and mine had been no different. The walls of the stairwell were splashed with gore, and from the dampness soaking into my clothes, I knew I was lying in a pool that had formed on the floor below the steps.

The cold was coming back and I tried to tell him about it, but couldn't draw the breath to do so. Thanks for coming, Charles. It's too late, but thanks all the same. Maybe you can track them down before they kill Bobbi.

My eyes rolled up and the dark closed in.

"Jack!"

The lids twitched. They were so heavy. At least this time it wouldn't hurt.

He was doing something, making short, choppy movements above me. "Stay with me, Jack. Damn your eyes, *stay with me.*"

Fingers forced my lips back. He pulled my teeth apart and the first drops seeped into my mouth. I gagged, fighting him.

"Stay with me," he hissed.

It was hardly more than a taste, enough to seize my attention, but not nearly enough to do me any real good. I couldn't let him risk himself.

"Stay . . ."

I turned my head away or tried to, but his other hand grabbed my hair and held me in place.

"*Stay . . .*"

Then I accepted it. Fully.

My teeth abruptly pierced his skin, and the red warmth flowed more freely. He recoiled—perhaps from pain, perhaps from revulsion at what I was doing—then recovered, knowing that I couldn't help myself. I still desperately wanted to *live*. The instincts born from my changed nature had taken over and ignored the faint, dissonant warning that I could kill him if I went too far.

I ignored it—and I drank.

A heavy engine driving a heavier load. Men distantly shouting to each other. The lazy lap of wash as the barge passed along the river three stories below. The city was slowly waking, or maybe it had never really been asleep.

Some long time earlier I'd found the strength to push away his lifeline, hopefully before it was too late.

My eyes were squeezed shut as much from the effort of recovery as to avoid looking at him. I wasn't quite able to do that just yet.

"Come on, Jack, no games. Are you still with us? Wake up."

His voice was thin, but conversationally normal. Some of the crushing weight on my soul melted away. I wanted to shout from the relief.

"That's it, open them so I know you're all right."

I did, but couldn't focus too well and didn't want to look at the stuff on the walls. The lids came down again like lead bricks. He, at least, was still alive. I was too shattered and sick to be very certain of my own chances.

He continued, trying to encourage me. "The bleeding in

your chest stopped. It closed right up once I took that bloody great stick out.''

He couldn't have meant it as a joke. My head wobbled from side to side as though to deny the thought. The cold and numbness were gone, but shock and weakness were left in their place. I could move again, barely.

''You'll be all right.'' He sounded very convincing, but I wasn't quite ready to believe him yet.

I drew an experimental breath to talk, and heard and felt a bubbling noise within. It developed into a spasm and I rolled on one side in a fit of coughing. One of my lungs had been pierced and was full of blood and fluid. This alarmed Escott, but I felt his steadying hand on my shoulder as I hacked some of it out. The business passed and I flopped back, exhausted.

I took another breath, shallow this time, to avoid coughing. It stayed inside without discomfort and wheezed out in what I hoped was a recognizable name.

He understood. ''Your friends told me where you'd gone. They've heard nothing from the kidnappers yet.''

I tried another breath, felt the cough beginning, and forced it to subside. ''Gaylen did this—''

''You needn't explain, I found out a great deal about Miss Dumont in New York.''

''Came back?''

''Yes, that's why I returned early. I thought things might be urgent, so I flew back. It only took five hours, but I'm sorry it couldn't have been faster.''

He was sitting, his knees drawn up and his back to the wall about a yard away, a handkerchief tied around his left wrist. With a wry expression, he retrieved a folding knife from the floor.

''Hadn't time to sterilize it. If I get lockjaw, it will be your fault.''

He tucked it away in a pocket and said nothing more of what else had happened.

''Did they give you any idea where they were going?'' he asked.

I shook my head. ''Took her away. Another woman with them. Malcolm—'' I had to stop for the coughing.

"That's all right," he told me. "I'll see to it, I'll do my best."

"No cops?"

"No," he assured me. "Do you think you can move?"

"Can try." One thin, stained hand gripped the stair rail and pulled, the other pushed against the floor. He helped, but it was too much. The cough returned and the convulsions doubled me over.

"Have to wait." I whispered. "Weak."

He looked away, uneasy. "You can't wait long, the sun will be coming up shortly."

"When?" I had no sense of time passing. The whole night must have slipped by.

"About thirty minutes."

It was no good, I needed hours to recover—and my earth. "My trunk. Bring it here. I have to—"

"Certainly, if you'll be all right alone."

There wasn't much choice. He could probably carry me down to his car, but I was in no shape to move. The trip could kill me if I were exposed to the sun in this weakened state. I nodded yes, and hoped I was telling the truth.

It took him a little longer than thirty minutes. Though I was in a shadowed area, I was too feeble to fight the daylight blaring through the broken windows. I slipped into a half-aware trance, eyes partially open and unblinking.

He did finally return with the smaller of my two trunks, loaded down with two bags of earth. I must have looked really dead then, for he paused to check for a pulse and heartbeat before putting me into the trunk. There were none to be found, of course, but he was optimistic.

As soon as I was lowered onto the bags inside I went out completely.

The next night I surprised myself and woke up.

Escott was perched on a chair, peering at me. "How do you feel?"

A reasonably important question, I thought it over while checking things from the inside out. "Alive," was the conclusion. I didn't mention the ton of iron wrapped tightly around my chest or that my head felt like a balloon ready to pop. My nose and throat hurt as well, but they were much less noticeable.

"Bobbi?" I asked.

He shook his head. "I have been trying."

We were both silent. If Bobbi were not free by now there was little or no chance of her still being alive. After what Gaylen had done to Braxton and then me . . . The emptiness inside yawned deeper and blacker.

Escott saw and guessed what was going on. "Jack, I need you thinking, not feeling. There's still a chance for her."

"Yeah, just give me a minute." It took longer than a minute to shut it all down. I had to make myself believe she was alive. Anything else had to be kicked out or I'd be useless. Bobbi was alive and needed help, and that was that.

Escott got up while I was adjusting things. We were in his bare dining room, the only place on the ground floor with just one window. The panes of glass were now covered with sheets of cardboard to block out the day's sun. He pulled it all down, stacking the stuff neatly on a packing crate and twitching the curtains back together. Outside, a steady rain was streaming down the glass.

I was on a cot set up near one wall, on top of a bedsheet on top of a layer of my earth. It felt much more comfortable and civilized than lumpy bags inside a cramped trunk. My stained clothes had been stripped away and most of the blood on my skin cleaned off. Modesty had been preserved by a blanket tucked up to my chin.

He came back and sat down. Instead of the handkerchief, there was a neat padding of bandage circling his wrist. The skin on his face was tight, with dark smudges under his eyes from no sleep. Last night and the following day had been no picnic for him, either.

"I'm glad you're better. You looked quite ghastly earlier."

"How bad was it?"

"Bad enough. The blood loss was massive—it was as though your death a month ago had caught up with you." His eyes shifted uneasily away from the memory.

I dimly recalled my hand clutching the stair rail and noting its thinness. In retrospect, it was not so much thin as skeletal. I looked at my hands now. They were normal.

The movement caused a tugging at my cheek. "What's all

this?'' There was tape on my face and a rubber tube leading into my nose. The other end of it was connected to an upside-down glass bottle hanging from a metal stand. The bottle was half-full of some recognizable red liquid.

He stopped looking so grim. ''It began as an experiment and proved successful. I borrowed the equipment from Dr. Clarson—remember the fellow who stitched me up—then made a visit to the Stockyards to obtain six quarts of animal blood. I daresay they thought I was more than a little mad, but they humored me and I returned here to set it up. You looked awful and I couldn't tell if you were alive or not, but thought it all worth a try. It did help you that time you were sun-blind. . . .''

I was astonished.

''You needed it. The first bottle was empty within a quarter hour and the others with decreasing slowness throughout the day, and each one filled you out a little more. With the lack of normal vital signs it was extremely encouraging. I originally considered trying a needle and tube in your arm, but decided against it. Your body, I suppose, has been adjusted to absorb and process blood through the stomach walls, and I was reluctant to tamper with the system by putting it directly into the veins. I'm still very much mystified by your condition. It really shouldn't work—not without a heart to pump and lungs to oxygenate, it really shouldn't.''

He looked as though I should have an answer for him. I shrugged and shook my head, just as puzzled. ''Beats me, but as long as it does work I'm not complaining. Where'd you learn to do all this?'' I tugged at the tube, which itched where I couldn't scratch.

''Please, allow me.'' He began gently pulling the tube out; there seemed to be a lot of it. ''I learned in a hospital when I was very young. I once thought I wanted to be a doctor, so one of my father's friends got me a job there, but it never worked out.''

''Why not?''

He rolled up the tubing and unhooked the bottle. ''Too squeamish,'' he said with a perfectly straight face, and carried the stuff off to the kitchen.

I sat up cautiously, my chest still aching. Some leftover fluid in the lung shifted and burbled with the position change.

When I didn't collapse into a coughing fit, I stood and followed him, but slowly, wrapped in the blanket like a refugee.

Near the sink were a number of similar glass containers, all empty.

"All that went into me?"

He turned on the tap, upended the bottle, and rinsed it out. The beef blood gurgled around the drain, and rushing water diluted it and carried it down. Involuntarily I thought of the walls in the stairwell and looked away.

"Nearly five out of six," he said. "There's one left in there if you need it." With his elbow he indicated the refrigerator. He'd been through a lot setting this up and then waiting to see if it worked. Faced with the same grim task and my inert and unpromising carcass, I might have given up before starting.

"Are you all right?" I asked him in turn.

He knew just what I meant. "A little light-headed when I move too fast, but otherwise there are no ill effects."

"Charles . . . I . . ."

He could see it coming and grimaced. "Please don't be an embarrassing ass about this. I only did what was necessary."

I nearly said something anyway, but held it back. He acted as though he'd done nothing more than loan me a book, and wanted to keep it that way. All right, my very good friend, if you insist. But thank you for my life, all the same.

The phone rang, and he answered.

"Escott."

The voice on the other end was familiar and not one I expected.

"Yes, he's up now. . . . He seems to be. What have you heard? Very well. We'll talk and I'll let you know." He put the earpiece back on the hook.

"Gordy?"

"You're surprised."

"The last time you saw him he was poking a gun at you."

"Forgive and forget. Besides, he never really wanted to kill me." Unconcerned, he crossed back with the bottles and busily loaded them into a cardboard box on the table. "From what you told me about him, I decided we needed his assistance. He has a large organization of eyes and ears and is more than willing to help us locate Miss Smythe. I called and told him everything that happened and he's been tearing this city apart since dawn. He just called now to inquire after your health, but unfortunately has no news for us.''

Next to the box on the table were some of my things—watch, pencil, keys, wallet, and notebook. He'd made an attempt to clean it all but the notebook was a loss. The pages were rusty brown and stuck together. If he were so squeamish, how the hell had he been able to—

''Charles.''

He paused, following my hand as I peeled a page open.

It was still legible. ''There, I wrote it down and forgot it. Can you trace license plates this late? Can Gordy?''

''Is it Gaylen's?''

''No, her bullyboy. That blond crazy, Malcolm.''

He remembered. ''Yes, Gordy and I went to his office, but could trace him no farther. He was very careful about his personal papers; the place was cleaned out.''

''This was to his Ford, the one he was in outside her hotel. Maybe there's an address other than his office.''

''We can try.'' His voice was level, but charged with hope as he got back on the phone, relayed the numbers to Gordy, then quickly hung up. ''Now we must wait. He'll call as soon as he has anything.''

There was someone else waiting. ''What about Marza?''

''She's still at Miss Smythe's hotel with Mr. Pruitt. She is upset, but in control, as when I talked with her last night. You'd left for the warehouse quite some time before I arrived, and I got only her version of things. I would be most interested if you could tell me what events led up to your being impaled in a stairwell in such a disreputable neighborhood.''

It was the way he said it that made it seem funny. I started to laugh. It was probably just a normal release of pent-up emotion, but it turned into a coughing fit. I forced it all back, holding on to my aching chest.

''You should lie down, you're not nearly recovered yet.''

''Nah, I'll be all right. Lemme get some clothes on and I'll tell you what happened.''

I wandered up to the bathroom and tried not to think about Bobbi while I bathed, shaved, and hacked out the last of the junk in my lung. In less than thirty minutes I was dressed and in his parlor, finishing my story to him about last night's events. I stuck to the bare facts and left out the emotions. The earlier laughter was long gone by now, and my hands were trembling when I'd finished.

With a pipe clenched in his teeth, Escott listened, with closed eyes, stretched out on the sofa. The only sign he was awake was an occasional puff of smoke from his lips. It drifted up to get lost in the dusk of the ceiling. Only one lamp was on in the room, a stiff brass thing on a table by the window. The rain had slacked off a little, but in the distance, the sky rumbled with the promise of more.

"Your turn," I said. "Why did you leave for New York so suddenly, and what were you doing up in Kingsburg?"

He removed the pipe to talk. "It wasn't sudden to me. I was here digesting Herr Braungardt's excellent meal and thinking over our interview with Gaylen. The more I thought, the more my eye kept drifting to my packed bag. There was a night train leaving for New York and I simply saw no reason to delay."

"So you left."

"When I got to the city and began looking into things, it became obvious that Gaylen's information was useless. The addresses were nonexistent and the phone number a blind. The address you gave me was real enough, but by then I had reversed things and was intent on backtracking Gaylen rather than Maureen. It did not take long once I located the right papers and records, and then the reasons behind the falsehoods began to emerge. That led me to Kingsburg. Ten years ago Maureen had Gaylen confined to a private asylum located there."

"What? She put her own sister in a nuthouse?"

He opened one eye in my direction. "You know you have a bent toward colorful language that I find most entertaining."

"And you're funny, too. Go on."

He shut his eye and continued. "It was an expensive place, the sort that the wealthy patronize when they have inconvenient relatives. The patients, no matter how lively, are treated with velvet gloves, but kept under strict watch. The usual sort found there are alcoholics and drug addicts, but occasionally they take in someone like Gaylen. Her daughter, Maureen, had her declared mentally incompetent—"

''But they—''

''Yes, you and I know they were sisters, but I imagine it would have looked odd if Maureen gave that fact to the doctors.''

''And if Gaylen insisted—''

''Which she did at first, according to the doctor I talked to, and that insistence only reinforced the reasons for her being there, at least for a while. It was there she became friends with another patient, Norma Gryder.''

''The woman helping them. Why was she there?''

''Morphine addict. They escaped together in 1931 and vanished.''

''Maureen found out and had to run to protect herself and me, to try and prevent what I walked right into.''

''It seems likely. Perhaps all this time they were keeping an eye on you through your ad just as Braxton had been doing. She would also need more dependable help than Norma could provide and would be looking for someone like Malcolm. When your notice was canceled they had to find out why. I should never have brought it to your attention.''

''You couldn't have known. They were worried, though. She was genuinely relieved when I showed up on the doorstep.''

''And genuinely horrified about Braxton, and she lost no time in trying to persuade you to this blood exchange when she knew I'd be going to New York. My return or an untimely telegram would have ruined it all for her, but your own instincts made you turn down her request, causing her to make it a demand. Either way, you lose.''

''Not me—Bobbi. Why didn't you send a telegram?''

''I did. One here and the other to Miss Smythe's hotel. Both must have been intercepted by Malcolm or Gryder. I received no replies and decided to take an aeroplane back. An interesting mode of transport, I quite enjoyed it, despite the noise.

''I checked with her hotel the moment I was back, and they told me she was out, then I went looking for you. This morning I called Gordy and he started his own investigation. We visited Gaylen's room, of course, but she was gone. She went to a great deal of trouble to set up the facade of a harm-

less and endearing soul, no doubt to arouse your sympathies
before making her request.''

''I suppose all that stuff about Maureen's death was a lie.''

''I don't know. I had no time to trace down those records;
perhaps on the next trip. At the moment we can do nothing.
The management at her hotel hasn't seen Gaylen since she
left yesterday evening. Her clothes are still there, but some
few personal items, toiletries and such, are gone, and I doubt
if she will return now. Gordy has men watching just in case,
but if she's anywhere, it will be with Malcolm and Gryder.''

''And Bobbi. It'd have to be isolated, maybe out of town.''

His pipe had gone out. He sat up and fiddled with it. ''Not
necessarily. You saw how isolated you were in the warehouse.
I also checked on it. The owners are bankrupt and because
of legal problems it's been unrented and empty for months.''

''Then who paid the electric bill?''

''There's a generator in the basement. Gordy has two men
waiting there as well, just in case Malcolm returns to dispose
of your body.''

''He didn't strike me as being that neat. What about the
kid?''

''Kid . . . Oh, yes, the Braxton shooting was given an
excess of coverage in the newspapers, but the police have
little to go on. Young Webber received a concussion, but is
recovering in hospital. He described Malcolm as his attacker,
which is in your favor, as the police are looking for you.''

''For me?''

''Several people could not help but notice your disheveled
appearance as you tore around the building looking for Miss
Smythe. The police want to talk to you and have inquired
after Miss Smythe, but Marza told them she'd left town to be
with a sick relative.''

''She could have come up with something better than that.''

''I believe it was Mr. Pruitt's suggestion.''

''Bright guy. With him on their side, the Communists don't
stand a chance.''

''Hmmm.''

''Has Matheus talked?''

''I wasn't able to see him, but did manage a brief chat with
a hospital orderly who is fond of gossip. The boy is feeling
better, but naturally upset at the inexplicable death of his

friend. The police have been in to see him, but no one else except his parents has spoken to him.''

''And everyone full of questions.''

''True, but what can he say?''

''Yeah, if he tells the truth about hunting down a vampire, they'll think he's nuts.''

''You had better hope they do,'' he said with meaning.

I took it. Either way somebody would be in trouble; me if they believed his story, and him if they didn't.

His pipe relit and drawing, he leaned back on the sofa. ''How much time passed between Miss Smythe's call and Malcolm's?''

''Ten minutes, maybe less.''

''There was no phone in the warehouse. I would guess they made the first call to prove they had her, secured her, and made the second call. Then they hurried to the warehouse to wait for you.''

I lurched out of the chair, ready to put some holes in the walls, but hugged my chest instead. It still hurt. ''Gaylen may have died by now. She wouldn't wait.''

''Yes.''

''She'll be like me, if it happens.''

''Not like you.''

''It won't be just her. From her talk she'll be trying to change Malcolm, too. If it works for him, they'll be the kind of monsters Braxton was after.''

''You told me that acquiring this condition is difficult and there is no way to tell until after death.''

''That's how I understood it. I'm thinking that it might work for Gaylen since it worked for Maureen. Malcolm I don't know about, but it's better if we include him as well, just to save us from any surprises.''

''Unfortunately, yes.''

There was one more thought left unspoken. If Bobbi were still alive, they would be keeping her as a food source. Oh, God.

The phone rang, I reached it first, but let Escott do the answering. Gordy was on the other end. Escott had once told me I had no real idea on the grip and influence the mobs had in Chicago. It must have been pretty strong—he had an address.

"I'm coming over," he said. "You got some iron?"

Escott said yes, but I shook my head and asked for the earpiece.

"Gordy, this is Jack. If what I think has happened has happened, guns ain't gonna work, at least not on one of them."

"So what can we do?"

"Can you get some shotguns?"

"No problem."

"And some extra shells?"

"No problem."

"And one more thing . . ." I told him what. Escott's brows went up in surprise and interest.

Gordy considered and again said: "No problem. I'm sending some boys over to watch the place 'til we get there. Sit tight 'til I come for you."

Almost as soon as we hung up it rang again.

"Hello? What? Oh, yes." He passed it to me.

I answered thinking it was Marza.

The masculine voice was a jarring shock. "Jack, I want to talk with you."

"Dad?" *Oh, hell.*

"What kind of trouble are you into?"

"Trouble? What's the matter?"

"That's something you can tell me. The cops were by here just now wanting to know where you are."

"Did you tell them?"

"Hell no. Not until I know what's going on. They wouldn't say and your mother's throwing a fit, so start talking, boy."

Hell and damnation. "Dad, this is just some kind of a mix-up to do with those two con men."

"I'm listening."

I suddenly felt six years old again with Dad towering over me, ready to get the razor strop. I had to consciously shake off the image and remember I was thirty years older and a lot taller. "Okay, what happened is that the little guy Braxton got shot and killed, and the kid thinks I'm involved, so he sent the cops to look me up."

A long silence.

"That's the truth, Dad. The kid saw me in the same building. They were following me to make trouble, and then someone bumped off Braxton. The kid got knocked out. He saw the killer, but not the killing. He knew I was there so he gave my name to the cops, and yours, too.''

The language that followed heated the lines up, and then he repeated the story to Mom, who began groaning in the background.

''Look, why don't you pick up one of the Chicago papers? They're full of the whole story—''

''I did. It's the 'Studio Slaying,' isn't it?''

''Yes, Dad.''

''What were you doing there, anyway?''

''I went to see the show.''

''Why couldn't you have seen the show on the radio?'' he said illogically. ''What are you going to do? Are you going to the cops?''

Double hell. ''I don't know.''

''What do you mean?''

''I mean this whole thing stinks.''

''You're damn right it stinks,'' he agreed, his voice rising.

''I mean I need some time to get things straightened out.''

''What things?''

''It'd take too long to explain. If my boss thought I was really involved with this I could lose my job, and I don't want to lose my job.''

''And I don't want the cops coming around here again.''

''I know. Look, could you just hold off giving them this number?''

''For how long?''

''I don't know.''

''Shit!''

''Dad, I've got good reasons for staying out of this, but I can't go into them now.''

He growled, hemmed and hawed, but in the end decided he could even if he didn't like it. Then we said good-bye.

I put the earpiece back. ''This is ridiculous. The kid sicced the cops on my parents to try and find me.''

''So I gathered.''

''What a pain in the ass.''

''Well, at least you have a father willing to help you.''

''Yeah. I guess I'm going to have to talk with the kid and make him change his mind about me.''

"Though it would seem the damage had been done. I do admire the way you did not quite tell all the truth and yet avoided a direct lie."

"Yeah, it must be all that journalistic training," I said, beating him to the punch line. "Except that bit about losing my job."

"I suppose if it came down to it, you could say that I am your 'boss.' Technically I am, at least on certain occasions, and you are correct; if an employee of mine turned up in this sort of mess, I would not understand."

"Tell me another one."

11

WE WERE READY when Gordy pulled up and touched the horn, but the weather wasn't the best for a long trip. Though I had a raincoat and Escott loaned me a hat, neither one was going to be much protection against a sky that had split open with a vengeance. I didn't like it and felt a sharp twist inside because it had been raining out on the lake like this the night I'd been killed. Such associations were hard to ignore.

Escott and I recognized the car; it was the same one that belonged to Slick Morelli, Gordy's deceased boss. It also stirred up bad memories, but it was just a car, so we got in. Escott sat in front with Gordy and I shared the back with some hard lumpy things. "Careful with that stuff," Gordy cautioned.

The stuff was covered with an old blanket. I pulled it back and Escott turned around to see. They were all from different makers but had the same basic look; sawed off, doubled barreled, and at short range, appallingly deadly. Gordy handed me an oddly light cartridge box.

"Check this and see if it's what you want. They're loaded with 'em."

I opened the box, got a cartridge, and pried open the end with a thumbnail. The contents spilled into my palm. Less than a quarter inch in diameter and dull brown in color, there was just enough light to see the grain pattern in each one.

"They look like beads," I said, noticing the tiny holes drilled in them.

"That's 'cause they are beads. One of the girls at the club had this necklace. They gonna work?"

"If they're wood, they'll work, but only at short range."

"They're wood. We'll probably have to go for point blank, then."

Escott looked uncomfortable. Gordy noticed.

"You know how this could end up; stay in or get out," he said in an even tone.

Escott locked eyes with him a moment, then put his hand over the seat for one of the shotguns.

It was enough of an answer for Gordy. He gave me an up-and-down. "You look like hell, Fleming."

That was his way of saying hello, how are you. I shrugged. "Where are we going?"

He started the motor and shifted gears. "A house on the south side. Any of the guys down there catch my boys in their territory they might get annoyed, so keep your eyes open. What kind of iron you got?"

"This," said Escott, pulling out a huge, odd-looking revolver. It had a ring in the butt, which tagged it as an army gun to me. The cylinder had a kind of zigzag pattern to it and it looked like the top part slid back, as though for an automatic. It even had a safety. I'd never seen anything quite like it and neither had Gordy.

"What the hell is that?"

"A Webley-Fosbery 'automatic' revolver."

"Maybe someday you can explain what that means. How 'bout you, Fleming?"

"This shotgun's enough for me." I tried to sound confident, though I hadn't really held a gun since the armistice. "Did Charles tell you they've got a sawed-off, too?"

"Yeah, but the range on 'em's not so good."

"It's good enough to kill."

"So duck."

Pressing deep into the backseat, I inhaled a lot of air and slowly released it. My nerves were turning up with some sharp and useless edges, mostly because of last night. It'd been a long time since I last felt so physically weak, and it was unsettling.

We slipped through the nearly empty streets. Some stores and a few bars were open, their customers huddled inside near the comfort of the lights. Now and again a face could be glimpsed framed in a window, eyes raised to the sky. Rain crashed down against the roof and bounced from the hood.

"Lousy night," Gordy commented. It occurred to me he was showing some nerves as well in extraneous conversation.

"Quite," agreed Escott, making it unanimous.

It got worse. The wipers were doing their best in a bad situation, but there was just too much water coming down. Gordy slowed the car, muttering. A few blocks later we hit a clear patch and made up the time, then he took an abrupt turn, parking halfway down a long, empty block behind another car. He got out to talk to the men waiting in it and returned.

"That one," he said, his eyes pointing to a white house half-hidden in trees. All we could see was part of its wide front and a couple of brick pillars supporting the porch roof. There were no lights. "No one's been in or out. They think it's empty."

"We'll see," I said. "Stay in the car while I go look."

"But—"

"Let him," said Escott. "He's very good at it."

I got out, leaving the gun, and strolled casually on the sidewalk until I was even with the trees. The area was quiet, with only two other houses back at the corner where we had turned. No curious eyes were on us, the rain had sent everyone inside to listen to the weather reports on the radio. It was a good location: private, fairly isolated, and still close to the city. They would feel safe bringing Bobbi here. I wanted them to feel very safe.

The wind kicked up and tugged my coat. The storm cell we'd driven out from was catching up, and I felt wet enough already. I stepped under the dripping trees and melted in with the shadows. I kept enough solidity so the wind wouldn't blow me away, but was virtually invisible, at least to night-dulled human eyes.

The front windows were dark and the curtains drawn. It looked as deserted as Gordy's men had reported. Around the side, one of the bedroom windows was raised a few inches. I eased close and listened, but the rain interfered with any sounds within. There was screening to keep out the flies and curtains as well, but not the kind you could see through. I moved around to the back of the house.

We'd found the right place. I recognized the panel truck parked next to the open and empty garage. I sighted on it, vanished completely, and floated over, re-forming with it between me and the house. The motor was cold, the key gone. The front interior was clean but there was a box in the back; a box about five and a half feet long, a foot high, and two feet wide. I lifted the lid and was not surprised to find three or four inches of dirt lining the bottom. What was disturbing was the clear imprint of a body in the earth.

Gaylen had not waited a moment longer than necessary. I wondered if she had killed herself or given that task over to Malcolm.

Going back to the house, I went from window to window, shamelessly peering in, but with no results. They were all closed, except for that one, and the curtains were firmly drawn. I found one unobscured basement window, and it looked like a discreet place for us all to slip inside.

When I returned Escott and Gordy were anxious for even negative news. "Malcolm's car is gone, but the truck's out back. Her box of earth is in it—it's been used."

Gordy didn't like my tone. "Whaddaya mean 'used'?"

"He means that these guns and the shells in them are no longer a mere precaution, but a necessity," explained Escott.

"She's a vampire, then?"

"Yes, and every bit as potentially dangerous as our friend here."

Gordy looked at me, considering the possibilities. I didn't look particularly dangerous, but he knew from experience I at least had endurance.

"She will appear to be about Bobbi's age now," I said. "Maybe younger, and she could kill either of you without even trying. These guns give us a chance against her at night, but only a chance. If you get a clear shot, don't hesitate; I can promise she won't. If you miss and it looks bad, do whatever you can to get away, and let me handle her."

"Are they in the house?"

"I don't know. It looks deserted. If it weren't raining I'd be able to hear something inside."

"We shall have to break in, then," said Escott. "But quietly."

"I've got a window picked out, but I want someone to back me up while I'm checking the joint."

"Just lead the way."

Loading our pockets with shells, we took the guns, concealing them under our coats as Malcolm had done at the radio station. I cautiously led them around and pointed out the window. Gordy let out a startled "Jeeze" when I vanished and re-formed inside. The catch was a rusty mess and nearly broke off in my hand when I twisted it free and pulled. As it was, they had to push from the outside while I dug my nails deep under the painted-shut framing. There was a sharp crack and a creak and it opened. We all stopped moving and listened, but no one came down the stairs to investigate. When it was wide enough, Escott came through feetfirst, and as soon as they touched the floor he pivoted around to get his shotgun.

"Come on, Gordy."

His eyes went around the opening. With him next to it for comparison it looked a lot smaller. "Are you kiddin'? I'll watch things out here 'til you can get the back door open."

Escott nodded. "Very well, we do need a rear guard."

Rain spattered our faces, and above Gordy's huge frame the sky burned with lightning. The thunder that followed seconds later made me wince from the sheer sound, and even Escott paused and frowned.

"Lousy night," Gordy muttered, showing his nerves again.

I told Escott to stay in the basement while I looked upstairs, and left him in charge of the guns. He didn't argue.

The basement door was hanging wide open, which was a bad sign to me. Most people keep theirs shut because a large opening into a dark pit makes them uncomfortable, but only when they're home. The door led straight up to the kitchen.

No one was there, but they had been. The table, counters, and stove were all stacked with dishes, pans, and leftover food; a small garbage pail by the back door had passed the point of no return some time ago. I held still and listened, but the rain on the roof acted like so much radio static.

The back door was locked. I didn't want to chance any noise letting Gordy in, he'd have to wait awhile longer.

The kitchen opened onto a dark living room. No one was hiding in the corners. In the middle of the floor stood Gaylen's discarded wheelchair.

I went back, passing Escott, who waited quietly near the top of the steps with a shotgun ready in his hands, his brows raised in a question. I shook my head and pointed down the hall to the bedrooms and went there.

The first door on the right was the bath, the second a small empty bedroom. The bed was unmade and women's clothing decorated the floor and furniture. A crumpled mass of fabric on a chair looked like the flower-print dress Norma had worn last night. It was still damp and smelled of the river.

The door to the second bedroom was shut. I pressed my ear to it. Even with the rain, I was certain to hear anyone on the other side, but the wood was thick and the thunder made me jumpy. I vanished, slipped through the door, and clung close to it while trying to substitute extended touch for sight.

On the right was something large and square, perhaps a bureau; on the left, space for the door to swing and another square object. Ahead was empty space. I could hear, but only in a muffled sort of way, and by then I was imagining sounds. I had to see what I was into and tried for a partial materialization.

Standing out starkly on the walls and ceilings were red splashes—a lot of them. My eyes dropped to the body on the floor. She was on her back, half-covered with a bedspread, her legs tangled in its folds. The red dress still looked new, the bloodstains blending invisibly into the bright color.

Blood was everywhere.

Everywhere. There was no head.

I must have made a noise or been too long. I was dimly aware of Escott quitting the basement and approaching. I had no memory of leaving the room, but he found me on my knees in the hall next to the open door.

"Jack?"

I blinked. I was staring very hard at a corner where the wall met the floor. There was dust in the crevice. I had to look at that and concentrate on it or I would see her instead.

He stepped carefully past me and turned on the bedroom light.

"Don't." The word came out of nowhere. It was wrong to put light in that room; light would make what was there real.

He flinched, caught his breath, then looked back at me, but my mind and eyes were focused on a meaningless detail to keep the unacceptable at bay. The light went out and he remained still for a while, getting his breath back to normal. After a time he stepped away from the door.

"Come on, Jack. Come with me."

It was something simple to respond to, something undemanding. I got up and walked. In the kitchen he pulled a chair out for me. I sat.

He unlocked the door and went out. His voice and Gordy's drifted in. I could guess what was being said, but didn't want to distinguish the words because that would make it real as well. I stared at a bent spoon fallen from the counter. My arm brushed against a tray on the table and tipped over a coffee cup. I righted it again. There was lip rouge on the rim. I recognized the color.

The crash inside was louder than the storm and brought Escott and Gordy right away, but by then it was over. The table and all the junk on it were now in a shattered heap with the wheelchair in the living room. I pushed past them into the rain. Water streamed down my face. It was a good enough surrogate for tears that would not come.

Escott and Gordy trudged into sight, their figures distorted by the water on the windows. They got in, the car shaking a little from their combined weight and movements.

"Jack."

It was hard to raise my eyes, and when I did, Escott didn't like what he found there. He didn't ask me if I was all right; he could see for himself I wasn't.

"Jack."

I shook my head and looked out a window that faced away from the house, a window full of darkness and rain. I watched a drop slither down on the inside and disappear into the frame and waited to see if another would follow.

"I'd like to take him home."

Gordy looked at me uncomfortably. "Yeah, go ahead. I'm

gonna stick around until she comes back for her box.'' He handed over the key and got out.

"Thank you.''

He didn't quite shut the door. "He gonna be all right?''

Escott slid over to the driver's side and put the key in the ignition. "I'll park it behind my building, you can pick it up later.''

The door slammed, he started the motor, and made a U-turn. I closed my eyes in time to avoid looking at the house.

The sky opened up in earnest as we crawled home. The streetlights did little more than mark where the sidewalks began, and lightning flashed overhead as though God were taking pictures of it all. Between the water hammering the roof and the thunder, conversation was impossible, but neither of us felt like talking. Escott refrained from the usual phrases of sympathy, his silence was infinitely more comforting. He would leave me alone or stick around, whatever was needed. He seemed to understand grief.

He pulled the car around the house, triple-parking behind the Nash and my Buick. He must have picked it up from the warehouse sometime during the day. He cut the motor and considered without enthusiasm the soaking dash to the door.

"I suppose we can't get any more wet,'' he said, but hesitated.

Maybe he was thinking about standing in the downpour and struggling with the stiff lock on the back door; it was that or the necessity of having to leave me alone for a few minutes. He opened his mouth again, but the sound died as his attention focused rigidly on something in the mirror. His head whipped around.

"Oh, good God,'' he whispered.

I stared out the back window. A pale shape lurched toward the car. Rain streamed past, blurring the view. The shape stumbled and fell against glass, and the face, anxious and white, looked inside. Our eyes locked with mutual incredulity.

Numbed only for a second, I tore out of the car, afraid she'd disappear, but she came into my arms, solid and real, moving, laughing, crying.

Alive.

Some joys are too much for the heart to hold and can even

supersede grief for intensity. The tears that had not come before now burned my eyes and finally spilled out onto Bobbi's upturned face.

We clung to each other in the car while Escott watched with a mixture of happy indulgence and indecision. He looked ready to leave us alone, but Bobbi saw his intent, hooked an arm around his neck, and held him in place with a hug.

"Good heavens," he mumbled, embarrassed and pleased, and unsuccessfully tried to suppress his smile.

She finally released him and turned back to me. Her face was swollen and red from crying, and her chopped-off hair was limp and dripping, but honest to God, she was the most beautiful woman in the world. Escott offered her a handkerchief and she gratefully accepted and blew her nose.

"I thought they'd killed you," she told me with a hiccup.

"We had drawn the same conclusion about you," said Escott.

"What do you mean?"

"We traced down Malcolm's house. There's a woman's body there, wearing your red dress."

"Jesus, no wonder Jack looked so strange."

"Who was it? What happened?"

"That was Norma. We had a fight and she lost."

"Could you be a little less succinct?"

"Easy, Charles, she's all in," I said, annoyed.

"No," she gulped, "it's okay. The other two left, the man and old woman."

"She's still old?" I asked.

"I don't know, I only heard her voice. I'd heard what they wanted you for, what they wanted you to do. . . . Did you?"

"Yes."

She paused, her thoughts on her face.

"I had to, Bobbi."

Her fingers brushed my temple, and I caught her hand and kissed it.

"I heard you," she said. "I think it was you. It was after she pulled me from the water, that's when they said you were dead."

"They were wrong. Charles found me in time to save my ass. Just tell me what happened to you."

"It's hazy; I was drugged a lot of the time. They kept me tied up in that bedroom all day, and once in a while the man would come in and check on me. The woman, Norma, sometimes shoved some cotton wadding over my nose and I'd hold my breath."

"Chloroform?"

She nodded. "I didn't think it was perfume, so I faked sleeping, and they left me alone most of the day. I spent the time getting untied. When it got dark I heard them again, the other woman, Gaylen—"

"What was her voice like? Old or young?"

She thought a moment. "Young, I think. I was still pretty woozy, but it was strong, at least. She and the man left, and then it was just me and Norma. When she came in to check on me she had the shotgun, but I hardly saw it because she was prancing around in my new red silk. It was a stupid thing to get mad about after thinking you were dead, but it just set me off. I jumped her, the gun came up, I pushed it away, and it—just—"

I held her tight. "It's okay, we know."

"God, I was sick and I had to get out. I grabbed one of her dresses and started walking. I didn't know where I was and the rain—"

"How did you get here?" asked Escott.

"Some couple in a car saw me, stopped, and offered a lift." She began to laugh—with relief, not hysteria. "I told 'em I had to walk home from a bad date and they believed it. They took me here, because I had to see Charles about you."

"Do you know where Gaylen went?"

"No."

"Probably the Stockyards," said Escott.

I agreed with him and looked at Bobbi. "Come on, let's get you inside before you freeze."

"Could we go to my place?"

"Anywhere you want."

"And Marza, she looked so awful when they grabbed me. Could you call her? Please, I know she's worried sick."

Escott fingered his waistcoat pocket. "My key—"

"Won't need it." I grinned and left the car, dashed up the back steps, and sieved through, re-forming again inside the kitchen. I opened the door and waved at them through the screen, showing off. They couldn't see me very well, what with the darkness and rain—

"Hey . . . Escott." A man's voice. Behind me.

Again, no warning.

They must have been expecting him to come in the front way and been waiting there, then heard the back door open and quietly come up from behind. It might have been avoidable with no rain or with the lights on, but then the right man would have been killed. I might have even stepped out of it, but my thoughts were elsewhere, and all the emotional shocks had made me sluggish. There was no time to react before something like a sledgehammer slammed into my back at kidney level. The breath was pushed right out of me. I staggered sideways against a wall and slid down, my back on fire.

Legs gave out and crumbled with no strength, right arm hanging loose and useless, left one twitching—my nervous system was shot all to hell. What was it, what was wrong with my back? My hand flailed around the source of the pain and my fingers brushed against hard metal. It was sticking out of my back at a firm right angle and I didn't realize what it was at first. When I did, I moaned and felt a sudden sympathy with Escott's squeamishness.

Two other people were with me, but only one was breathing. I kept my head down and went very still.

"Is he dead?" She was across the kitchen. Any closer and she'd see who I was.

Malcolm's hand pressed my wrist. He was close enough, but it was dark and he didn't have her night eyes—not yet. "Yeah, let's go."

I had to wait. No matter how badly I wanted them dead, I had to let them get clear and hope Escott and Bobbi stayed out in the car. I might be able to protect them from Malcolm, but not from her.

The front door slammed shut behind them.

Get up, go after them. Push against the wall, get the legs under the body. Stand up, get control, *walk*.

It was more of a drunken reel. The table got in the way.

Rest a second. It's not that bad. Now *move*.

I shoved the table away and went to the front of the house,

trying to ignore my back. I made it to the door and twisted
the knob. They were down the steps and walking quickly to
their car parked down the street. Her coat was too long, but
her figure fit it; it might have been one of Norma's spares.
Her hair was full and dark, her walk light and strong. I didn't
have to see her face; it would look like the photo she'd given
Escott. Her skin firm and smooth again, an image of a girl
in her pretty youth.

Their heads were down because of the rain, so neither of
them saw it coming.

A narrow alley ran between Escott's house and the next;
kids were always charging through it in their games. Malcolm, no gentleman, was on the inside of the walk and closest
to the opening when a noise like thunder, but much louder
and briefer, happened there. Raindrops were caught and frozen for an instant in the flash before smoke and darkness
obscured them.

It had been Escott. He'd seen something from the car and
had gone around to ambush them. Unfortunately, Malcolm's
body was in the way for the crucial second and took most of
the blast.

He was thrown hard against Gaylen. She screamed from
surprise or pain or both, and they went down together. She
rolled clear, her coat full of small holes. He pitched onto his
face, his head and part of one shoulder hanging over the curb
in the runoff water.

Gaylen got to her feet, dazed and staring at Malcolm, then
looked down the alley. She took a half-step toward it, but
lights were coming on in the surrounding houses. Malcolm
moved and moaned, pushing himself up and reaching for her.
She hesitated; there was blood all over his left side, head to
toe, but he was somehow still alive. He sobbed her name.
She made her decision and got him standing and helped him
unsteadily toward the car. They were too busy to notice as I
followed in roughly the same condition. I glanced down the
alley in passing, but Escott had sensibly left.

She started the car and began rolling away. It paused undecided at the end of the street, enabling me to catch up, but
not long enough to get inside. I grabbed the spare-tire cover
and got my feet up on the bumper's narrow edge, with most
of my weight resting on the slick angle of the trunk. It was

not the most comfortable or secure position I'd ever been in, much less in a rainstorm with a knife in my back.

The gears were grinding, I dug in with my hands and held on tight. The metal began to bend under the pressure. I tried to vanish and slip inside the car, but the knife was screwing that up somehow. I tried to find a way to hang on with one hand so that I could pull it out, but things were too precarious. Literally and figuratively, I was stuck with it.

Dirty water flew up in my eyes, blurring the spinning pavement. I squeezed them shut, not daring to spare a hand to wipe them. Headlights flashed briefly, then peeled away. A horn honked. The Ford sped up, skidded on a corner, and straightened with a jerk. My foot came loose from the fender. The damaged muscles in my back protested the sudden movement and again at the effort required to put the foot back again. Wind caught Escott's borrowed hat and sent it spinning. My hair got soaked and dribbled into my eyes. Bobbi had said I needed to cut it.

Bobbi—

Not now, I couldn't think of even her now. I had to hold—

A short skid, more headlights. A truck coming from the other direction; its spray blinding, its roar deafening.

A speed change. Brakes.

We slow and stop. Stoplight.

I stick a foot on the road for balance and reach around. Can't find it—there—close the fingers—*pull*.

The initial pain returns. I nearly fall, nearly scream. Bite my lip instead. There's no end to the damned blade.

Pull.

Fingers slipping, gripping, no time to baby it out.

Pull.

It's a goddamned sword. . . . There . . . the edge catches on something. . . .

There.

Gears. Car lurching forward. Grab at the wheel cover. Rest.

It didn't hurt so much now, but the nerves were suffering from the aftershock. I looked at the thing. It wasn't a sword, just eight inches of good-quality steel and heavy enough not to easily break. A solid chef's knife that was meant to be slipped under Escott's ribs so he couldn't tell anyone what he learned in Kingsburg. After the first hideous shock he wouldn't have felt much, maybe just a little surprise as the floor came up. Malcolm was an efficient killer, he liked to do it quick and then get away before the fuss started.

We made another turn, and the streets looked familiar. How'd that story go about the man walking backward so that he could see where he'd been? We were approaching the neighborhood where Malcolm's house was, where she had left her box of earth, where Gordy and his men were waiting.

12

THE CAR CRUISED past the correct turn and took the next one a quarter mile down the road. The shotgun blast had made Gaylen cautious. Someone knew about her and her changed nature and knew how to fight her. She was going to be careful not to approach her box openly. We rolled into an area thick with trees and darkness. Branches and leaves stirring constantly in the wind made it all seem alive and aware. We stopped cold in the middle of a deserted mud-washed road, the motor died, and their voices rose up in the relative quiet.

"Don't leave me here!"

"I'll be right back. I have to see that it's clear."

"God, I'm dying. You can't go now."

"You'll be all right." Her door opened.

"No! Do it now! You said you would—you promised! Gaylen!"

She got out. I was flat on the ground by the rear passenger tire pretending to be a rock. The door slammed shut on Malcolm's protests. From under the car I saw her feet slip on the mud, regain balance, and walk away. When I no longer heard her I stood up.

Malcolm was on his side across the length of the seat and hardly noticed when his door opened. He was still alive, and that was all that mattered to me.

His wounds were scattered and colorful and he was bleeding freely in several spots. The little skin showing through the blood was white and clammy with shock. He and Gaylen had been outside the lethal range of the wood pellets, though. His claims of dying were premature, at least for the moment.

"Gaylen, please—"

"She's gone, all you've got left is me." I wanted him to *know*, to see it coming.

He didn't know me at first, I was only an unexpected intrusion, then his eyes rolled fully open and he started to scream. My hand smothered his mouth and part of his nose.

"You said you wanted it. Does it matter where it comes from?"

He couldn't move. He was that scared and hardly flinched when my hand slid down his face to close around his neck.

"You want to be a dead man like me? I can do that for you, Malcolm." My fingers tightened.

He struggled for air, imagining my grip to be stronger than it was.

"I'm not as good as you are, though. It won't be quick, and believe me—it's gonna hurt."

Simple words he could understand, and now simple actions. I brought the knife up so he could see. The blade was clean and shining now, the edge was so sharp that it hurt to look at it. He recognized the thing and realized the mistake he'd made in Escott's kitchen. I let it hover next to his face. He shrank back into the car seat, and when he could go no farther, the first pathetic mewlings of sound began deep in his throat.

"Where do you want it first? Your eyelids?" I pressed the flat of the blade against his temple, the razor edge brushing his eyebrow. "I could cut them away, top and bottom."

He jerked at the touch of the steel, causing a tiny nick in the skin. I drew back and let him recover. His breath was coming too fast, and I didn't want him passing out.

"That'd hurt, but there are better nerve centers to play with. I want you to know what I went through in that stairwell. I want you to know what you gave Braxton and Bobbi. You think you're hurting now—in a minute you're gonna wish it was this good."

I threw the knife in the backseat and used my bare hands and, God help me, I was laughing.

* * *

I crawled from the car like a drunk and leaned against it, still shaking a little from what I'd done. Maybe I should have been sickened by my actions, but nothing so normal as that touched me now.

The wind was damp and cool as it washed over my face.

I'd stopped in time. He was still alive. Somehow I just managed to shake free of the insanity that had taken me over. Malcolm hadn't been so lucky. I'd paid him back for all that he'd done and then some. I was free of the nightmare. He would always be its prisoner.

I sucked clean, moist air deep into my lungs and let it shudder out again, flushing away the last stink of his terror.

No regrets. None.

I pushed away from the car and went after Gaylen.

The rain had almost stopped, but the leaves above continued to drip, creating a false fall. I couldn't count on that to muffle any noise I made, and stepped carefully on soft grass whenever possible.

She'd heard his screams and was coming back to investigate. I saw her just in time, put a fat tree between us, and sprinted, closing the space. I got within ten yards and froze, peering out from a fork in the branches.

She stopped short of the car; one of her sharp new senses had tipped her off and her head snapped around, on guard for an unknown threat.

The old woman was gone. It was one thing to know that fact, quite another to see it. Her face was so very like Maureen's, especially now with her anxious expression. But she was someone else, not the gentle woman I had loved.

I stepped out from behind the tree and walked swiftly toward her.

The body and its inner functions may have changed, but her mind was still human-slow to react. I was absolutely the last thing she expected to see, and with good reason, since she'd watched me die. She was still rooted in place when I caught her arms. The touch confirmed my reality. There was some struggling, then she abruptly stopped and smiled, quite calm. That smile made me freeze in turn and I knew then why Maureen had confined her sister to an asylum.

"What are you going to do?" she asked. "Kill me?"

I held her fast. "I can try, and after what you did to Bobbi,

I'll enjoy it. There's a lot of wood around here . . . haven't you noticed?''

She had. She was still smiling, though. Then her face rippled, faded, and became a shapeless *something*. The hair on my scalp went up. My hand no longer clutched arms, but closed through cold tendrils darker and thicker than any fog. Her body was gone and in its place was a floating blob of about the same size. She had vanished, even as I had done a hundred times before.

But I could *see* her. She might not know that. It was some kind of advantage to me if I could keep fooling her.

The gray thing hung in the air for a few seconds, then moved away like an amoeba swimming in fluid. It fell in on itself, shaping and growing solid again. She was laughing.

''You didn't expect that; I thought you would have. I can do everything you can. Did you think I'd just *let* you kill me?''

''Do you think I'll let you go? If I don't get you, Escott will. Malcolm missed, you know. Did you see him in the alley? His gun? You felt it. That wasn't rock salt in the cartridges.''

''I'm not worried about him.''

''Aren't you? You tried to have him killed tonight, but the next time you'll have to do the dirty work yourself. Malcolm's finished.''

''I don't need him now.''

She vanished again, or almost. The shape swung to one side and behind some trees, but didn't wander far. I kept staring at the spot she'd been in, even after she materialized, turning only when she made a sound. It was to test me. Apparently I'd passed. Pleased, she vanished again.

There were noises behind me, near Malcolm, but off to the left. I followed their direction, stopping, listening. A loud snap. A foot skidding over damp leaves. Silence.

A glimpse of movement against the wind.

The gray thing moved closer, coming across open ground to get close to me. It seemed larger.

I circled as though searching, but with my head turned enough to keep an eye on her. She would sense my presence and movement. I made it easier for her by stopping next to a tree and waiting.

She went solid and swung the broken branch at my head. I dropped a split second early, turned, and dived for her midsection. Her club broke against the tree; she still clutched a two-foot length as we went down. I pulled it from her, raised, and struck.

The angle was bad; there was no force in the blow, nothing near what was needed. The raw edge caught her shoulder, not her head. She yelped and the splinters tore her dress and scraped her fresh skin, and then I was holding on to nothing again as she turned into living fog.

It slithered along the ground and rose into a rough human shape. I remembered to move around as though confused. A face began forming, and when there was enough for ordinary eyes to see I brought the branch down on its middle. That did no harm and she only retreated again.

Her direction was good, she was moving toward the house. She must have tired of teasing me and wanted to get on with her original business before she made a mistake. I let her get ahead and followed, keeping a prudent distance.

The backyard to Malcolm's house came into sight, its width sloping down at us, the trimmed grass giving away to weeds as the ground tilted sharply. The land did the same again from our side, forming a broad V shape. Down the middle, swollen and fast from the rain, was a brown stream. It wouldn't be very deep, two or three feet at the most, and in some spots no more than four feet wide. As far as she was concerned it could have been the Chicago River. Without help she'd find it nearly impossible to cross.

She stopped short at the very edge of the bank, the gray pseudopods probing and undecided. She was held back by the invisible barrier of free-flowing water. She went solid, with her back to the stream and her eyes on the woods to see my approach. I was hunched down behind a bush, keeping very still, and she missed me. Now she glanced side to side for a bridge of some sort, a fallen tree or stones sticking up, but nothing so convenient was at hand.

She turned again, checking for me and considering the car. She could go back for it and reach the house from the front, but would it be any easier? It was a long way back and I might be waiting near it. The truck with her box of earth was less than a hundred feet away, its nose pointing to the street, all ready to go.

Gaylen made up her mind and eased one foot tentatively in the water like a swimmer testing the temperature. She didn't like it, pulled out quickly, and again looked for an alternative. Nothing presented itself, so with a grimace she tried once more, right foot, left, the water churning up around her knees, then higher. For all her need of speed, she might have been wading through partially set cement.

When she was in far enough, I broke cover and closed on her with the club. She heard me and turned, or tried to; her feet couldn't keep up with the changing situation. The branch swung, she caught my arm, and no doubt at that moment tried to vanish. The confused surprise was plain on her face.

Had she been floating freely in the water, I'd have lost her, but her contact with the stream bed negated that option. The mud and earth beneath her feet held her solid.

I dragged free and struck again. She deflected it, but the force she needed threw her off balance, and she gave out a little scream and splashed full length on her side. The next scream was louder and filled with anguished pain. She fought to get up and out.

The branch caught her flailing hand, and she grabbed my arm successfully with the other and held fast, either to pull me in or make me pull her out. My own balance was tenuous on the loose, slippery bank. The fall was inevitable, but only my right arm and leg went in. They were more than enough.

I'd crossed free water before: above it dematerialized and rushing out of control to the nearest shore or clinging to the inside of a boat or sitting solid in a car to feel only its tug from one riverbank to another, but never by direct contact. It was a tremendous shock, like being dumped in the Arctic in winter. The actual temperature of the water had nothing to do with the freezing ice it felt like to me. I was different now and uniquely vulnerable to this element. I was instantly weakened. No wonder she'd screamed.

She clung to me, knowing I wouldn't go in any deeper if I could help it, and I inadvertently pulled her out a little as I tried to get free. My left hand closed on her wrist, squeezing and turning, trying to break it. Her grip on my shoulder loosened, then she took a chance, jerked free, and slammed her fist into my jaw. It was a solid hit and rattled my brain. I slipped deeper into the fiery cold on top of her.

It was utterly numbing. Our muscles were freezing up, our movements slowing to nothing. Neither of us could vanish and neither would let go. I pushed her under while trying to get back up on the bank. Breathing was no longer necessary to her survival, but such instincts are not easily overcome in a few hours. She pushed her body against the stream bed and her face came up, her hair matted and her teeth bared. With a free hand I hit her as hard as I could.

Her bones should have shattered under the blow. She felt it but ignored it. I hit her two more times before she knocked my hand away and stabbed my neck with stiffened fingers. She caught the Adam's apple, and I gagged a moment, then shoved her under again, hoping the cold would slow her down more than it was slowing me.

I used the leverage to free one leg from the water. The iciness abated a little, and I concentrated on holding her beneath the surface. She wouldn't drown, but a lengthy immersion might weaken her.

The branch was gone, lost in the swirling water, and there was nothing large or sturdy enough to take its place. Fingers closed on my ear and twisted hard. I hit at her face again and connected with a nose and eye ridge. It surprised her and broke her grip. My ear stayed attached and I seized her hand before it could do anything else. I had to look to see that I had it, for I was losing feeling fast.

Voices. Lights twitching above and to the right.

Gordy and one of his men had heard her scream and were investigating. They carried shotguns. It took them a full minute to find us; I was too busy holding her under to call out. My arms were nearly dead and I couldn't tell if my fingers were doing their job properly. At least her struggles had slowed.

Then my knees slipped in again and she exploded to the surface.

Her eyes were wide with flat, blank panic, and that gave her more strength than I was prepared or able to deal with. She wanted only to escape from the near-petrifying cold. Twisting and clawing halfway out of the water, her hands dug for purchase in the mud, tearing gouges in the bank. Wrapping arms around her middle, I kept her down, but she was kicking and I was already weak and battered.

Gordy was standing on the far bank, a flashlight disclosing the scene. His gun came up uncertainly.

"It's me!" I yelled, realizing he didn't know me for all the mud.

He knew my voice, crab-walked down the slope, and waded across, making it look easy. Gaylen's knee caught me under the rib cage, knocking my breath out. I couldn't warn him to stay back. One of her hands shot out and got his ankle. He yelped and fell, his body acting as an anchor as she began to pull free of the water.

I grabbed her a little higher, throwing my weight on top and smashing her face in the mud. We slid down the bank, our legs still in the stream. It was freezing agony, but safe. As long as she was held in it she couldn't vanish and escape.

Her face lifted, she spit mud and pleaded with Gordy. "Please help me, he—"

I flipped her over, cutting off her helpless-damsel act. She was extremely strong, but when it came down to it, I was bigger and just able to hold her in the water. The man that had come with Gordy stared with openmouthed horror as I shoved her down again. Maybe Gordy had told him something, maybe not. He was unprepared for this kind of savagery and looked ready to run. Gordy stopped him.

"Hitch! Stay here and cover her." He got up, stepped back into the water, and kept his distance.

Gaylen fought her way up again, but this time she saw the gun. She remembered what I'd said earlier.

Gordy loomed over us, the muzzles centering on her chest. She tore and kicked against me.

"Fleming?" he asked.

Gaylen's eyes turned on me, frantic and helpless and with all the torment and wanting in the world in them.

I thought of Braxton staring sightlessly at his own blood on the tiles.

I thought of Bobbi being mercilessly shoved into the river water. The image was blinding.

"*Yes,*" I choked.

She was screaming, but without sound, even as I had screamed in the stairwell. Gordy put the barrels to her chest.

There was no color in his face. The tendons in his hands were ridged to control the shaking. He was familiar with violence, but this was different.

The night roared once and went silent.

The rubber blade squeaked annoyingly as it dragged over the nearly dry glass.

I was so goddamned tired. I was tired and sickened and cold enough to lie down and die, but he put his hand out and pulled me from the water, away from the red stains before they—

The window was a good thing to stare at; the movement of the wipers was soothing and hypnotic, even the noisy one. You could stare for hours at the fan shapes being renewed with each swinging stroke and not think of anything at all. You could forget the wetness and the clinging clothes and the earthy stink of mud.

"That shot'll bring the cops," Hitch had said uneasily, his eyes on me as I flopped bonelessly to the ground at his feet.

No time to rest. Things to do first.

Malcolm. I told them where to find what was left of him and what to do.

Back and forth. The squeak changed as some of the rubber loosened and trailed after the wiper like a piece of black string. First straight, then curled under on the return stroke. Back and forth.

"It's in the living room," Gordy told him. "Wipe it clean."

"Yeah, boss." He fled to the house, then stopped just short of it as a car pulled up and braked in the driveway. It was Gordy's, and Escott and Bobbi spilled out.

Gordy stared at her, his big face slack with stunned recognition. "Bobbi . . ."

Understanding his surprise, she paused long enough to give him a fierce hug, then knelt next to me, asking if I was all right. I couldn't answer and held on to her. Escott was explaining things to Gordy and was asking what had happened, until the sight of Gaylen's mangled body stopped the flow of words.

We all looked.

"Jesus," Gordy whispered, and stepped back from the bank.

The tangled hair was still dark, but the skin was changing. The smooth texture was sagging around the jaw, growing puffy under the eyes. Wrinkles formed as we watched.

It was as though your death . . . had caught up with you.

"She's dying," I said.

"She's not dead?"

"We take a lot of killing." I knew what she was going through and took no pleasure in the knowledge.

"Charles, get Bobbi out of here."

He came and gently took her shoulders. She shrugged him off.

"I want to stay."

"Please, go with him."

"But—"

"I know, but you can't. We have to leave, and fast. I'm all right, I promise, but I want you out of here."

She didn't like it but saw the sense. She kissed me hard. "I'll be waiting at my place."

"I'll come as soon as I can."

She smiled. It was a wan one, but still a smile, and she let Escott pull her away.

"What about her?" said Gordy, nodding at the stream when they were gone.

"We can't leave her for the cops. We can't chance an autopsy—not on her. And that truck with the box in it has to go."

"I'll get the boys to fix things."

Hitch came back then with another mug named Jinky and the shotgun used to kill Norma. Gordy sent them across the stream and into the trees.

"Put his mitts on it, and for Chrissake make sure he ain't got no spare shells."

"Yeah, boss."

"And clean off that knife."

"Yeah, boss."

While they were gone we did what was necessary and did it fast.

The trail of rubber flapped and twisted, vibrating and adding its noise to the squeak. Hitch, who was driving, finally shut them off. We made a turn and the blanket-wrapped thing on the floor shifted with the direction change. I moved my feet so it wouldn't touch me.

Silly thing to do.

For the hundredth time Hitch checked the mirror. He was more worried about looking out for cops than not seeing my reflection. He made another turn and we swayed. His speed was cautious, but his driving technique clumsy. He didn't like what was in the back with me and Jinky.

Couldn't blame him.

Jinky was nervous as well and complaining. "This just ain't done, this cartin' around. Plug 'em and leave 'em, I sez."

"Shut up, Jinky," Hitch said wearily.

He shut up and kept looking sideways at me, uneasy from my silence. His hand never strayed far from the bulge under his armpit. Maybe he was picking up on my feelings of death. I looked at him once, he blanched, and the fear smell came off him, sharp and stinging.

Gordy was in the front passenger seat and turned his head, noticing something was wrong. I kept looking out the window.

"How's your mother, Jinky?" he asked out of the blue.

Jinky was gulping. "Wha . . . oh, she's okay."

"She's doin' okay. Still got that dog? What's its name?"

"Peanuts . . . yeah, she's still got 'im."

Gordy, not a great conversationalist, kept him talking until he calmed down. After five minutes, Jinky looked less likely to make a fatal exit out the door. I shut my eyes and pretended to nap, half expecting to fight off an army of ugly images from the recent past but finding sweet, warm darkness instead.

We drove north along the lake for a long time. I thought vaguely we were going to Wisconsin, but Hitch made a last turn onto a muddy, rutted road that curved into thick trees. The car bounced and slewed. The thing at my feet shifted again, but this time I didn't bother moving.

A little later, the four of us were slogging through more mud and wet leaves. While Gordy and Hitch carried the rope-tied bundle, Jinky and I used the flashlights. Jinky came along because he didn't want to be alone.

Twenty feet of dock and a boathouse waited for us at the shoreline. Gordy unlocked the boathouse. I couldn't easily go in since most of it was over the water, so I missed seeing them load the thing into the boat. Without any delay they rowed free of the house and out onto the lake.

I sat on the damp ground and watched them. They didn't start the motor until they were small specks in the distance. Human eyes could not see them in that dark, but Gordy was taking no chances.

Jinky alternately paced and squatted, wanting to stay near me for the company, but not wanting to get too close. He'd seen Malcolm, after all, and maybe Hitch had been talking to him.

Jinky was shivering; the wind off the restless lake was cool. He paced around, hands in pockets, jingling the change there. "We used to use this place a lot," he said out of nervousness. I let him talk; his voice took me out of myself. "We used to run some pretty good stuff through here from Canada. Mostly for the boss 'n his friends. Stuff that was too good for the speaks, they said."

The boat was at the edge of sight. The wind carried the thin buzz of the motor to us. The boat vanished.

He must have been wondering what I was staring at in the gloom. "Got hijacked once," he continued. "Early out. That was fun. Then we started packin' big rods and that hotted things up. We went to a lot of trouble over that fancy hooch and for what? You get drunk just as fast on the homemade stuff, faster even. Richer, too. Half those mugs never knew the difference."

The motor buzz was irregular now, the wind affecting it.

"There was this girl I had then, always after me for some of the fancy stuff. I took an empty bottle that still had the label on and put in some of the local make and some tea for color. She never knew the difference, but sure knew how to say thanks. Not too smart, but she was a lot of fun."

The buzz changed and grew. I blinked the flashlight a few times to give them a direction to aim for and kept it up until they were close. The motor cut and they rowed the rest of the way in. The bundle was gone and so was the boat anchor and its length of chain.

They got out and Gordy locked up. "Where to?" he asked me.

My throat was clogged; I had to clear it first. "Bobbi's."

He nodded.

The ride back seemed shorter.